MUSICAL CHAIRS

MUSICAL CHAIRS

Kinky Friedman

WILLIAM MORROW AND COMPANY, INC.
New York

Recognizing the importance of preserving what has been written, it is the policy of William Morrow and Company, Inc., and its imprints and affiliates to have the books it publishes printed on acid-free paper, and we exert our best efforts to that end.

Library of Congress Cataloging-in-Publication Data

Friedman, Kinky.
    Musical chairs / Kinky Friedman.
        p.   cm.
    ISBN 0-688-09148-2
    I. Title
PS3556.R527M88   1991
813'.54—dc20
                                                    90-45678
                                                    CIP

Printed in the United States of America

First Edition

1 2 3 4 5 6 7 8 9 10

BOOK DESIGN BY M & M DESIGN

This book is dedicated to the memory of
Floyd E. Potter, Jr.
Friend, teacher, tireless defender
of Texas wildlife

and to the memory of
Joan B. Potter
Who had that lost human
talent for finding something
to like in everyone

Homo Erectus
Got to connect this
Bone that I discovered yesterday
Tyrannosaurus
Lived in the forest
Died because its heart got in the way

—From "Homo erectus," by Kinky Friedman and
Panama Red

MUSICAL CHAIRS

1

It was Christmas Eve and all the salamis in the window of the Carnegie Deli had been hung with care. It was two o'clock in the morning and I was drifting by the window like a secular ghost in the rain when suddenly, between two salamis, I saw something that made me stop on a dime and pick it up. Standing in the middle of the restaurant, bathed in that incandescent, celestial light you only see coming out of heaven or a jukebox, was Leo Steiner.

In Leo's case, I thought I knew where the light was coming from. Leo was dead.

At least I hoped he was dead—we'd buried him almost a year ago.

Leo had owned and operated the Carnegie from 1976 to 1987, during which time he'd managed, using an equal mixture of pastrami and charm, to turn the place into a cultural institution, a veritable haven for wandering Jews of all creeds and religions.

Leo was the man who first made me believe that New York could be my home.

Now Leo was holding some menus and laughing

11

and talking to Adlai Stevenson, Jean Seberg, and Thurman Munson, one of those rather unwieldy parties of three, apparently, and trying to find them a nonsmoking table not too near the kitchen. For a moment I thought of what my father says whenever a waiter or maître d' gives him a table anywhere near the kitchen. My father says: "Why don't you just put us right *in* the kitchen." Neither my father nor the waiter ever seems to find anything funny in this line, but, at the moment, it was about the most humorous thing I had going.

I was beginning to wonder, as I stood out on the frozen sidewalk watching this unworldly scene unfold, if I hadn't been T-boned by a runaway Volvo and just didn't know it yet. But I could see that I wasn't in heaven and, quite fortunately, it didn't look a hell of a lot like Kansas. The celestial, half-blinding light from inside the Carnegie Deli continued to pour rather eerily out onto the street. Could it indeed, I wondered, be reflecting from the cherubic cheeks of some large luminous buttocks?

I rubbed my bloodshot orbs and looked away for a moment to that dead Dixieland of the spirit that, just when you don't really need it, will sometimes rise again. My gaze fell upon a bag lady, her earthy possessions gathered around her in ragged splendor, sitting on the curb with her feet in the gutter, warming her hands over a steam vent. When she smiled at me I saw in her face all the regrets of my life.

I looked between the salamis again and Leo and his cool customers were gone. It was just another storefront now, I thought, and Christmas Eve was just another night to me. Chestnuts might've been roasting on the open fire for some Americans, but, right at the moment, my own nuts were about to freeze off. I hailed a hack and headed for 199B Vandam.

I watched New York slide by beneath streetlights that had seen it all and still wanted more. From the cab it seemed like a forgettable familiar film caught in the projector in an old movie house when you were a kid. A body lying on the sidewalk, people walking over it. A skinhead sullenly aiming south, kicking at pigeons. A new Mercedes with tinted glass windows and a vanity license plate that read "GREED." I wondered where the hell the angels were. Maybe they were hanging out in Herald Square.

By the time we got down to the Village, the third McCartney song in a row had come to an end.

"What happened?" I asked the driver. "Paul McCartney die?"

"It's a tape," he said.

2

The period between Christmas and New Year's can be a rather lonely time for those of us married to the wind. Old people living alone tend to leap from their top-floor balconies in greatly increased numbers, sometimes taking until Purim to hit the pavement. Young people who feel alone see the holiday season as a pretty good time to end it all before it begins. They hang themselves while listening to albums by Whitesnake, overdose on St. Joseph's baby aspirins, or just wander away, having always dreamed of someday seeing themselves on milk cartons.

It's not a very good time either for the "in-between people," as the Koreans call the children of mixed ancestry left over from the war. They stay home alone sift-

13

ing the ashes of their childhoods, dreading becoming o-l-d, and wondering if this could signal the fearful, muted arrival of middle age.

It could.

I was sitting in my loft the day after Christmas smoking a cigar and killing a medicinal shot of Jameson's Irish whiskey when I found myself vaguely wishing I was a Young Republican. I never liked Young Republicans much but I'd never seen an unhappy Young Republican and I kind of wondered what their secret was. I wasn't really feeling sorry for myself but I wasn't feeling much of anything else, either.

I stroked the cat, poured another shot, and looked at the calendar. I'd sort of penciled in a New Year's date with Winnie Katz, the girl who ran the lesbian dance class in the loft above me. Of course, with a lesbian, you never really knew how things stood, or lay, as the case may be. There was some fine, slightly twisted silk machinery in their minds that no man would ever be able to observe intimately. It was hard enough understanding normal broads which, in itself, was about as likely as making eye contact with a unicorn.

Winnie and I'd been kind of on-again-off-again for the past year or so, and anytime I heard the lesbian dance class starting up over my head I knew we were off-again.

"At least," I said to the cat, "I'm not playing another New Year's Eve gig at the Lone Star Cafe." The last time I'd done that had been several years back and the results had been most unpleasant, not to say painful.

The cat didn't say anything, but looked at me with a rather jaundiced expression. She'd been burned out on country music for some time now. The last thing she'd really liked was "I've Got a Tiger by the Tail" by Buck Owens. I never cared for Buck Owens myself, though I had to admit he didn't much sound like a Young Republican.

The cat and I had rather diverse musical tastes but

14

somehow we managed. We'd gotten along in a cold, drafty loft at 199B Vandam Street, New York City, for almost five years together. That's more than you can say for most urban couples.

When I thought about it, there'd been an absence of music lately in both my life and the cat's. I killed the shot and thought about it, took a reflective puff or two on the cigar, and thought about it some more. Because of my years on the road as a country singer I had come to hate the sound of the human voice singing. That was understandable, I figured. Sonny Bono never lets his young wife play rock 'n' roll music. Elton John never goes to concerts unless they are his own. Of course, his close friends call him Sharon, but the point is that too much of a good thing can get pretty tedious.

Things for me, however, hadn't always been this way. I took a nostalgic puff on the cigar, blew the smoke upward toward the now silent Isle of Lesbos, leaned back in the chair, and drifted daydreamily off to a girl in a peach-colored dress. Her eyes kept staring at me like they belonged in a Mexican picture of Jesus.

She was out of the picture, so to speak. She'd married a highly successful shoe distributor in Seattle and was now about nine months' pregnant with twins. That was about as out of the picture as you could get. I had, however, suggested to her that if one of the twins turned out to be a girl, they might consider naming her Kinkadora.

Suddenly, there was a ringing in my ears.

They say if there's a ringing in your left ear it usually means someone's saying something bad about you. They say if there's a ringing in your right ear—which is, of course, a far more rare occurrence—someone's saying something good about you.

As it happened, no one was saying anything about me. The two red phones were ringing on my desk. I watched them ring for a long time. Then I picked up the blower on the left.

"Start talkin'," I said.

"Kinky, this is Tequila. I'm here in New York."

"Tequila," I said with a fairly undisguised lack of enthusiasm. Tequila'd been a guitar picker with my old band, the Texas Jewboys. In the thirteen years since the band had broken up I hadn't seen or spoken with Tequila and there'd been a damn good reason for it. Trouble followed the guy like a tornado honing in on a mobile-home park.

"Wondered if I could crash at your place for a couple days. I got to talk to you about something. You're some kind of big private dick now, aren't you?"

"That's what she told me last night."

You never know what kind of paint-by-the-numbers hell you're going to get yourself into when you pick up a blower these days, but having done so, reluctantly, I also, reluctantly, gave Tequila my address. He said he'd be right over.

"By the way, Tequila," I said, "what do you need a private dick for?"

"Oh, I forgot to tell you," he said. "Somebody's trying to kill my ass."

3

One of the things I didn't need in my life just at the moment was a ghost from Christmas past. I stoked up the espresso machine and the cat and I walked around the kitchen looking into empty cabinets, seeing what provisions I didn't have for a housepest I didn't want.

"Well," I said to the cat, "at least he won't be staying long." The cat didn't say anything but she raised her eyes to the ceiling in a look of disgust. Cats, as a rule, hate housepests of any kind because they view them, most of the time correctly, as agents of change. To a cat, all change is extremely unwelcome. They are lovers of the status quo who do not embrace strange people with strange habits intruding upon their orderly world. Cats, as a group, are a little to the right of Judge Bork.

I walked into the bathroom to throw some cold water on my face and I happened to glance in the mirror. Maybe it was the lighting but it looked like I was beginning to resemble Judge Bork. I hadn't shaved in a few weeks apparently and I damn sure wasn't going to start now just because I had a housepest coming over. After all, he wasn't Prince Charles; he was a burned-out, paranoid guitar picker with a dark streptocumulus cloud the size of Bangladesh hanging over his head. And he thought somebody was trying to kill him. Should be a nice visit.

I sat back down at the desk to wait for Tequila. I found a half-smoked cigar in the wastebasket that had a kind of nice, earthy look to it and fired it up. Cigars, like love, are often better the second time around. There are other parallels and analogies between cigars and love and I might've drawn quite a few of them if I'd been in a romantic or philosophical mood, but I wasn't. I was waiting for Tequila.

Stupid name, Tequila. All the time I'd picked with the guy on the road I never knew his real name. What, I wondered, would make a guy want to call himself Tequila? Why not pick a name like Kinky?

I was jolted out of my reverie by a muffled shout from the street. I got up rather grudgingly and walked over to the kitchen window. I opened the window just enough to lower the temperature in the loft another forty degrees. If it got any colder I could grow orchids in hell.

I looked down into the frozen, gray, viscous afternoon and saw a large black hat seemingly levitating about five feet four inches above the sidewalk. Tequila was not tall but he did wear a big hat. Possibly because he didn't want the pigeons to shit on his lips.

I reached up to the top of the refrigerator and took down the puppet head with the parachute attached and the key to the building wedged in its mouth. It was a friendly Negro puppet head that I'd picked up at a flea market on Canal Street once while waiting for my meticulously selective friend Ratso to Christian the guy down on a pair of dead man's shoes.

The puppet head was about the only housepest that the cat or I were ever likely to abide on anything like a permanent basis. It always had a smile for everyone and a little twinkle in its eye that seemed to say "Have a nice day" without, of course, being so drivingly tedious as to actually *say* "Have a nice day."

I threw the puppet head out the window using the big black hat as a target. The colorful parachute drifted through the drizzle in slow motion like some exotic jellyfish floating just across Jacques Cousteau's nose. I figured even Tequila could work out what to do with the key and find his way up to the fourth floor. I closed the window, went back over to the desk, poured a small jolt of Jameson's into the old bull's horn, killed the shot, and waited for my most unwelcome housepest.

"I never should've given the bastard our address," I said to the cat. The cat said nothing, but it wasn't hard to see that she was irritated. Her eyes had turned from a peaceful green to a rather dangerous-looking yellow.

I heard somebody stumbling on the stairs. I heard voices in the hallway. I looked at the cat and the cat looked at me and I tried, only partially successfully, to

18

dodge the little feline daggers that were clearly coming my way. More voices in the hallway. I took a patient puff on my cigar.

I waited.

There are those who say heaven belongs to those who wait. Obviously, they've never tried to buy theater tickets.

4

It was taking Tequila a hell of a lot longer than your average American to find the loft. Maybe he'd run into a bass player from L.A. lurking somewhere in the hallway and they'd gotten into a jam session. I killed the cigar deep in the heart of a Texas-shaped ashtray, sighed rather deeply, and glanced uneasily at the door. Nothing.

I was just starting to get up and walk over to the door when I heard a loud, persistent rapping like a rather repellent raven on Methedrine. I went to the door, opened it, and there he was. Hat, coat, gloves, knapsack, duffel bag, guitar, face like a road map with more lines than I remembered, topped off with a twitchy little Richard Speck smile.

"Hey, brother," he said as he threw his arms around me in the kind of hug you get only from a fellow road musician or a favorite Jewish aunt. It all came back to me now. I could see that gritty, dusty, long-ago road zigzagging its way like life itself. From Austin to Nashville. From Nashville to L.A. From L.A. to New York. Punctuated by every one-night stand along the painful parade route to eternity.

"Good to see you again, Tequila," I said with a truthfulness that surprised me. "Long time between dreams."

The cat was checking out Tequila's guitar case, which was covered with stickers from every band he'd ever picked with, the way some elderly couple might plaster the back of their RV with things like "We Saw Niagara Falls," "We Visited the Grand Canyon," "We Don't Believe in Anything That Can't Be Reduced to a Bumper Sticker." I walked over to the counter to pour us both a shot.

"You look good, Kinkster," Tequila said, nodding his head like an approving parent.

"Clean living. You don't look too bad yourself," I said.

He looked like shit.

Tequila not only had the ambience of the road about him, he seemed to have a lot of the road physically on him. And in his eyes I could see the dulling pain of being out of the limelight once you'd gotten used to it.

"Been ridin' the couch circuit for a while," he said, like he'd been reading my mail. He seemed to shiver for a moment and then sneezed three times in rapid succession. When he'd run through his repertoire I handed him the glass and he raised it in a toast. "To the Texas Jewboys," he said.

"May they rest in peace," I said.

I told Tequila that my loft was his loft, showed him the couch, and gave him a big green beach towel from Hawaii, which he promptly sneezed into several times.

"Gettin' a cold?" I asked.

"No, man. I think I'm just allergic to cats."

He shook his head and wiped his nose on the beach towel. I was glad it was green.

"Jump in the rain room," I said. "Take a hot shower. I've got to go out for a minute and get some groceries."

"It's a thought," said Tequila. "Wash off some of this Tennessee mud and Georgia clay."

"Make room for some New York pigeon shit."

Tequila smiled. It always made his eyes look even sadder when he smiled.

When I heard the water running I put on my coat, grabbed a few cigars, and headed out into the darkening afternoon. I left Tequila in the loft, closing the door softly like you would for a pilgrim in a sanctuary.

5

There is a difference between the street and the road. I thought about it as I walked down one and remembered the other. Shadows seemed to shiver around me as I went down Vandam and hooked a left somewhere before Seventh Avenue. I must've wandered for a while because by the time I got to the little corner store that specialized in beer, cat food, and perma-logs, I felt like a shadow myself, only there was nowhere for me to fall. The afternoon, like a well-rehearsed magician's trick, had turned into the night.

The guys who ran the store were of a heavy, rather uncertain ethnicity. They looked Italian, Greek, Lebanese, or Pakistani, depending on how you were feeling at the time.

That evening they looked Pakistani. I wasn't wearing seven gold chains with evil-looking icons around my neck but I was feeling somewhat Pakistani myself. Nobody was from here anyway, I thought. Nobody, spiritually speaking, was ever from anywhere. Every place and every person was merely a station on the way. This was the legacy of the road.

I bought a can of 9 Lives tuna for sixty-seven cents. I bought a weird thing that could have been a Vietnamese salami, some coffee, toilet paper, and a few more cans of 9 Lives tuna for sixty-seven cents apiece. I didn't want Tequila telling anybody I didn't take good care of my housepests.

I paid for the stuff and headed home through the gloom. In my memory, I saw a clear picture of a dusty station wagon pulling an overloaded U-haul trailer. Like *A Thousand Clowns,* it was crammed full of people and it rolled easily across the Arkansas of the mind. We'd just tennis-shoed the bill at the Little Rock Holiday Inn and were racing to Dothan, Alabama, to open a show for B. J. Thomas . . .

A doorknob distributor or a circuit rabbi or a traveling nipple-jewelry salesman may think they know the road and perhaps they do. It's their territory, they say. But a country musician's attitude toward the road is that of a jet-set gypsy. The road does not belong to him; he, like Jack Kerouac, belongs to the road.

I stopped off at a liquor store on the way home and picked up a bottle of tequila for Tequila.

By the time I got back onto Vandam, the road had receded to a lukewarm memory and I knew I was back on the street. I trudged the final few blocks of urban tundra, groceries in hand, past garbage trucks, bag ladies, people in a hurry. A bright-red Porsche with its burglar alarm blaring was parked downwind from a garbage truck. Porsche probably belonged to one of Janis

Joplin's friends. It did not seem out of place in the frozen, reeling emptiness of New York night. Nothing ever did.

I commandeered the freight elevator with the one exposed lightbulb up to the fourth floor. It was an uneventful trip. There wasn't even an elevator operator to say "Nice ride" to.

In front of my doorway someone had dropped a guitar pick. Probably Tequila, I thought. But it was funny that I hadn't noticed it on my way out to get the groceries. I turned the pick over and saw that it said "Kinky Friedman" with a Star of David dotting the *i* in *Kinky*. I thought of what Robert B. Parker, my adult pen pal, had once said about the way I signed my letters to him: "Anyone who dots their *i*'s with a Star of David can't be all bad."

In 1974 I'd had the picks made and given them to the band and a few close friends while they'd lasted. The picks, that is.

I turned the pick over in my fingers and smiled wistfully. *Had* to be Tequila, I thought.

When I opened the door to the loft I heard the shower still running. When I went over to the counter to set down the groceries I noticed that the kitchen floor was wet with water flooding out of the bathroom. When I shouted "Hey, Tequila, keep the damn curtain inside the tub!" there was no answer. Like a fairly pissed-off modern-day Jesus, I walked on the water all the way to the bathroom, pounded loudly on the door, and shouted, "Tequila!"

Nothing. Not even a sneeze.

I listened for a moment and thought about my hotwater bill. I opened the bathroom door and the loft suddenly felt like a Navajo sweat lodge. I cut a determined swath through the blanket of steam, trying to focus on anything other than the hot white gauze that kept wrapping itself around my orbs.

I spotted the green beach towel still hanging on the hook. The shower curtain was halfway open and the water flowing out of the tub was a blushing pink slowly going to red like a Hawaiian sunset. What was not very pretty was the jagged hole that was visible waist-high through the curtain.

I took a few steps closer and saw the dark form of a body lying in the tub. One quick glance caused the hair along my forearms to wave like miniature fields of grain. I couldn't say for sure but I made an educated guess about the object that was plugging up the drain.

The thing looked a hell of a lot like what was left of Tequila's head.

"No, McGovern, I can't meet you at The Corner Bistro," I said into the blower on the left. The loft was crawling with cops of all shapes, sizes, and personality profiles, one of the more unpleasant being Detective Sergeant Mort Cooperman, who was standing by my left elbow glinting at me through the cigar smoke.

"Why not?" McGovern wanted to know.

"There's been a little, uh, urban hunting accident over here." I took a nervous puff on the cigar. Cooperman made a little gesture of irritation and I shrugged helplessly and pointed to the blower.

"Is there a story in it?" I heard McGovern ask.

"Oh, I don't know, McGovern," I said, casting a sideways look at Cooperman. "There's about seven hundred cops in the place and there's a stiff in my rain room. Might make a nice little human-interest feature for the Sunday magazine."

"You knew the guy?" asked McGovern.

"I'm afraid so," I said.

"Anybody I knew?"

"I'm afraid not."

"Maybe I ought to get to know him. Every other stiff I've become involved with through you has always led to a good story."

"This one'll be a little harder to get to know, McGovern. His face's been blown off."

"I'll be right over."

"Shall I chill the red wine or the white?" I asked, but McGovern had already hung up. It's safer to get between a pit bull and a throat than it is to stand between a newspaperman and a story. I cradled the blower and turned to find Cooperman still glaring malevolently at me.

"You know something, Tex," he said, "you must be a magnet for deep shit. Last time I was here there was a croaked Kraut. Time before that, it was something else. What was it, Fox?"

Detective Sergeant Buddy Fox was standing nearby in the kitchen, apparently studying his gaunt, sinister features in the shiny reflection of the espresso machine. "Spliced spics," he stated succinctly.

"Yeah," continued Cooperman, "you got a real problem here, Tex. You're livin' in a two-bit loft that seems to want to be a killing field when it grows up."

"And it ain't doin' bad," said Fox with a sandpaper chuckle. He stopped admiring himself, turned, and walked across the loft to the living-room couch, where two cops were crouching and tentatively toying with

25

Tequila's pathetic possessions, gypsies poking at camp-fire embers.

"I know it's a little difficult," said Cooperman, "to make an identification when the party you're identifying ain't got a face, but let's share the experience, Tex." He headed for the crime scene at a casual clip and gestured brusquely for me to follow him. I got up stiffly from the chair. I'd never quite realized how far the desk was from the bathroom door. To Cooperman, I knew it was just routine, but there was something inside me that wasn't all that eager to go back into that rain room. Sooner or later, of course I'd have to.

For one thing, the faster I cooperated with Cooperman, the faster the cops would bug out for the dugout. For another, I had to urinate like a racehorse. Of course, when I thought about my going face-to-bloody-pulp with Tequila again, it seemed mildly preferable to just go outside and take a whiz on an electric fence.

As I took the long walk toward death's steamy threshold, the protective state of shock seemed to wear off and left me to deal coldly in the down-home, night-marish casino of reality. For the first time since the murder I consciously thought of what Tequila had told me over the phone. "Somebody's trying to kill my ass." I entered the bathroom and forced myself to look in the tub.

I didn't know who the somebody was but they'd done a pretty damn good job.

7

Cooperman led me through the crime scene with all the panache of a used-car dealer. There were, according to Cooperman, some interesting dissimilarities between the wound in the victim's body and the wound in the victim's head. The blast that had caught Tequila in the lower chest had been fired, apparently, from a greater distance. There was no evidence of powder burns, which Cooperman explained was called "tattooing," in the chest wound. The head wound, on the other hand, was delivered from a much closer distance and did evidence clear tattooing, as Cooperman, with only faintly concealed pleasure, made a point of emphasizing. Much of Tequila's head was beginning to resemble the extra-lean section at the supermarket meat counter. No eyes, no nose, and definitely low in the fat and cholesterol department. I fought back a sudden tendency to gag.

Cooperman picked up on my discomfort and, with this added encouragement, plunged headlong into a closer examination and explanation of the chest wound. He pointed out the plastic particles from the shower curtain that were clearly visible in the bloody mess. I nodded and tried not to throw up my toenails.

"Isn't this a job for Quincy or somebody?" I asked.

"Yeah," said Cooperman, "Quince'll be along any

27

minute. While we're waiting, suppose you and I have a little chat. What's this guy's name?"

"Tequila."

"Tequila?"

"Tequila. Guitar player used to be in my band. Hadn't seen or spoken to him for thirteen years until today."

"Well, this is what sometimes happens when old friends get back together, isn't it, Tex? It's never quite the same as it used to be." Cooperman winked at me and nodded toward the body in the tub. "You kill him, Tex?"

I explained to Cooperman how I left Tequila in the loft, went out for a while, walked around, bought groceries, bought the bottle of tequila, came back, and found the body.

Cooperman made some notes in his little notebook and flipped the page over the top. A few more characters started to drift in and out of the bathroom. They were talking pro football. I made a move to leave but Cooperman stood his ground with his little book.

"What was his real name?" he asked.

I explained that the only name I'd ever known him by was Tequila. Cooperman laughed unpleasantly to himself.

"That's nice," he said. He shook a Gauloises out of his pack and lit it up with a Zippo. He inhaled and studied me for a moment. Then he said: "Not that we don't trust you, Tex, but where did you buy those groceries?"

"It's a little corner store somewhere over by Tenth Street. Run by Greeks, or Italians, or Pakistanis, or—"

"Make up your rabbit mind, Tex," said Cooperman gruffly.

"Lebanese," I said.

After what seemed like forty days and forty nights Cooperman and I finally left the dumper. We wandered

28

into the kitchen where he sat down at the table and stared at me and I busied myself with the espresso machine so I wouldn't have to stare back at him. He was asking me about how I'd first met Tequila when a rotund little man with an ill-fitting leather coat came rolling into the room like a sentient bowling ball. Without breaking stride he nodded to Cooperman and headed toward the door of the bathroom, which, in terms of activity, was beginning to resemble a recently molested dirt dobber's nest.

When the little man disappeared into the bowels of the rain room Cooperman looked up and smiled the nearest thing to a real smile I'd seen from him in several years. It didn't noticeably warm the loft. It looked more like he was halfheartedly auditioning for "good cop" and didn't much care whether they gave the part to somebody else.

"That," said Cooperman, "was Quincy."

The smile disappeared quicker than a rain forest. Cooperman was now glaring at the doorway to the loft which was mostly filled with a large uniform and the even larger form of McGovern.

"Mike McGovern, *Daily News*," said McGovern, holding his press card and introducing himself like a huge, rather shy, adult Mouseketeer.

"This is fucking terrific," said Cooperman with disgust. Then he rather grudgingly pulled a chair out for McGovern. Like most cops I'd run into, he was ambivalent about the situation. He loved and needed the press. It was reporters he hated. I poured three espressos, collared a nearby bottle of Jameson's, and managed, with some little risk factor, to get them all over to the table in one trip.

"You should have been a waitress in a hash house," said McGovern. This was followed by his hearty Irish laughter which was always a little too loud. Particularly on this occasion.

"I thought about waitressing for a while," I said as

I sipped my espresso, "but the opportunities and benefits in the dental hygiene area finally won me over. Sorry we're out of whipped cream, McGovern. I could've served you an Irish coffee."

McGovern poured an extremely large portion of Jameson's into his espresso. "That's all right," he said.

8

The espresso was hot and bitter and the conversation was starting to turn that way. McGovern could see that the rain room was indeed the storm center of quite some little activity, could see the flashes from photographs being taken, could see plainclothes dicks and uniforms drifting in and out like human flotsam and jetsam in a tide of events he was not being allowed to be a part of. Apparently, McGovern was not to be privy to the privy, and this did not go down well with the polite, but very large, Irishman. Every time McGovern would make a comment like "So there really *is* a stiff in there," Cooperman would respond with a grim "Sit tight" and stare malevolently into his espresso leaves. And I still had to urinate.

This rather unpleasant Hispanic standoff continued through another round of espresso and several direct shots of Jameson's fired point-blank down the necks of McGovern and myself. Cooperman, of course, did not drink on the job, but it was difficult to see what the job was unless you wanted to count restraining a large and increasingly angry Irish journalist, which I guess, in all fairness, you could say was a job. But Cooperman loved his work and must've said "Sit tight" about five times before Fox finally walked over and interrupted the tension convention with a little tension of his own.

"Sorry to bust up your little tea party here," he said, "but we've found something in the luggage. If these two fine gentlemen don't mind, I think you ought to come have a look." He smiled a vaguely serpentine smile in the direction of myself and McGovern and motioned with his head for Cooperman. Cooperman got up and followed Fox over to the other side of the living room.

Fox's gesture with his head, I reflected, was somewhat reminiscent of the way the natives of Borneo pointed things out from time to time. In Borneo, it's considered quite rude to point with your hands, so the people there point with their heads or stick their lips out and point with their lips. By the time the U.S. Peace Corps forcibly returned me to my own culture, I'd gotten pretty good at pointing at things with my lips. Unfortunately, this particular talent did not have great application in the Western world.

I wondered for a moment whether all cops and all natives of Borneo made similar gestures with their heads. Was this significant? Could there be other similarities between the two tribes?

Of course, I decided, there were things the two did not have in common. The natives of Borneo are a gentle, peace-loving people. Also, they are almost never rude. In defense of cops, however, it must be said that during a murder investigation, etiquette, as well as a number of other things, often quite rightly must go overboard. One of those other things was my bladder, and I was just thinking of the possibility of urination in one of my landlord's potted plants when I saw McGovern get up determinedly from his chair and start moving like a surly aircraft carrier toward the rain room.

Very unpleasant, I thought.

31

Halfway there I caught up with McGovern, but my efforts to stop his forward progress were somewhat similar to a valiant young water spider trying to reason with a right-wing hippopotamus. In a last-ditch effort I got between McGovern and the bathroom and attempted to establish eye contact with my friend who, more and more, was taking on the behavioral traits of an escapee from the gorilla house at the Bronx Zoo.

"McGovern!" I shouted in a hoarse stage whisper. "Hold the weddin'! The body's not going anywhere!"

Concerning this last, I was very wrong. What finally stopped McGovern was the sight of a small parade of men trooping out of the bathroom carrying a body bag. McGovern and I stood aside and watched in silence as they carried Tequila across the kitchen and out the door of the loft.

"Well," said McGovern, "that's that."

"Not quite," said Sergeant Cooperman, looming surprisingly close to my left shoulder like an unpleasant parrot. "Want to tell me again why you agreed to let . . . uh . . . Tequila stay here?"

"I already told you," I said. "Tequila called. He needed a place to crash, he said. He'd been ridin' the couch circuit for quite a while apparently. So I told him he could stay here for a few days."

"Isn't that interesting," said Cooperman.

"Not especially."

"Oh, I think it is," said Cooperman smugly.

"Why is that?" I asked with just the slightest qualm of anxiety.

"I've got to call the boss and I'll want you and McGovern here to witness this, but we've found something a little unusual in . . . uh . . . Tequila's duffel bag."

"Like what?" I lit a fresh cigar and took a tentative puff or two.

"Like twenty-five thousand dollars in cash."

McGovern's eyes got a great deal wider. Then a large smile spread across his face. I don't know what my face looked like but an involuntary intake of breath caused me to choke momentarily on my own cigar smoke. Always a bit of a social embarrassment. When I did recover my poise, my mind was whirring with the implications of this latest finding.

"Well," asked Cooperman, "what do you have to say for yourself, Tex?"

"He could've stayed here all week on that," I said.

9

"Music's a gift," said McGovern, shouting over the jukebox at the Corner Bistro. "It brings people together! It makes people happy! You're blessed, man, you're blessed!"

"Yeah," I said. "Maybe I could play rhythm guitar for the Dalai Lama."

It was after two in the morning and I was just grateful that I'd finally had the chance to grab my Republican by the neck and then get the hell out of the loft. I thought for a while I'd need a forklift to get Cooperman out but he finally left, promising, like MacArthur, to return, and, like MacArthur, I knew he'd probably be pretty tedious about it when he did.

McGovern motioned to Dave the bartender for another drink. McGovern was drinking a Vodka

McGovern. Dave, of course, was more than a little familiar with this drink: a rather large helping of vodka, soda, fresh orange juice, and a squeeze of lime. Not a woosie little piece of lime peel. It had to be a *squeeze* of lime. The Vodka McGovern was one of the few things in this world that McGovern could be said to be truly meticulous about. He could always tell you and always *would* tell you if it was wrong. Dave, according to McGovern, made just about the finest Vodka McGovern in Manhattan. Dave put another one together with the speed and agility of a neurosurgeon, placed it before McGovern, and looked questioningly at me.

"I'll have a diet hemlock," I said.

I didn't enjoy having a friend of mine, even one I didn't like all that much, go to Jesus in quite this violent a fashion. And how did I know whether or not I liked Tequila? I hadn't really seen the boy in thirteen years and now it looked like it might be a while before I woke up next to him in hell.

The jukebox had thankfully gone silent and the place was starting to thin out. I was trying rather unsuccessfully to rid my mind of the image of Tequila's bloody body lying in my bathtub, and McGovern and Dave were standing across the bar from each other just to the left of me talking about Portugal.

Strangely enough, I was starting to miss Tequila. I took the guitar pick out of my pocket and gazed at it as if it were a tiny mirror to my memories. McGovern had asked me an excessive number of questions about Tequila and had found it rather irritating that I knew almost nothing about the murder and not a hell of a lot more about the man. Of course, performers often tend to shroud their origins in mystery because it makes for better press. Then they start believing their own press and pretty soon they can't remember who they actually are. Back when I was touring with the Jewboys I used to give a different age and place of birth in every interview. Tequila, now that I thought about it, had probably had something of the same idea and that was why nobody really knew dick about him.

"It was about one hundred eighty miles west of Jib," I heard Dave saying.

I turned to McGovern. ' Jib?" I asked.

"Gibralter," said McGovern. "Dave once owned a bar on the southern coast of Portugal. When was that, Dave?"

"Sixty-eight."

"What was that place called? The City of Light?"

"It was a little fishing village," said Dave, "called Playa de Luz. Means 'Beach of Light.' "

McGovern was moving smoothly through his fourth Vodka McGovern and I was drinking whatever it was that Dave was putting in front of me. It might've really been diet hemlock because it was taking a while to kick in.

"Of course it's not the City of Light, McGovern," I said. "The City of Light is either Paris or heaven or wherever Jerry Lewis isn't."

McGovern laughed his hearty Irish laugh. The one that was just a little too loud for indoor use. I made the mistake of mentioning it to McGovern.

"Well, isn't there such a thing," he said not quite innocently, "as hearty *Jewish* laughter?"

"I'm afraid not, McGovern. The Jews have very little in this world to laugh about. Almost as little as the Irish."

"That's why we laugh," said McGovern.

Two rounds later Dave had told us all about Playa de Luz, the bar called Godot's, the little terrace that extended out over the Atlantic, the ex-French Foreign Legionnaire who helped him run the place, and the large old hound dog named Dingus that, much to his regret, he'd had to leave behind in Portugal. The southern coast of Portugal was so beautiful and the people were so great, Dave explained, that eventually he got tired of it and had to come back to New York.

I watched the vague, dreary, late night with David

Letterman shadows move by the windows of the Bistro and wondered wistfully whether any people in Portugal were standing at a bar talking about New York. Probably not, I figured.

Suddenly I felt as tired and used up as the year itself. By my latest calculations there were five more days to go till New Year's and I wasn't at all sure that the current year or I was going to make it. And Tequila was seeping back into my mind again or maybe he'd never left. Besides the tragedy of the whole thing, I still felt some lingering shock that somebody would blow a guy away in my bathtub while I was out shopping for groceries. It was an invasion of privacy.

I thought of the huge caseloads the NYPD routinely handled and I was not optimistic about Cooperman's chances of ever nailing the killer. I thought of Tequila again. How ragged but righteous his face had looked. How he'd hugged me.

As I listened to Dave and McGovern droning on in the near distance I felt like a child hearing his own secret messages in adult cocktail chatter. A child staying up late. Listening to muffled voices in the hallway.

10

There was something I probably should've been doing besides tying and macraméing my nose hairs, but I couldn't figure out what it was. There is a time after the death of someone you know that leaves you shocked, confused, and as rattled as a tin can tied to a cat's tail by a mischievous little neighborhood boy with a cute cowlick in a painting by Norman Rockwell. Life might've been a magazine but if this state of ennui and troubled inactivity went on much longer we'd both be out of circulation. A friend of mine had been whacked right under my nose and I had to do something. I just didn't have a clue as to what that something was.

When I woke up it was Monday morning. A numbing cold had invaded the loft, a dreary mask of gray urban oblivion had descended upon the city, the garbage trucks were grumbling loudly outside my window, and I realized I was not in Portugal. I also realized that I was freezing my balls off.

The cat was curled up tighter than a fossil snail on top of my stomach and did not seem to be eager to move. I lifted my back off the mattress a few times and made a couple of false starts toward getting out of bed but the cat wasn't buying it. One fast sit-up, I thought, would've probably shot the little booger right off the bed and onto the floor but there was no telling what she might've grabbed on the way down. It wasn't the most serious quandary I'd ever been in in my life but it was a problem.

Even if you hate cats it's usually not a good idea to try to shove one off your stomach. Cats like stomachs, they don't like to be shoved, and, if you try to shove one off your stomach, it won't like you. Not that it liked you a hell of a lot to begin with.

If you love cats, the problem becomes even more difficult because you have to contend not only with the logistics of removing the cat from your stomach but also with the expression in its eyes, which, under the circumstances, could be that of betrayal, anger, or even shocked disbelief. Painful for any cat lover. Distressing for any sensitive American. More than most New Yorkers would care to deal with before breakfast. A foot away, a face full of freeze-dried feline hatred staring down past your irises into the back of your head, coldly observing the weather-beaten remnants of your dreams.

By grabbing the comforter on either side of the cat and gently but firmly stretching it tight, then wriggling slowly to my right, I was able to slip out from under the problem. I put on my purple bathrobe with cat hairs all over it and the cigar hole burned through it, walked purposely over to the espresso machine, fed it with a little of my special Kona-Kilimanjaro mix, and turned on the juice and cut the damn thing loose.

I lit my first cigar of the morning with a kitchen match, took a few puffs, opened the window, looked out at the gray people scurrying here and there across the gray morning. It wasn't a bad feeling not to be one of them.

I glanced into the bedroom. The cat had not moved a muscle. This was good. If I could round up a reasonably well-preserved bagel and a can of tuna, the cat and I could have a late power brunch together. Sort of get the week off on the right footing.

I looked back out the window again, thought gray thoughts. Getting out from under a cat was one thing, I reflected. Getting out from under some of the other problems in life could prove a bit more tedious. Like the ramifications of having an old friend blown from your rain room all the way to kingdom come and then finding twenty-five thousand dollars in his duffel bag. That one could turn out to be a little gnarly. The case was full of loose, untidy threads, I thought. If things didn't go well I could always open up a tailor shop.

I turned and glanced briefly at the solitary, unopened bottle of tequila still sanding like a lonely sentry on the kitchen counter. If things didn't work out with Winnie for New Year's Eve, I could always have a date with that bottle, I figured. I walked over to the espresso machine, which was humming and steaming and beginning to make little Jimi Hendrix noises, drew myself a cupful, walked back over to the window, and looked at some more gray.

I was semiconsciously humming "Oh, What a Beautiful Morning" when I noticed two figures coming toward my building from across the street. I'd just gotten to the line "The corn is as high as an elephant's eye" when I noticed that one of them was Winnie Katz.

I took a slight step backward so that I could see the parties in the street but they couldn't see me. It was a technique I'd learned from *Rear Window*. The girl walking next to Winnie was one I hadn't seen before. She had a huge, gorgeous mass of reddish-blond moss, only a portion of which was shoved under a cute black cowboy hat, and slightly Oriental-looking orbs that were so green they shined like smuggled emeralds. Both girls looked flushed and radiant as if they were coming back from a break after a workout or something.

I leaned forward over the sill as Winnie was negotiating the lock on the front door of the building and from four floors up I could see that even among dancers' asses, this girl had a dancer's ass. Maybe the nicest one I'd seen since a few years back when a little Palestinian friend of mine had gone to the arms of Allah. Some guys had all the luck.

They were just two broads walking into a building in New York City, but as I watched the big metal door swing open I saw something that caused a little louvered cat door in my heart to swing shut.

They entered the hallway holding hands.

It was the first time I'd ever been jealous of a broad and I wasn't even sure which one I was jealous of. I took a bitter sip of espresso, closed the window, and walked numbly back toward my desk like a journeyman fighter who'd just had his bell rung again.

It was about that time when I first noticed that both my phone book and my puppet head were missing.

39

11

A power brunch with a cat will take you only so far in life. After that you've got to go out and make things happen for yourself.

I went into the bathroom to take a Waylon Jennings Bus Shower in the sink and to think about shaving. During these unsavory ablutions I registered for the first time the fact that Cooperman had taken my shower curtain as evidence. At this moment, Quincy and his personable Japanese assistant, Salmon Skin Roll, might be poring over the curtain in the lab looking for whatever vestigial brain cells Tequila hadn't already fried with the Texas Jewboys on the Left Coast. I couldn't imagine what else they could be doing with the curtain. Fingerprints maybe. I didn't know a hell of a lot about guns and I didn't really want to, but I did know that running a ballistics test on a shotgun blast was about as practical as pissing up a rope.

I left the cat in charge and snaked my way through the bleak afternoon until I reached the din and racket of Canal Street. I'd been on Canal Street many times in the past but this was the first time I'd ever gone there shopping for a shower curtain. Almost makes you feel like a young suburbanite buying decorative things for the home until you stumble on a large Samoan selling used dildos on the sidewalk. You can buy anything on Canal Street if you're crazy enough to want it.

The first store I went into sold pornographic books,

hassocks, handcuffs, and World War II incendiary bombs. It was sort of a country store in the city. There was a fat guy in charge wearing a Giants warm-up jacket. A large dog was lying on the floor. Part German shepherd, part mutt, with big brown eyes that looked almost as sad as Tequila's. Jewish shepherd, I decided.

"Do you have any shower curtains?" I asked.

"Louie!" he shouted to the back of the store.

A guy who looked like a human groundhog gradually emerged from somewhere in the musky, raincoat-wrapped, extended bowels of the shop.

"Shower curtain!" the fat guy in the warm-up jacket shouted.

Louie turned at about a 78-degree angle and made a beeline for the far corner of the place. I edged past the nose of the Jewish shepherd and followed Louie, my Virgil of Canal Street, into an era that had ended before I was born but was constantly being brought back from the dead by trendy Americans, if only sartorially. I felt a little uneasy, like a kid just before he gets lost in a museum.

For a moment I thought of my friend Ratso, the editor of *National Lampoon*. He was loyal, seedy, parsimonious to a fault. This was his kind of place. Practically his whole wardrobe was lying around on open tables and in cardboard boxes. Ratso'd been a lot of help to me in the past on a number of pretty unsavory cases. I would've liked to have talked to him now about Tequila, but Ratso was in California working on some kind of screenplay for a while. This was Ratso's kind of place, but he wasn't here.

In a few minutes I had the curtain and was heading back to pay the fat guy. He was now fairly busy picking his nose with a camouflage handkerchief and examining the contents.

"Find what you were looking for?" he asked.

"Yeah," I said, holding up the shower curtain. "These little boogers are hard to come by."

41

"So are these," he said as he shook out the handkerchief.

I paid the guy and walked out into the pale, refracted light of the last decade of the twentieth century and didn't even blink.

I walked up Canal, took a right on Mott Street past the Chinese dwarf-painting pastel pictures, and realized that Big Wong's was closed on Mondays. Big Wong's is always closed on Mondays. In all the excitement of shopping for a shower curtain, I'd forgotten.

I went two more blocks up Mott Street and turned into one of those twenty-four-hour places that Jack Kerouac used to hang out in. I didn't see Jack but my waiter looked a lot like Allen Ginsberg.

When you go into an all-night place in the afternoon there's a certain carryover of spirit sometimes that kind of warms the soul. There were few patrons at this time of day but you could almost hear the leftover conversations and smell the whiff of sweet-and-sour stale perfume wafting in with the wontons.

I used an entrance line that my old pal Dylan Ferrero, road manager of the Texas Jewboys, had often used in the past.

"Sirhan Sirhan," I told the waiter, "party of one."

I put the shower curtain on the table, gave my order, and smoked a cigar while I waited for the food. Another nice thing about twenty-four-hour Chinese restaurants is that they don't give a damn whether you smoke a cigar, put a shower curtain on the table, or hang yourself from the shower rod.

I thought about one bleary night about a year ago in Chinatown when Goat Carson was sucking up a large oily-looking plate of snails at three o'clock in the morning and reminiscing about dancing with Judy Garland at the Salvation Club just two weeks before her death. He said she looked like "a marshmallow with two little toothpicks for legs." I thought, strangely, about the last time I'd hugged Tequila.

My mind drifted macabrely to the little particles of plastic shower curtain embedded like highway reflectors in the wound to Tequila's body. The wound that had not evidenced the tattooing effect. I thought of the wound to the head that had evidenced tattooing but had contained no embedded shower-curtain particles. There was meaning in this somewhere but I couldn't figure out what it was. Not for the life of me.

If Cooperman did not come up with something fairly soon I was very much afraid that I was spiritually obligated to get involved in this one myself. And this one looked like it might go a lot deeper than the water running over the tub.

"What you got in package?" the waiter asked.

"Curtains for somebody," I said.

12

By the time I got out of Chinatown it was pushing five o'clock and there was a long line of honking four-wheeled penises struggling to get the hell out of Manhattan. Many of them were on their way to God's country. New Jersey. The sooner the better, I thought, as I lugged the shower curtain up Hudson like a weary circuit preacher hugging a ragged Bible.

When I got back to the loft there was one note under my door, one message on the answering machine, and one cat who did not seem particularly pleased to see me.

43

"Honey, I'm home," I said to the cat.

The cat did not answer. Cats can be clever, wily, ruthless, and brutally persistent, but the ability to understand facetiousness is not a quality that is often found on their dance cards.

I decided to ignore the cat and open the note at the same time. Kill two birds and get stoned. The note was from Winnie. It said to call her. I did.

"Hello . . ."

"Win, it's Kinky. About New Year's . . ."

"Let's discuss it later."

I lit a cigar and waited. There wasn't a hell of a lot of later, I thought. When she spoke again it was in a softer voice.

"I'm sorry to hear about what happened to your friend. He seemed very nice."

"You met Tequila?"

"We met in the hallway when he was looking for your loft. He seemed like such a lost little lamb."

I took a disbelieving puff on the cigar, thought of Tequila with twenty-five thousand simoleons in his duffel bag, coughed politely a few times, and rolled my eyes at the cat. Never eat at a place called Mom's, I thought, and never underestimate the charm of a road musician.

"Lost little lamb," I said. "Go on."

"He said you were the only one he trusted."

"Guy was in worse shape than I thought. What else did he say?"

"He said that he'd come all the way from Sixteenth Avenue and now he was lost in the hallway. That's in Brooklyn, isn't it?"

"The hallway?"

"Sixteenth Avenue, shrimp dick."

Because of the fact that they don't have a shrimp themselves, lesbians may, at times, become a bit acerbic with the opposite sex. There were slightly adolescent things I could've said to Winnie at the time, like "You'll eat those words," or "Someday you'll come to realize, quite literally, probably, that I have a giant prawn." Fortunately, my roots are firmly enough grounded in my manhood that I can be gracious about these things and need not resort to such petulant, pre-pubescent rejoinders.

"Mr. Shrimp Dick, to you," I said as I calmly cradled the blower.

I had other fish to fry. I had a phone message to check on that could conceivably represent the call that could change my life, I had a shower curtain to hang, and, if those things weren't enough, my mind was already beginning to worm its wandering way down to Sixteenth Avenue.

If Winnie wasn't willing to walk beside me, she could get the hell out of my way.

So could everybody else.

13

The shower curtain was a piece of cake, the phone message was a piece of work, and Sixteenth Avenue, I soon came to learn, was a piece of real estate you'd better not buy if you ever wanted to play monopoly again. But first things first.

As any good bisexual interior decorator will tell you, having the rain room in order often can set the mood and decor for the rest of the house. It is commonly called the centerpiece on the table of interior decoration. Having the curtain strung nicely across the shower rod gave me such a sense of peace and completion that I took a bottle of Jameson's over to the desk and poured a celebratory shot into the old bull's horn. I broke out a fresh cigar, lopped the butt off in my desk-sized guillotine, fired it up with a kitchen match, took a few relaxed puffs, then killed the shot. Then I played back the message on the answering machine.

It was not music to my ears.

It was Cleve.

Cleve was a former road manager of the Texas Jewboys, a former musician, a former manager of the Lone Star Cafe, and a current occupant of the monstro-wig ward at the Pilgrim State Mental Hospital. He was there for murdering not one, not two, but three country singers as well as seriously injuring my scrotum. For a while I thought I might have to become a traveling falsetto yodeler, but, as they say in Hollywood, time heals everything. Even your scrotum.

It wasn't that Cleve actually caused trouble anymore. It was just that he was sort of a harbinger of trouble. Whenever he called with some new idea for reviving and revitalizing my somewhat dormant musical career, I soon seemed to find myself quite predictably in a world of shit. This time I hadn't even needed Cleve's help to get there but he called anyway. I figured I'd get it over with and call him back. He answered on the first ring and he knew who I was as soon as I spoke. At least his hand-to-ear coordination and the voice-identification centers of his brain were functioning.

"Kinkster!" he shouted in the brittle, barely modulated tone of all seriously ill people. "Your pet shark here has a whale of an idea this time!"

"I'm sure you do, Cleve," I said. If they ever let him out of there there'd really be hell to pay, I thought.

46

I puffed a couple of preparatory puffs on the cigar and then said: "All right. Spit it."

"We do a reunion tour of the Texas Jewboys!"

I sat in a stony silence. The idea was so far off base, even Luis Aparicio would've gotten picked off for nurturing it.

"Cleve," I said in what I hoped was a calming, rational tone, "the guys in the band hated each other's guts, they've been scattered to the winds for thirteen years, and, at our peak popularity, we barely had the commercial success to make a national tour, much less a reunion tour more than a decade later. And on top of that, I'd rather go on a lifelong bean-curd diet than go back out on the road again."

"I anticipated there would be problems," said Cleve.

I smoked the cigar and looked at the cat, trying to pretend that no conversation had taken place. It worked for a few seconds, until Cleve started going over the imaginary itinerary in his mind with me. He'd anticipated there would be problems, I said to myself as Cleve recited the names of various American cities as if he were reading them off the moving destination roll on the front of a Greyhound bus stopped at a little station on a rainy afternoon before the world went digital and something was lost.

"Cleve," I said hopelessly.

"New York, Boston, Philadelphia, Washington—"

"Forget it, Cleve."

"Chicago . . ."

I knew from experience that when Cleve got a hot new idea it usually required a fired-up Gurkha unit to disabuse him of the notion. I wasn't up to the task and I knew it so I did what everyone does with the criminally insane. I agreed with him.

"Sounds like a winner, Cleve. We'll have to talk about it."

"Oh, I've already talked it over with most of the

47

guys. They're up for it. A few may require a little arm-twisting but that's what you have your pet shark for. I also talked to a reporter about the idea and he sounded very interested."

"It wasn't Bob Woodward, was it?"

"I don't remember his name. Said he'd call back to flesh it out. You don't have Tequila's number, do you?"

Tequila's number was up, but there was no point in disturbing Cleve's precarious emotional architecture with the truth. There wasn't going to be any reunion tour anyway. I figured my musical career had pretty well bottomed out and might be in position to rise modestly again if Cleve could pull his lips together for a while. I shuddered at the thought of the possible media fallout of having a career comeback being put together by an agent/publicist operating out of a mental hospital. I'd worked very hard to get my career to bottom out and I wasn't going to have somebody blow it for me now.

"Tequila's going to be on the road for a while," I said.

"Well, when you see him, tell him to give me a call."

"Sure thing, Cleve."

"Detroit, St. Louis . . ."

After I'd hung up with Cleve I paced around a bit and noticed it'd gotten very dark in the loft. I turned on a few lights here and there but it didn't seem to make much difference.

14

All that night I remained physically at Vandam Street but mentally my address was somewhere along Sixteenth Avenue. I had Noxema or amnesia or whatever you call it when you can't sleep, so I didn't. I sat up with the cat and drank Jameson's and thought about Tequila.

In the early hours of the morning I took a long shot and called Cooperman. I hadn't heard from him since Tequila had gotten himself capped. Not that I expected all that much from the NYPD. I never had liked or trusted cops, especially New York cops, but I had to admit they were better than L.A. cops, who were recruited from little towns in Alabama, looked like Hitler Youth, and crucified you for jaywalking. New York cops, at least, never cared much what you did. There hasn't been a moving violation issued to anyone in New York City for at least twenty years. Killing one person in New York is all right, but you can get your wrist slapped if you ice two people. If you smoke more than two people you might find yourself organizing reunion tours.

"Sixth Precinct," said a bored and grumpy voice. I identified myself, asked for Detective Sergeant Cooperman, and was put on hold.

I held.

At 2:45 in the morning it beat having a nightmare

49

about a large green whale landing like a helicopter on Vandam Street with Texas state troopers pouring out of its mouth to arrest me for retroactive obscenity in a show I did in Dallas in 1973. Cooperman came on the line after I'd just about given up on him, like a verbal bulldozer knocking down Tom Joad's farmhouse.

"You're in luck, Tex. I'm here. What in the fuck do you want?"

"I was just calling, Sergeant, to inquire if there's been any progress on the Tequila situation."

"Yeah, Tex. We got him ID'd. Name's . . ." Here there was a pause of about half a minute in which I could hear Cooperman riffling through papers and cursing all Americans who'd come to New York from the great state of Texas. People in Texas didn't generally hold New Yorkers who'd moved to Texas in very high regard either, but this didn't seem like the time or place to communicate this information to Cooperman.

". . . Kirby McMillan," said Cooperman.

"Kirby McMillan?"

"Kirby McMillan."

I was going to say "Kirby McMillan?" again but I thought better of it. Tequila as Kirby McMillan would take some getting used to. Of course, now there was all the time in the world to get used to it.

"Fairly Yuppie name for a country guitar picker," I said.

"Aw, you know these country entertainers, Tex. They got all kinds of funny names. Used to know a guy named Kinky once. Wasn't much of a guitar picker so he thought he'd turn to crime-solving. Sort of a mid-life career change. Well, he had a little beginner's luck at first. Then one day he got in over his head and—"

At this point I put the blower gently down on the desk, took a cigar out of my porcelain Sherlock Holmes head, lopped off the butt, and lit it with my latest Bic, a hot-pink little number that I'd bought from a Negro

50

with no legs on the Bowery. It worked fine, I'm happy to report.

I'd heard Cooperman's whole, rather tedious megillah on a goodly number of occasions and it always started the same way, rolled along for a seeming eternity, and then ended with something grotesque and horrible happening to Kinky. The only place where Cooperman provided any variety at all was in what particularly sordid and macabre ending befell the perpetrator. In this case, me. It was kind of like watching a fairly familiar soap opera where you know the characters and what they usually would do and you only really watch for the little twist at the end.

I picked up the blower just in time to hear Cooperman saying: ". . . found his left arm—the one with the Ubangi tattoo—floating in the East River still holding on to that little pickaninny puppet head, and his right arm—the one he picked the guitar with—was found crammed into the mouth of that big lizard on top of the Lone Star Cafe . . . had all its fingers cut off . . ."

"And they found the body," I injected, "in the trunk of a fifty-seven DeSoto at JFK."

"Newark," said Cooperman.

"Look, Sergeant," I said, "a woman I know in the building has told me—"

"The dyke upstairs?"

"—has told me that she spoke to Tequila just before he came into my loft. He told her he'd come all the way from Sixteenth Avenue."

"Now, isn't that interesting."

"Yeah. It's Brooklyn, isn't it?"

"Yeah. It's Brooklyn. It's also Bensonhurst. It's also the Gambino family's backyard."

"Maybe they'll invite us over for some barbecued cannolis."

"This is a red-hot potato, Tex, and it's not my fucking beat. I'm gonna lateral it off to the OCCB."

51

"What's the OCCB?"

"The Organized Crime Control Board."

"Yup. All the initials check out."

"Twelve million people in this city don't fucking get involved, Tex. You don't want to end up visitin' the fish, you goddamn sure better see you're one of them."

"I'll do my best," I said. "You guys didn't by any chance take my little black book with phone numbers in it, did you?"

Cooperman laughed a hoarse, gravelly, but seemingly genuine, laugh. It sounded like somebody shoveling a light layer of snow off a driveway.

"Don't flatter yourself," he said.

15

I never got around to asking Cooperman whether or not he'd taken the puppet head but it was probably just as well. There were a lot of ways not to get involved with this thing and all I had to do was find one and run with it. It didn't seem like that tough a job. But life sometimes is like a kitten with a ball of yarn. It starts out going harmlessly along in one direction and before you know it, it rolls under the couch and you reach under there to get it and before you know it, you're staring into the limpid blue eyes of a twelve-year-old member of Future Hatchet Murderers of America who's hiding from imaginary Iroquois and he kills you and before you know it, the kitten is using your scrotum for a bean bag. Next thing you know, you're on Paul Harvey, page four.

Essentially, I'd known all this since I was eight years old playing baseball in my backyard. Still, I figured if I was careful enough, I could explore around the edges of the thing without actually becoming involved. This notion proved to contain a small amount of pilot error on my part, but we all have a different interpretation of what "not getting involved" means. That's what makes for horse racing. It's also, unfortunately, what makes for waking up next to a horse's head.

It was Tuesday morning. Tequila'd been croaked on Sunday. There were four days left in the old year and something told me each of them would be tie-dyed with his blood.

In the aftermath of the murder I had, perhaps, not been thinking as clearly as I might've. It was now very apparent to me that I had *not* misplaced my little black phone book. Nor did I need my local pointy-headed ACLU representative to tell me that the cops legally couldn't've lifted it. The conclusion was inevitable. Tequila's murderer had goniffed my phone book. I found speculating *why* to be a moderately frightening experience.

On impulse, I walked over to the refrigerator and stared somberly at the empty space on top where the puppet head usually resided. You could probably concoct numerous reasons why a killer might steal a little book with phone numbers and addresses in it, but what rational homicidal maniac on the planet would goniff somebody's puppet head? It was one of those senseless crimes.

In desperation, I looked into the dark, cobwebby space between the back of the refrigerator and the wall. Once my eyes adjusted I saw a little black face smiling up at me. It was like finding an old friend you thought had been lost from your life.

I picked it up, dusted it off, and put it gently back

53

on top of the refrigerator. As a test, I opened the refrigerator door and slammed it shut hard. I repeated this Butt-Holdsworth Home for the Bewildered–type behavior several more times but the puppet head did not move. Its smile did not even noticeably quiver.

I never like to lift anything heavier than a Freudian slip, but, subconsciously, I sort of knew something was forebodingly wrong. By the time I consciously figured out what it was, of course, it was too late.

16

Friday evening I was coming home from miniature golf or something when I found Ratso's body lying on my doorstep.

Ratso was not even supposed to be in New York. He was definitely not supposed to be sprawled facedown in my hallway. He was supposed to be in L.A. working on screenplays and getting acclimated to the Southern California life-style so he could move out there and eat yogurt happily ever after. At the moment, that didn't look like a real viable possibility.

"Who did it, Ratso?" I shouted. "What happened?"

Ratso said nothing. He just lay there like a large, ill-proportioned doormat.

I thought fleetingly of the many times Ratso and I had teamed up together to tackle cases that the NYPD had already consigned to its "open" file. I thought of

Ratso, my old pal, in his seedy sartorial splendor sally-
ing forth in a spirit of stumbling ingenuousness. If the
soul of Dr. Watson could be said to be alive today, it
surely dwells in the large and sometimes rather unhy-
gienic temple of Ratso's body. Now I was very much
afraid that I was witnessing the final destruction of that
temple.

"Get up, Ratso!" I whispered hoarsely. "You don't
know where that floor's been."

Ratso didn't move.

I thought of what all New Yorkers say to comfort
themselves when confronted with the death of someone
they know. "He's not really dead," I told myself. "He's
just not currently working on a project." It didn't help.

I crept closer, reached down, and tried to find signs
of a pulse in Ratso's wrist. He didn't seem to have any
veins. I remembered what William Burroughs had once
said to the shoeshine boy in New Orleans: "If I had
veins like that, I'd have myself a party."

I felt around a little closer to his hand and pressed
my thumb down harder. I felt faint flutterings like the
kind that might emanate from a beautiful butterfly in
some idiot's collection when nobody's looking.

I knew it wasn't wise to move someone like Ratso.
You could further injure the victim and, very possibly,
you could injure your scrotum. I unlocked the door, ran
to the blower, and dialed 911. I gave them everything
but my shoe size and they said they'd be right over. I
stepped over Ratso, went back down the stairs, left the
front door of the building open, climbed back up the
stairs, stepped over Ratso again, went to the counter,
and poured a rather shaky shot of Jameson's.

As I killed the shot I heard a grinding, growling
noise that sounded like it should've been coming from
my stomach but wasn't. It was coming from the hallway
and it was not a very pleasant thing to hear but, in this
instance, it sounded as comforting as the music from

55

the harp in the lobby of the Omni Berkshire where you can have tea and crumpets, talk about Ambrose Bierce or pork-belly futures, and hear otherworldly notes peacefully penetrating your soul whether you like it or not.

The noise from the hallway came again. It sounded quite a bit louder this time, like a dog working Yorick's skull. You couldn't keep a good rat down, I thought, as I poured a celebratory shot of Jameson's into the bull's horn. I killed the shot, walked over to the door, and very carefully slid Ratso into the loft like a large sack of incoming mail. I was rewarded with a series of grunts and grinding noises but no words. It was one of the more pleasant conversations I'd had with Ratso in a long time.

Eventually, the paramedics showed up, checked Ratso over, and determined that he had a concussion and a broken jaw. They put him on a stretcher and carried him down to the meat wagon. I got in back with Ratso and off we drove to St. Vincent's.

I won't trouble you with the tedium of the next few hours. Filling out forms, calling Cooperman, greeting Cooperman at the hospital, telling Cooperman I didn't know a damn thing about what had happened.

But in spite of all that, I was glad I'd accompanied Ratso to the hospital. If I hadn't, they probably would've admitted him as Ratso Doe or something. Also, it wouldn't have been too pleasant if I'd stood at the kitchen window and watched them take him away alone in the meat wagon.

Every time you watch a meat wagon drive off, it takes a little piece of you with it.

17

It was after four in the morning when I got back to the loft, and by the next day at this time it would be what is designated by certain Western cultures as the New Year. In certain Eastern cultures it's business as usual. Kill a Jew for Allah. Kill a Sikh for Buddha. Poke the prisoner's eyes out with bicycle spokes. Worship a cow. Shun a pig. Have sexual relations with a chicken. In the West, of course, we had all we could do just to kill an evening for Christ.

Ratso had now been at St. Vincent's for several hours. I was sitting at the kitchen table smoking a cigar. The cat was sleeping on my lap. I just wished there was a place I could bring the old year, leave it out on the lot. Don't know who they'd sell it to. Some hapless, death-bound American teenager might like to kick its tires. Maybe an old, friendly Caribbean yardman from somebody's childhood. Might've been the kind of year he'd like to drive around in.

I didn't know if it was hot or if it was me and I didn't really care. I put the cat down on the kitchen table and walked over to the window. I tried to raise it but it was jammed. Always live in a house that's older than you are. You may get a stuck window now and then but the wisdom of the ages will seep into your very being. Of course, many may prefer windows that open.

I walked over to another window and tried to raise it. It was jammed, too. I looked over at the cat to see what she thought about the situation. She was sitting upright on the kitchen table staring directly away from me. Still miffed that I'd gotten up while she was sleeping on my lap. She didn't understand that if you wait for a cat to wake up you'll never be vice-president of Dow Chemical.

I took a closer look at the windowsill and the window jam. Then I walked around quickly and checked the other windows in the loft. Every one in the place had been nailed shut.

They say when the Lord closes the door He opens a little window. But if it took Him all night to pull three little nails out of Jesus, He was going to be working His buns off on this job. I walked into the kitchen puffing on the cigar. I looked at the cat.

"I just hope He does windows," I said.

18

"If I had a hammer," I thought, "I'd hammer in the morning. . . ."

I didn't have a hammer.

When you don't have a hammer you can't open windows that've been nailed shut unless you're close friends with Uri Geller. I didn't even know who to call at this hour. I thought about Pinocchio's father, Geppetto the carpenter, but he wouldn't've believed me. The only other carpenter I could think of was Jesus, but all the lines were probably down because of heavy calling from television evangelists.

In a rising panic I thought of places I could go to get away from some seriously unthreaded individual who was nailing my windows shut. For some reason I thought of my old college friend Joe Kboudi, who'd retired from the human race about twenty years ago and now owned a record store called All That Jazz in Steamboat Springs, Colorado. Joe skied every day. Lived in a house he'd built with his own hands, and, though he'd never been married, claimed to have been divorced twice. I thought of the way most people lived in New York and Joe's life-style suddenly seemed pretty damn good. "You ever tried cross-country?" I asked the cat. Apparently she hadn't.

Flying by Jewish radar, I walked over to the door of the loft, opened it, and took a good long look at the lock. I didn't see anything unusual but the light in the hallway wasn't that great. I got out my hot-pink Bic, fired it up, and took a closer look. Inside the tumbler, the pins were scratched. I could see where the metal gleamed bright against the dull surface of the inside of the lock. Clearly someone had picked the lock, come inside, and nailed the windows shut. But why? I thought about this all the way over to the bottle of Jameson's.

I poured a shot. It was cold as hell outside and, whether the windows were open or closed, the loft was usually cold in winter and hot in summer. Yet here it was the end of December and I was feeling hot in the loft. It didn't take a detective to determine that I must be feverish. I put my hand to my forehead, then put my hand to the cat's forehead, then checked my own again. I was definitely feverish. Maybe I was coming down with the Epizoodic or something.

I wondered very briefly if someone had released

some kind of deadly microbes in the loft. I discounted this possibility for three reasons: one, the cat wasn't sick; two, the forced lock and nailed-down windows were a rather crude modus operandi to be associated with the placing of deadly microbes; and three, life rarely imitates James Bond. Life is grainier and not quite as diverting. The popcorn, however, is always better with the movie.

So, if it wasn't microbes, why would someone force their way in and nail down the windows? Even given that the windows were an overdramatic touch, if the party had wished to kill me, why not wait *inside* the loft to accomplish it? Especially after picking the lock? Why wait outside on the staircase where, I surmised, the perpetrator was lurking when Ratso's untimely arrival surprised him?

I was starting to sound like Cooperman, I realized to my slight discomfort. Well, why not? I was obviously becoming more professional with experience. And, I noted, what seemed to be absent from the methods of the intruder was exactly that professional touch. Among professionals, of course, I wasn't a professional, but, compared to this guy, I was smoother than Lord Peter Wimsey. Of course, Lord Peter Wimsey wasn't a professional either, but he was an aristocrat, so you couldn't tell the difference.

Coming as quickly as it did after the murder of Tequila, the break-in could very well be connected. Possibly the killer thought Tequila had certain information which he'd imparted to me. That scenario seemed particularly unfortunate. I'd hate to die for withholding information I didn't have.

I sat around drinking and smoking and stroking the cat for a while, and eventually, the fever seemed to diminish. By just before dawn it was gone. Jameson's will cure anything if you drink enough of it.

Suddenly, I felt a great need to talk to someone about this latest episode. I couldn't call Ratso till the late morning at the earliest. Rambam, my private-investigator friend, would surely have an angle on it, but he was jumping this month with a crack Guatemalan airborne unit called "Los Cobras." Maybe that's where I should've been. It sounded safer at the moment.

I settled on calling McGovern. He picked up the phone on the eleventh or twelfth ring and he didn't sound real happy about it.

"Leap sideways, McGovern," I shouted. "MIT— MIT—MIT!" "MIT" was our special coded signal for the Man In Trouble Hotline in case something happened to either of us and nobody came around to check on us until the body had decomposed. McGovern had read on the wire where a guy in Illinois had died in his apartment and wasn't discovered for six months. The purpose of the Man In Trouble Hotline was to avoid such a situation if possible.

Finally, I heard McGovern's groggy reply: "MIT— MIT—MIT . . ." To an untrained ear, the conversation might've sounded like a mating call between two large, rather ill birds.

"McGovern, I've got a problem. I had to call someone."

"Why me, lord?"

"Because you're my friend and you have a very large head that contains a great deal of knowledge. Also, you're the only one who'll listen."

"Makes sense." If it made sense to McGovern, I thought, I was really in trouble.

"Okay. Tequila gets blown away in my rain room a few days ago."

"I covered the story," said McGovern irritably.

"Right. Well, before he went to Jesus he'd mentioned something about coming from Sixteenth Avenue. That information plus the large amount of cash that was found made Cooperman turn the whole case over to the OCCB. You know what that is?"

"Too bad it wasn't the OTB," said McGovern. He

61

laughed rather loudly for that hour of the morning. Then, just as abruptly, he stopped just short of driving off in a 1947 snit. "Of course I know what it is."

"Well, get this. Tonight I get home and find Ratso, who's supposed to be in California, knocked colder than a stuffed flounder at my doorstep with a broken jaw and a concussion. I notice the lock's been picked and when I check the windows, they've all been nailed shut."

"Holy shit! The last time that happened was in the thirties. You ever hear of Legs Diamond?"

"Yeah. He was a bad Broadway show."

"That's how they killed Legs Diamond. He kept getting away from them so they nailed his windows shut, came in, and blew him away."

I was starting not to like the Sixteenth Avenue aspects of the case. I was beginning to feel that not only were the windows nailed shut but the walls seemed to be doing a pretty fair impersonation of closing in on me. Kind of claustrophobic in the loft. It was hell not to get involved when you didn't know what it was you weren't supposed to get involved in.

"Hey, Kink. I've got a good idea for you."

"What?"

"Have you thought about going to Portugal?"

19

A long time ago my mother told me a story about a friend of hers who once spent the night at a big hotel in St. Louis. When I was a child all hotels seemed very big and St. Louis seemed very far away—almost as far away as childhood seems to me now. Be that as it may, here is what all of this has to do with the windows. The woman in the story left her window open while she slept that night and somehow a bird got into the room. The bird dived and flew around the dark room, waking the woman up and scaring the hell out of her. For the rest of her life, I was given to understand, the woman could not eat chicken, turkey, or any kind of fowl. If she did, the reaction, apparently, was always the same. Projectile vomit.

The Legs Diamond death scenario being operative that night, I figured no bird, roach, or Stealth Bomber would be getting in under the windows. All I had to do was get up and bar the door. I did.

In the morning, I could call the super about the windows. If I wanted faster action I could go down to Canal Street and buy a hammer at the same place I bought the shower curtain. See if the guy was still picking his nose with the same camouflage snot rag.

Around dawn or so I killed the lights, got into bed,

and went to sleep more easily than on any night since Tequila had nodded off forever.

I'd check on Ratso in the morning.

I'd fix the windows in the morning.

I'd explore the Egyptian ruins of my social life in the morning.

But before the morning came something else did. It belonged to the ugly, unwelcome, sifting-the-ashes-of-childhood department, and it told me in no uncertain terms that no matter what happened in the morning I was very soon karma-bound to reap an ill-winded, inexorable harvest of hate.

20

Scientists don't know where dreams come from. Of course they don't; that's why we call them scientists. But, in all fairness, very few other Americans know where dreams come from either. Dreamers, for instance, don't know where dreams come from. Of course they don't; that's why we call them dreamers. But there is one man who does know where dreams come from. He's a guy I went to high school with who I used to call Wally but who now operates under the moniker Dr. Wallace P. Mendelson. Wally wrote a book called *Human Sleep and Its Disorders* which he once sent me a copy of. The problem with the book is that it's a very learned, well-researched, scientific study, and by the time you get to the part that tells you where dreams come from you're usually on the nod.

In layman's terms, Wally's main contention is that dreams and nightmares, more often than not, are caused by gas. It is a thesis I am not prepared to argue with, having had in my life many dreams, many nightmares, and, of course, rather large amounts of gas. Wally levels a few fairly fetid blasts at the school of frilly Freudian lingerie thinking and I can't say I disagree with him. I say only that my nightmare came from somewhere pretty unpleasant and it didn't get in through the windows.

My friend Captain Midnite always maintains that the first time he met me I was hanging from a cross outside the Nashville Holiday Inn. That was where the dream started. And, like many dreams these days, it got worse.

To my left from high upon the cross, I saw the Day-Glo skeleton of Ernest Tubb sinuously weaving its way up lower Broadway singing, "I'd waltz across Texas with you in my arms." To my right all I could see was a huge sign that read: BAPTIST BOOK STORE. I looked straight ahead and saw the lights of the city of Nashville below me. It reminded me of the old Tom T. Hall song "I Flew Over Our House Last Night." As my friend Dave Hickey says: "I like all of Tom T. Hall's songs and both of his melodies."

There wasn't a hell of a lot else to see. It might be exciting to Jerry Falwell or somebody like that, but I think most people would find hanging around on a cross all night pretty goddamn boring. I decided to come down and maybe get a big hairy steak in the little restaurant that Midnite always referred to as "Hillbilly Heaven," and which, as things evolved, was an extremely appropriate name. But I'm getting ahead of my dream.

It must've been the late sixties or early seventies, judging by the taillights, yet when I went inside Hillbilly Heaven the ragged group sitting around the table stared back at me with eyes that were timeless as the rain. They were too degenerate to be King Arthur's boys, and, though several of them looked rather like Dorothy Parker, they lacked the sophistication to be confused with the Algonquin Hotel crowd. Nonetheless, they were destined for their place in history. This band of brigands was the Texas Jewboys, soon to travel across America, racing to stay one step ahead of angry Jews, Negroes, rednecks, and women in their relentless effort to piss off everybody.

Captain Midnite himself was sitting at the head of the table discoursing to the group about Billie Jean Horton, the woman who had had the misfortune to be married to both Hank Williams and Johnny Horton. "People say Billie Jean was a witch," intoned Midnite. "They say she killed Hank Williams and Johnny Horton and stunted Faron Young's growth."

Billy Swan took out his glass eye and dipped it in his drink. Willie Fong Young, the "Singing Chinaman," made a lurch like a lizard's tongue for the waitress's left breast. Not all the Texas Jewboys were Jewish, but all of them were Jews by inspiration.

Next thing I knew I found myself blithering down a vaguely familiar street in Nashville with a couple of the guys in the band and a bottle of Jack Daniel's approximately the size of Webb Pierce's guitar-shaped swimming pool. I took a slug from the bottle and the water from the pool all sloshed over to one side. Through the pool, which was now inside the bottle, I could see the dark form of the German battleship *The Bismarck* sailing directly toward my uvula at an unpleasantly brisk clip. The background music for this part of the dream was Johnny Horton singing "Sink the Bismarck." I passed the bottle to the drummer, Major Boles. He made the observation that his come count was redlining and passed the bottle to the bass player, Brian "Skycap" Adams. They were talking to a broad who looked a lot like the green-eyed blonde I'd last seen holding hands with Winnie Katz. Probably the same one who was going to shoot me out of the saddle for the New Year's date, I thought, but there wasn't time to dwell on it. The street was running with blood.

Tequila's face floated by in the gutter like a discarded fright mask. Workmen were hammering on a sign that read: WELCOME TO MUSIC ROW. The hammer blows came irregularly, sounding like gunshots. The blood was rising rapidly in the street, slightly discoloring my brontosaurus foreskin boots.

Music Row, I said to myself. Music Row.

It was only after I'd wakened from the dream that I realized what should've been obvious to me some time ago. What was now called Music Row in Nashville had for many years been known to all of us by another name.

"Music Row" had once been Sixteenth Avenue South.

21

New Year's Eve came around relentless as a tedious housepest. You can coddle a tedious housepest, pretend you like him, ignore him, but he'll still be hanging around like a bad smell unless you get a forklift and get him the hell out of there. New Year's Eve was the same way—unforgivable and unforkliftable. Like Exxon or a twenty-four-hour Chinese restaurant, New Year's Eve didn't care if you sang, danced, or hung yourself from a shower rod. The only remedy was to sleep through the bastard like a bad dream, and I'd already had one of those too many the night before.

At least the super had showed up and, for a small honorarium, had unpried the windows, which was a good thing because I was beginning to worry a little that my entire loft might be developing a crucifixion complex. It was a couple of minutes after ten—less than two hours before the arrival of that smarmy, smirking little rug rat in a diaper that symbolizes all our hopes and dreams for the future—when I opened the bottle of tequila.

The fact that Sixteenth Avenue South in Nashville could've quite logically been what Tequila'd been talking about before he died, rather than Sixteenth Avenue in Brooklyn, was still on my mind. The fact that I, with the New Year coming, felt myself being spiritually sucked into the vortex of Kirby McMillan's (a.k.a. Tequila's) murder case was also on my mind. About the only thing, in fact, that was not on mind was Georgia.

Then I took the first strong shot of tequila, felt my scalp tingle, and felt the brain under that scalp grow as empty and as blank as the blue eyes of a bimbo in love. Tequila'll do that to you. It'll send you to a different planet than a white wine cassis.

After another shot or two, with the lemon neatly quartered and the salt sprinkled sparingly on the back of my wrist to cut the bite the tequila was taking out of my heart, an entirely new scenario was filling my mind, a bold new attitude taking over my being. I was on a planet with Tom Mix, John Wayne, Steve McQueen, and my old friend Tom Baker, and, I was pleased to observe, I felt I belonged there.

Cleve's crazy dream of a giant Texas Jewboy reunion tour didn't seem so bad to me suddenly. I could see us back in '73, '74, '75, at Armadillo World Headquarters in Austin, Liberty Hall in Houston, Max's Kansas City in New York, the Troubadour in L.A., electrifying the crowds with avant garde insanity. In all its old glory, I thought, the band was really something. Of course, it's hard to be avant garde on a reunion tour. But, after all, we were cultural pioneers. Before MTV. Before Watergate. Before Christ. Before—

There was a loud noise in the hallway. It did not sound like applause. It sounded more like the wail of a wildly distraught woman. I killed another shot of tequila, which was going down a lot more smoothly now, and I lit a cigar. The noise did not seem to be going away.

I licked some residual salt from the back of my wrist, took a few irritated puffs on the cigar, and, very reluctantly, headed for the door. That hallway was going to get me into trouble yet.

22

"Of course you couldn't've known she was a lesbian, Kelli," I said reassuringly. "They don't have lesbians in Texas." We were standing by the counter after I'd coaxed the young blond, green-eyed dancer into the loft, coaxed her name and port of origin out of her, and coaxed her into taking several stiff shots of tequila. Now, if I could coax her into bed with me, the New Year might yet come in with a bang.

"It's not that," said Kelli, wiping two blue tear-drops from her green, green eyes. "I've been a dancer all my life. I've got an ex-boyfriend in Texas who's been harassing me and threatening to come up here. I just got rid of him and now this woman thinks she owns me. I thought she was a friend."

I handed her my snot rag and she dabbed at her pretty eyes again. "With friends like that," I said, taking a patient puff on the cigar, "who needs lesbians?"

She nodded as if she understood whatever the hell it was I meant. I thought very fleetingly of the first time I'd seen her from my kitchen window. She was crossing Vandam Street, I reflected, on those muscular, perfectly formed dancer's legs. She'd really knocked the helmet off my Nazi love puppet. It was a good thing, too. You never get a second chance to make a first impression.

Kelli smiled a little and seemed to loosen up a bit. She took out a pack of Merits, shook one free, and let me light it for her. I liked dancers who smoked Merits. I liked broads who smoked anything; you could get on a coffee-and-cigarette wavelength with them on rainy days after you'd done a little horizontal hokeypokey and then in the evening go out to romantic little Spanish restaurants and get drunk with colorful, bohemian friends. Also, broads who smoked tended to bitch less about my cigars.

As Kelli and I developed a rapport of sorts, midnight was slipping up on Vandam Street. There was definitely some kind of organic chemistry between us.

"Actually," I said, "I really do know a lot about dancers. Do you know how you can tell when your date is a dancer?"

"How?" she asked in beautiful, breathless innocence.

"When she does splits on your face," I said.

Black and white images of black and white people were seething, snaking, and shimmering all across the screen of my black and white television set. They were

70

all watching a ball drop. Like a baby's untried, trepid testicle descending into the netherworld of Times Square, it appeared about the same size, shape, and consistency as a fairly healthy boysenberry. Kelli and I watched this rite with varying degrees of fascination.

"We should be there," said Kelli.

I remembered being there once. Thirty seconds after the ball fell, a group of black youths, as they're called, beat a seventy-nine-year-old Frenchman to death with his own cane right in front of his granddaughter. I got there just as the black youths were vanishing into the crowd and they were beginning to load one stiff Frog into the meat wagon. Though a noninvolved passersby eagerly provided me with a blow-by-blow description of what I'd missed, I did witness a burly white youth picking up a funny-looking little beret from the sidewalk, putting it on his head, and blowing a noisemaker that seemed to stretch out like the tongue of an avaricious anteater and reach all the way to the beaches of Normandy.

"Happy New Year," I said as I poured out two shots of tequila.

We were clinking our glasses together in a toast and I was staring into the rather promising depths of Kelli's green eyes when there came the sound of someone knocking at my chamber door. A woman's voice could also be heard and the voice was saying my name. The voice sounded a lot like Winnie Katz's.

"Oh, God," said Kelli. "Not that—that creature!"

"Who?" I said ineffectually. "Where?"

It wasn't my idea for Kelli to hide in the linen closet. It just seemed like the appropriate thing to do under the circumstances. Try putting yourself in her place. You're a young dancer from Texas and a large, athletic, cranked-up New York bull dyke is standing at the door ready to huff and puff and do a few other unpleasant things if she discovers you're here.

She'd probably drill you like your friendly neighborhood dentist. Of course, dentists, like bull dykes, like many other Americans, spend most of their lives drilling in the wrong places and that's why they not infrequently commit suicide. I have very little sympathy for people who take a brodie. I agree with my friend Nelda from Medina, Texas, who, whenever she hears of someone taking his own life, always remarks: "Wish I could of handed 'em the gun, the chickenshit!"

I opened the door to the hallway.

Winnie was wearing a smile I could not read and something that looked like a teddy for cooler weather that I could not take my eyes off of and she was holding a large bottle of some kind of château de cat piss.

"Happy New Year!" I said. I had a rather distinct feeling that it wasn't going to be one for very long.

Winnie brushed past me into the loft at about the same time that Kelli sneezed in the linen closet.

"What was that?" asked Winnie.

"What?" I said. "Where?"

Kellie sneezed again. It was a cute little sneeze and I wanted to throttle her for it.

What happened next was not all that pleasant but it was better than what happened after that. But let me tell the events in the order they occurred, for there is a place for everything under heaven . . . turn, turn, turn. I turned, all right. Just in time to see Winnie yank open the door to the linen closet and Kelli come flying out like a belligerent blond bat for her throat. Was this my innocent little dancer from Texas?

I didn't have a hell of a lot of time to wonder. Winnie did not shirk from the action and soon they were kicking and flailing, and choking, and scratching, and cursing, and screaming, and carrying on, in general, like a married couple. The cat and I both jumped repeatedly out of the way and finally I stood on the sidelines wondering whether to be jealous, smug, or ambivalent. I won't repeat some of the things that were said, for they certainly belong to the argot of the gutter.

Kelli threw my "Imus in the Morning" coffee mug at Winnie and it crashed into an expensive-looking picture of a ballet dancer that belonged to the Greek woman I subletted the loft from. That's the way it goes. Winnie picked up my porcelain Sherlock Holmes head in which I kept my cigars and rocketed it at Kelli's skull. It was a large object and, when Kelli ducked, it smashed into the wall above the refrigerator, sending the puppet head and a small covey of expensive cigars flying off in all directions. Great material damage was done to the loft.

The skirmish seemed to go on forever but, in reality, lasted for only a few minutes. It ended when the two combatants, the cat, and myself all suddenly realized that the four of us were not alone in the loft.

A large, fairly deranged-looking man was standing just inside the doorway and watching the action with eyes that glittered dully like pinballs. He had a tavern tan and it appeared as if he'd been sleeping in his hat and coat for a couple of years. He had no facial hair except for a rather evil-looking "white man-hater" that grew from his lower lip like a black orchid and made him look like a drunk who'd missed the mark on Ash Wednesday. He sprayed evil around the place like a blue-balled tomcat.

"Let me guess," I said. "You're Kelli's boyfriend from Texas."

"Wrong," he said as he took out the gun. "I'm Winnie's husband from Sing Sing."

23

Lately the atmosphere of the loft had seemed to Vaseline violently back and forth between long periods of enormous ennui and brief, intense intervals of frenetic activity, both polarities being rather unpleasant. The cycle had appeared to begin the day I went out shopping for a bottle of tequila for Tequila, each of which vessels, of course, were now empty. Whether Winnie's husband from Sing Sing was really Winnie's husband from Sing Sing was something we could discuss later if there was a later. Whether he had decked Ratso, deep-sixed Tequila, and done some unauthorized carpentry work on my windows could also be given consideration at a later date. As far as the Texas Jewboy reunion tour went, we'd have to put that one on Hollywood hold for a while. Take a spiritual raincheck.

I looked at the man with the gun and saw that his dark, furry white man-hater was bobbing up and down and that meant he was flapping his lips. His voice was soft.

"Don't worry, baby," he said to Winnie. "I'm not gonna kill you. I'm just gonna give you something to remember me by every time you look in the mirror."

From a pocket in his overcoat he extracted a clear bottle about three-quarters full of a clear liquid. I noticed for the first time that he was wearing gloves. His orbs were starting to run through a few REM movements I hadn't seen before.

Winnie and Kelli were visibly shaken and I wasn't feeling too good myself. I looked at the two of them and registered that there was something very beautiful and arousing about a woman in a high state of danger and vulnerability, no doubt one of the things that delights the aesthetic eye of the rapist. They were both chalky-white, like statues of minor Greek goddesses smiling with fear.

I made myself focus on the bottle in his hand and wished I'd paid a little more attention in high school chemistry. I did remember that almost all acids have a kind of dirty clear color and have to be kept in brown bottles or they lose their potency. I made a judgment call that the bottle was not the McCoy. If this was true, the only little problem was the gun.

The cat hopped up on the desk next to where I was standing. As she walked to the far end, an idea crossed my desk as well. I picked up the cat and held her protectively, stroking her head as if to soothe her. I hoped to hell she'd cooperate. The cat hated to be picked up.

"That ain't the pussy I'm gonna hurt," said the man with the gun. I looked in the direction the gun was pointed and saw, incredibly, that the two girls were now hugging each other. Women.

I waited till the guy started futzing with the cap of the bottle, then I threw the cat in his face. With the same motion I went for the gun. The cat made a beautiful four-point landing on the guy's mug and promptly put down some rather sharp roots.

Two hours later, it was all over. Just me and the cat. Cooperman had un–hog-tied the guy and taken him away, the girls had left together, and I was still slightly shaken by the revelation that the gun hadn't even been loaded.

"Well," I said to the cat, "that was great teamwork. Now I'll just clean up the guy's urine sample or whatever the hell it is from the kitchen floor and we'll go to bed."

I've only owned one rug. It was a beautiful, very expensive Persian, one given to me some time ago by a little Armenian friend. I speak of it in the past tense because when I finally got over to look, it was still smoking with a hole in the middle roughly the size and shape of the Louisiana Purchase.

24

Sunday morning, the first day of the New Year, I was wandering my weary way over to the St. Vincent's Hospital Broken Jaw Ward. Thirty-seven years earlier, to the day, I reflected, Hank Williams had died on a one-way ride to Canton, Ohio. Maybe in a hundred years, I thought, there'd be a St. Hank's Hospital in New York.

Maybe not.

As I walked through the Village I noticed that people had already started chucking out their Christmas trees onto the curb. When I was a kid we used to collect them and build Christmas-tree forts to protect ourselves from wild Russian boars, imaginary Iroquois, or the bullet-heads from the next block. Now that we live in an adult world, of course, the currency of old Christmas trees has fallen off a bit. It was kind of ironic, I thought. Now was the time that we really needed Christmas-tree forts.

Ratso looked green for some reason. Maybe it was the lights. Maybe it was the Jell-O.

"You're always visiting me in hospitals," I said. "I thought I'd visit you in one."

"Hrrmghh," he said. It was painfully obvious they'd wired his jaw.

"What's the matter, Rats?" I asked. "They give you a charisma bypass?"

"Yechhuuum!" Ratso said, a bit more demonstratively.

"Well, maybe it's a blessing this happened," I said. "You've seen what Hollywood did to F. Scott Fitzgerald. They weren't very nice to the Lone Ranger, either. Wouldn't even let him wear his mask at county fairs. Mind if I smoke?"

Ratso made a noise in his throat that I took for an affirmative. I checked the hallway, saw that the coast was clear, lopped the butt off an English Market Selection Rothschild Maduro, and fired the little booger up.

"Well, I don't see Big Nurse out there," I said. "All I see is Big Nerd." I looked at Ratso and smiled a warm, lighthearted, engaging smile. The muscles in his jaw rippled a few times like an overly zealous B-movie star and his lips twitched a bit grotesquely. I decided that must be the way people with wired jaws laughed.

"Screenwriting's like putting together lawn furniture," I said. "Not a hell of a lot of creation there. You should stay in New York with me and we'll put those little gray cells to work on this latest case that seems to have fallen into my lap like a bowl of matzo-ball soup. Of course, I guess that makes me a spiritual *shlemazel*, right? The *schlemiel* is the one who spills the soup, I believe. The *shlemazel* is the one who gets the soup spilled on him. Or is it the other way around? I knew I was one of those guys."

77

At this point I laughed in good-natured self-depre-
cation. Ratso made another noise in his throat. Sounded
like a slow, and very unpleasant, child learning how to
chuckle.

I took it as a positive sign. I sat back in my chair
and puffed on the cigar a bit. The Maduro cigar is of a
very dark color and brings to mind obvious racial as well
as Freudian implications but has a nice, toasted aroma
that I felt could only enhance the ambience of the ster-
ile, spiritless room.

I filled Ratso in on what had happened at the loft
both before and after his little accident. I started with
the circumstances of Tequila's death that Sunday evening exactly one week ago. I mentioned the business
about Sixteenth Avenue, the missing phone book, and
the temporarily missing puppet head, and then I fast-
forwarded to the Friday night I'd found Ratso lying on
my doorstep. Ratso reacted to all this in stoic silence,
which is about the only way a person with his jaw wired
shut can react. If he had any thoughts he kept them to
himself.

Finally, I briefed Ratso on the events of the previous night, featuring Winnie's husband from Sing Sing.
When I'd gotten to the part about finding the giant hole
burned in the Persian rug by the acid, I saw the first
smile come to Ratso's lips since I'd entered the room.
It was a painful thing to see, but there it was. It looked
kind of like a frozen Jackie Kennedy funeral smile.

"Here, Ratso," I said, handing him a blank page
from the little notebook I carried with me. "Write
everything you saw about the person who did this to
you." I handed Ratso a pen and he was scribbling ma-
niacally on the page when the Big Nurse finally did come
in and began to gag on the cigar smoke. She gave me
the old fish-eye, then wheeled in my direction and came
toward me at a surprisingly accelerated pace for such a
large woman.

The nurse did not quite actually chase me around the room. She only appeared to do so as I lunged for the bed, grasped the paper Ratso was extending toward me, asked "Is that everything?," received a curt nod from Ratso, then ran around the back of the bed about two steps ahead of the huge, increasingly ominous-looking white-clad Fury with a stethoscope around her neck about the size of the Holland Tunnel. I speed-walked to the door as quickly as dignity would allow.

Out on the street, I took in the grim, cold, debris-blown visage of the New Year as a man about half my age plundered a nearby garbage can. I didn't know if he happened to be one of the wonderfully weak-willed generation of Americans we seem to be breeding lately, an outpatient from the Butt-Holdsworth Home for the Bewildered, or a guy kind of like myself who had run out of people to see and places to go. He was a small part of the wretched refuse from that teeming shore that, unfortunately, now seemed to be our own. Shore, that is.

I walked up the block to a French laundry that was now run by a Chinese family. I waved to a little Chinese kid inside and he waved back. I didn't know if they still sautéed pinafores, or whatever French laundries were supposed to do, but at least this one was friendly.

I stopped a little upwind from a guy urinating on a brick wall, flipped my cigar into the gutter, and took the crumpled page out of my coat pocket. The page on which Ratso had written everything he'd observed about his attacker. It was broad daylight but I semiconsciously stepped under a streetlamp to read it.

On the page was a somewhat crude, childlike drawing of a fist, the four knuckles of which had been tattooed with the letters L-O-V-E.

Almost precisely my sentiments for the season.

25

The phone book was still missing when I got back to the loft and so was some of my eagerness to jump into the quirky quagmire of the case without at least testing the water with my big toe. A week had gone by since Tequila's human contents had been punctiliously poured into the River Styx and there was still nothing new unless you wanted to count the New Year which, as far as I could see, didn't look too damn good.

Whether Ratso stayed in New York or went to California, it didn't appear as if he'd be able to be much help for some time to come. Working on a murder case without my faithful Dr. Watson would be lonely going, but, as my old friend Tom Baker used to say: "There are worse things in life than being lonely." Unfortunately, Tom failed to impart to me what these things were prior to his unscheduled exit.

The action seemed to be coming at fairly regular intervals right into my loft. If I leaped into the middle of things, I wouldn't have to jump too far.

I lit a cigar, sat down at my desk, and took the jump.

The first thing I needed to check on, even before I waded through Tequila's murky background, was the matter of the tattooed fist. Winnie's husband from Sing Sing, though he'd been wearing his little glovies the night I'd seen him, looked like a logical candidate for that kind of decorative self-expression. Tattoos of that nature, L-O-V-E on one fist and H-A-T-E on the other, were common in prisons and biker gangs, though they were not very popular yet among Young Republicans.

The point to settle was whether Winnie's husband from Sing Sing was also Ratso's attacker. Once this was established, a nice sliver of light might possibly be shed upon the identity of Tequila's attacker as well. All three violent incidents had occurred at my loft within one week. I didn't know if the crime rate was down in the city, but it seemed to be up in my apartment.

I puffed purposefully on the cigar for a moment, weighing the tedium of talking to Winnie with the unpleasantness of calling Cooperman.

Winnie won.

Not that I have anything against cops; cops are important and lesbians are important. It's just that if you don't really need a cop, sometimes it's better to make do with a lesbian.

I made myself a cup of espresso, got settled back at the desk, took a few tentative puffs on the cigar, and called Winnie. The ceiling seemed pretty quiet at the moment. When I got Winnie on the phone and asked her about her husband from Sing Sing, she seemed subdued and almost apologetic about the events of the previous night.

"I haven't seen my *ex*-husband, Bud, in eight years, fuck-face."

"Sir Fuck-face," I said.

"If he had the Gettysburg Address on the tip of his dork I wouldn't've known it."

"David Allen Coe has a snake tattooed on the tip of his penis," I said. I glanced briefly at my cigar but didn't take a puff.

"Who's David Allen Coe?" she asked.

I took a somewhat chargined slurp of espresso. I

have found that one of the rather disconcerting things about lesbians is their almost total lack of appreciation for country music.

"Country singer," I said.

"What do you have tattooed on the tip of your dork?" she asked. "A liver fluke?"

Out of the blower came a sexy, almost-growling lesbian laugh. I chuckled along to show that I was a good sport and that my masculinity wasn't threatened.

"Jewish people aren't allowed to have tattoos on the tips of their penises," I said calmly. "If they do, then their penises have to be buried in Gentile cemeteries. Of course, sometimes we'll just take the tattooed tips of the penises, wrap them up, and send them over to Russia. The Russians plant them over there. Grow little dictators."

Winnie did not laugh. She said, "That's precious," then she hung up the phone.

I was not making a lot of headway, as it were. All I'd learned was that the guy was her *ex*-husband and his name was Bud. I was not surprised that he wound up in Sing Sing. Guys named Bud usually do get into some kind of trouble. Even Robert Young's son on *Father Knows Best* got himself into trouble apparently, according to the *National Enquirer*. And if you're in the *National Enquirer* and you're not an astrologer or a Brazilian midget, you're definitely in trouble.

I took a sip of espresso but it was already tepid. I took a puff on the cigar but it'd gone out. I reached for my phone book but it wasn't there.

Sometimes, even if your name isn't Bud and you're not a Brazilian midget, life can be tedious.

26

Later that Sunday evening, as darkening shadows fell rather gingerly across the garbage trucks parked on Vandam Street, I reached out and touched Sergeant Cooperman. He was not greatly pleased to hear from me. During the course of our brief conversation I managed to pick up several semicogent pieces of information. Sing Sing was now known as the Ossining Correctional Facility. I conveyed to Cooperman my regret that a colorful, poetic name like Sing Sing should be changed to a dull, almost prison-gray, bureaucratic one such as the Ossining Correctional Facility. Cooperman belched lightly into the phone.

I also learned that Cooperman would have Bud's Department of Corrections file checked for tattooing on his knuckles and would get back to me on the matter. Finally, I learned that Bud would not be getting out anytime soon, a fact I heartily disbelieved, knowing the ridiculous release policies of New York area prisons and mental hospitals. I was a *Post* reader and I remembered the story about the guy who cut off his mother's head, was held briefly for observation, then was released and promptly cut off his ex-wife's head. The headline, I believe, had been TWO HEADS ARE BETTER THAN ONE. I thought fleetingly of Cleve for some reason.

The conversation ended rather abruptly when

Cooperman got a ten-four or whatever they call it and hung up on me just as I was saying "Good-bye, Sergeant. Thank you."

When you're left stranded with a blower in one hand and a cigar in the other, it's always a good idea to cradle the blower and light the cigar. I performed those acts. The cat did not applaud.

I still missed my phone book. Even if there'd been someone to call, there was no way to call them. Maybe I should've done what my friend Don Imus does every New Year's Eve. Throws his phone book into the fire. I'd had mine for so long it was starting to read like the *Book of the Dead*. It's all very well to sit back and let people call you, but when you're attempting to conduct an investigation into a murder, that particular passive dog usually won't hunt.

I took the guitar pick out of my pocket and studied it on my desk. Yep. They'd spelled my name right.

I thought of the painstaking process that was going to be required to gather the phone numbers of the people who'd been in and around the Texas Jewboys. They were the ones, I thought, who were most likely to still be hanging on to one of these guitar picks after thirteen years.

Some of the people and some of the picks could be accounted for, I reflected, and some of them couldn't. For instance, I'd given one to my Peace Corps buddy John Morgan who'd once used it—successfully, I might add—to get backstage at an Eric Clapton concert. Later, both Morgan and the pick had gone mysteriously missing and I suppose there were times you could've said the same about Eric, but that's rock 'n' roll. I'd finally found out what had become of John in Borneo, but the circumstances had been of such a peculiar nature that the subject of the pick, or Eric Clapton, had, of course, not arisen.

But what bothered me most was the fact that the

water'd been running when I left the loft last week and I hadn't noticed the pick in the doorway on my way out. So it was logical to think that whoever'd whacked Tequila had also dropped the pick, and I was rapidly coming to realize that, if Tequila hadn't dropped it on the way in, it might've been placed there on purpose. The person who'd done that, I theorized, had also taken my phone book. The bastard. But *why?* What numbers could possibly be in that book that a murderer would want to get his bloody hands on?

I thought about it as I fed the cat a late-night snack of tuna. I thought about it as I sat at the kitchen table alone smoking a cigar. I thought about it as I listened to the rhythmic thuddings of the lesbian dance class as it started up somewhere over my head in the night sky of New York.

I was still thinking about it later that night in bed when I got the phone call from Dylan Ferrero, the first road manager for the Texas Jewboys. Dylan told me that Raymond Boatright, the keyboard player for the band, had just been discovered dead from an apparent drug overdose in Dallas. An autopsy was to be conducted.

Boatright had been found, according to Dylan, sitting in his apartment, looking over an old scrapbook of the Texas Jewboys.

27

There was a time in rock 'n' roll, during the late sixties and early seventies, when the death of a band member was considered to be a very fashionable and fortuitous thing. After the demise of said dead individual, the band would succeed to far greater heights than they'd ever dreamed of or, in fact, usually deserved. Now, with the legacy of Nancy Reagan's persuasive "Just Say No" program and George Bush's equally effective antidrug policies, drugs and, for that matter death, are not as popular as they used to be. They're both still around, however. If you want them, you can find them.

For myself, I stopped snorting cocaine several weeks ago, when Bob Marley fell out of my left nostril. Haven't touched it since. Cocaine, that is. I still touch my left nostril every now and then when I think nobody's looking. I was touching my left nostril that Wednesday morning while standing at my kitchen window and, sure enough, somebody was watching.

It was a figure with a very large head, standing out there on the freezing sidewalk. The head was looking up at me. It was either McGovern or a very good McGovern impersonator, and it didn't matter which because it didn't look like it was going away.

"Stop pickin' your nose," it shouted as I opened

the window and threw down the puppet head. The puppet head made a graceful little trajectory, temporarily blotting out McGovern.

Trajectory. I thought of something Kelli Tuck, with her perfectly formed, muscular dancer's legs, had mentioned to me on New Year's Eve. Her father, Grady, had a theory he called "life as trajectory." Just as NASA, when trying to land a rocket on the moon, for instance, would aim a little above the target. Grady believed you should always aim a little higher than your dreams.

I watched as the puppet head, with its colorful parachute, completed its own little trajectory and fell directly in front of McGovern's face. I watched as he reached for it and missed, and the puppet head bounced painfully several times, puppet head first, onto the heartless, Paleolithic sidewalks of New York. I watched as the little head rolled off the sidewalk and the large form with the large head scuttled after it like a giant sun being drawn suddenly into the gravitational orbit of a small, black tennis ball in the gutter.

So much for life as trajectory.

It might work in theory, but in practice, I always felt you'd meet with less disappointment if you adhered to Tom Lehrer's attitude toward life. "Life," said Lehrer, "is like a sewer. What you get out of it depends upon what you put into it."

Scant moments later, McGovern and I were sipping carefully at two very hot espressos. It was not theories of life that the two of us were discussing. It was theories of death.

On the table between us McGovern had thoughtfully provided his rather lurid *Daily News* account of Tequila's murder. I scanned it until I came to the phrase "brains down the drain," and then, like Hercule Poirot, placed it perfectly symmetrically back on the table between us.

"That's somewhat graphic, isn't it, McGovern?"

"You should've seen the *Post!*" McGovern laughed his loud, hearty Irish laugh. It would always be too early in the morning for that laugh.

"McGovern," I said with some heat, "not to take away from the *great* writing you've done in the past . . ."

"Lots of it about you."

"Of course. Not to take away from *that*—but if I took a Nixon at Grand Central Station and read the men's room walls, I could save thirty-five cents."

McGovern looked hurt and I instantly regretted the remark. But he took a sip of espresso and brightened immediately.

"You'd only save a dime," he said.

"Why's that?" I asked. I lit my first cigar of the morning and waited.

"It costs you a quarter to take a dump at Grand Central," he said. Then he laughed even louder.

Suddenly, McGovern became very serious. "It's hard to believe a guy was murdered right here in your loft just ten days ago."

"No harder than believing in never-never land," I said. I took advantage of the absence of Irish laughter to refill both espresso cups and to mention to McGovern the news Dylan had told me several nights before.

McGovern stared at me thoughtfully. I shrugged amiably and took a puff or two on the cigar. "Just one of those little coincidences of life," I said.

"Or death," said McGovern.

It was a coincidence, all right. How strange after all these years that Raymond Boatright and I should suddenly be on the same wavelength. I'd been up here in New York pondering, resisting, wrestling the notion of going back out on the road with the band. Raymond, so far away in terms of time and geography, digging up strikingly similar bones. A scrapbook of the Texas Jew-boys.

88

We drank our espresso in silence. The cat jumped on the kitchen table and McGovern patted her head like he was very gently dribbling a basketball. McGovern loved everything, but he hadn't had a lot of luck with animals. He'd once sat his large Irish buttocks down on a couch without looking and seriously injured his girl-friend's lap dog.

"You know," he said, "the first shot that hit Tequila was a gut shot. It was fired right through the curtain and probably didn't kill him. Then the killer throws the cur-tain open, sees who his victim is, or, possibly, thinks he's been recognized, and finishes Tequila off almost point-blank to the head."

I puffed patiently on the cigar and waited. You had to wait a lot when McGovern was theorizing.

"That first shot," he said, "the one fired through the curtain—"

"Get to the meat of it," I said, irritably.

"That first shot," said McGovern, "was meant for *you.*"

28

I didn't really buy Mc-Govern's theory but I thought about it all the way to the bottle of Jameson's. McGovern was a large, colorful, kind, humorous American, but he was also a very smart American. He was the only person at the *Daily News* who'd been a Nieman Fellow at Harvard, one of journalism's highest accolades. He was also the only Nieman Fellow who'd never finished high school.

And McGovern thought the first shot was meant for me. I poured the kind of shot I liked a hell of a lot better and killed it. Nice way to start the day. Drink a shot of Jameson's and begin to realize that somebody'd been trying to kill you. Not that I hadn't been aware of that possibility. It was just that when McGovern said something he believed deeply, it always carried great spiritual force.

I poured another medicinal shot to settle my nerves. It was very early for me. Almost eleven o'clock. Maybe I'd go out to an Indian restaurant. Were any Indian restaurants open yet? Did Indians eat breakfast? What'd they order—blintzes *vindaloo?*

I was getting set to kill the second shot when the two red phones connected to the same line rang at once on both sides of my desk. They always rang at once, of course. That's what happens when you connect them to the same line. But it creates an urgency and an importance that I kind of like. You feel like you're doing something vital, like manning the crisis hotline for the National Bulimia Society.

I carried the shot of Jameson's over to the desk and, picking up the blower on the left, heard the unmistakable, grating, gravel voice of Sergeant Cooperman.

"No initials, Tex," he said. "No L-O-V-E, no H-A-T-E. Not even M-O-M."

"That's too bad," I said. The thing had looked too easy anyway.

"What's wrong, Tex? You wanted initials? You got a thing about initials?"

"Not really. I never like to say 'fuck' in front of a C-H-I-L-D, but that's—"

"You know, Tex, I've had to come over there twice this week. Three times could be the charm. What you need is to get out of the city for a while. Talk that little bull dyke upstairs into going on a vacation with you. Take her to Niagara Falls."

Possibly because of Cooperman's homophobic nuance I thought of Oscar Wilde and what he'd reportedly said upon seeing Niagara Falls: "Second greatest disappointment for American brides." They weren't makin' fagolas like Oscar Wilde anymore. They were making a hell of a lot of homosexuals these days, especially for a group that couldn't reproduce itself. But none of them were as clever or as funny as Oscar Wilde. Of course, nobody else was either.

"I hear Portugal's nice," I said to Cooperman.

"Look, pal, let me tell you something. I don't know what's goin' on, but you're definitely in the middle of a mess that's probably gonna turn out pretty fucking ugly. In fact, it already has. We ran the prints on this Kirby McMillan Tequila character and came up with nothing. Also, the OCCB's come up empty so far."

"What about Bud from Sing Sing? I mean the Ossining Correctional Facility? Ratso got decked in the hallway last week by a guy with L-O-V-E initialed on his fist. So obviously, it wasn't Bud. But who says Bud couldn't've been hanging around here the week before and knocked off Tequila?"

"I says," said Cooperman. "He would've had to have had a fuckin' out-of-body experience. He wasn't released from prison until New Year's Eve."

After I'd hung up the blower with Cooperman, I fed the cat some tuna, took the two espresso cups off the kitchen table, and walked them over to the sink where they'd feel more comfortable in the company of some friendly cockroaches and all the other unwashed crap. I looked around the loft and it suddenly appeared to my mind's myopic eye that the place seemed dusty, cold, empty, and unlived-in, like an attic that didn't want to think about its memories.

I left the cat in charge, grabbed a few cigars, put

on my old cowboy hat and hunting vest, and bugged out for the dugout. I took Vandam to Hudson to Eighth Avenue, and by the time I walked into LaBonbonniere and waved hello to Charles, the proprietor, my nose hairs were hanging down like frozen stalactites.

There was a new waitress there with an interesting mouth and about twenty-seven bracelets and legs that reminded me a little of Kelli's. She asked me what I wanted and I ordered bacon and eggs, honeymoon style.

"What's honeymoon style?" she asked as she adjusted several of her bracelets.

"Straight up and hard," I said. I don't remember whether she laughed or not, but the fat lady at the nearby table didn't appear to find it all that amusing.

I studied the fat lady as I ate my breakfast. She weighed in at almost three hundred pounds and the guy across from her, whom I took to be her husband, looked just like your normal guy. You see a lot of fat ladies like that who all seem to have average, fairly nice-looking husbands. I asked my friend Dr. Jim Bone about it once and he said it was the Jack Sprat Phenomenon.

Something was definitely wrong with the picture at the nearby table and I guess the Jack Sprat Phenomenon explained it as well as anything, but it didn't account for what was wrong with the picture in my mind. Nobody lives forever, but two members of the original band, the Texas Jewboys, had just gone to Jesus inside of one week. When I got back to the loft I planned to call Dylan and get an update on Raymond Boatright's death, but Tequila's croaking was starting to really puzzle me. Something was all wrong about it, that much I knew. Something I'd seen but I hadn't really observed.

I drank my coffee and looked out the window onto Eighth Avenue and thought of all the things that happen every day that we don't appreciate the significance of as they occur. For instance, it is recorded that on Tuesday, July 14, 1789, the day the mobs stormed the

Bastille, King Louis XVI of France wrote in his diary the word "Nothing."

I drank more coffee and looked out the window as history slowly ticked by on the already ancient street outside. The past and the present are deeply intertwined, I thought. History is what happens when one of them gets a little ahead of the other. When a couple of kids on skateboards rolled by I closed my eyes for a moment and it almost sounded like a streetcar.

29

"Linguini and yogurt?" I said.

"Don't you like it?" I heard Kelli ask in a tone that was almost maddening in its childlike innocence.

"Of course I like it," I shouted. "Everybody in America likes linguini and yogurt." I blew some cigar smoke up at the lesbians and made a face at the cat. The cat didn't respond but I knew damn well she wouldn't like linguini and yogurt. Linguini and tuna, maybe.

"So save your appetite. This should be really good. The dinner's at the home of some friends of mine, some dancers I'd like you to meet."

"I've already got a pretty good appetite," I said, "for you doing splits on the bridge of my nose." Kelli chuckled indulgently. So did I.

It was moving in on two-thirty when I hung up with Kelli. The plan was for me to pick her up around eight at her place on West Eleventh Street, and then together we'd venture into the East Village for linguini and yogurt. I'd already had my hip card fairly well punched in the funk department, but this promised to be the kind of experience very few Americans would ever get to have in the course of their lives. I owed it to myself. I owed it to my country.

Going over the day's correspondence, I noticed that I also owed quite a bit to Con Ed, New York Telephone, and the rather unpleasant Greek woman I subletted the loft from. I couldn't go on, I suddenly realized, being an unemployed youth forever. You can't eat a jukebox. My bank account was beginning to resemble that of Dr. Martin Luther King at the time of his death. I thought fleetingly of rounding up the Texas Jewboys and going back out on the road. Then I thought of Tequila. And Raymond. There'd been several incarnations of the Jewboys, and there were guys who'd gladly fill in for the two of them, but it wouldn't be quite the same. Of course, if I was the kind of person who wanted everything the same I wouldn't be going to the East Village tonight for linguini and yogurt.

I decided not to worry about money. Like I'd always said: "Money may buy you a fine dog, but only love can make it wag its tail." Unless I missed my bet, that tail was damn well going to be wagging the dog later tonight on Vandam Street.

Around five-thirty, when I thought Dylan would be home from teaching his fourth-grade class in San Antonio, Texas, I reached him on the blower.

"How was school today?" I asked.

" 'Teach your children well,' " he said. Dylan had the endearingly exasperating habit of frequently speaking in rock lyrics. It wasn't as bad a habit as, say, picking your nose, but sometimes it required the even-mindedness of the Mahatma on the part of the listener.

"Anything new on Boatright's autopsy?"

" 'Don't send me no more dead flowers, baby, no.' " How did he teach?

"The autopsy, Dylan. Anything?"

" 'Nothing was delivered,' " he said.

After some weedling and cajoling, I was able not only to understand Dylan but to, at least temporarily, wean him from his lyrical mode.

"So it looks like an intentional drug overdose," I said. "That's too bad." It was too bad. But lately I was fresh out of sympathy for drug overdoses, intentional or unintentional. Too many people who'd wanted to live on this rotting grapefruit of a dying star had already been indiscriminately eighty-sixed. Somebody up there was asleep at the switch.

"It's pretty strange, hoss," said Dylan. "Ray wasn't one for suicide. And he knew the dangers of drugs pretty well from all his years on the road."

"It's always the best swimmers who drown," I said.

Dylan also revealed that he'd gotten a phone call the day before from Snakebite Jacobs, the horn player for the Jewboys, who was living in New Orleans. Snakebite, apparently, had heard from Boatright in the days just prior to his death, and Raymond had sounded fine.

"In fact," said Dylan, "Ray had asked Snakebite for your phone number but Snakebite didn't have it. He also wanted the number of somebody else in the band."

"And who would that be?" I asked with a slight sense of dread.

"He wanted Tequila's number. You don't know how to reach Tequila, do you?"

"No," I said.

After I hung up I looked over at the cat. "I could've given him 1-800-CROAK," I said.

95

30

The East Village is like any other village except that it's seedier, funkier, and more violent. It is inhabited largely by witches, homosexuals, and drug addicts, and, of course, the few bad apples that you'd find in most any community.

"There better be one hell of a lot of linguini and yogurt," I said as we ankled it up seven flights of dark, dank stairs in the middle of nowhere. "What I'd really like is a big hairy steak."

"That's disgusting," said Kelli, turning up her cute, health-oriented nose as we made our way down a hallway almost big enough for a conga line of pygmies. Strange music was emanating from behind a shabby door. Sounded like somebody'd left their Ravi Shankar record out in the sun too long.

Kelli knocked.

I knocked.

We both knocked.

Eventually, the door was opened by a rather peevish pansexual with green hair who said, *"Entrez-vous."* We did.

The place was lit by candles and redolent with incense. Judging from the appearances of the fourteen men and the one woman who were there, it had the mildly

96

unhealthy ambience of a cheerless, homosexual Haight-Ashbury.

"I'll just help myself to the linguini," I said as the men and the woman began to gyrate wildly around the small room, all of them with their eyes closed.

Our host ignored my needs. Instead, he spoke patiently to Kelli and me, as if we were students in Dylan Ferrero's fourth-grade class. "Kundalini yoga," he said, "is a very old East Indian form of yoga. It involves shaking your body up and down in order to excite and encourage energy to go up and down your spine." He closed his eyes and gave us a very sick little demonstration. I gave Kelli a very thin little wintry smile.

"Kundalini yoga," I said, nodding my head sagely.

"Kundalini yoga?" she said to the thing with green hair, but he was now spinning around with his eyes closed and couldn't be bothered.

"The green moss is about the only normal thing about the guy," I said. "So much for linguini and yogurt."

"I'm sorry," Kelli said. "I must've been listening to these New Yorkers with a Texas accent."

"*These,*" I said, indicating the fourteen men and one woman who were now madly gyrating around the room, "are *not* New Yorkers. *These* are creatures from a distant doughnut. Their sexual identity is a multiple-choice question."

"They do have some nice moves," she said.

"It's a marvelously self-expressive form," I agreed. My head was aching and I was about ready to pass out from hunger, but you've got to humor a dancer if you ever hope to have her help you do the horizontal hustle.

Eventually, Ravi Shankar expired, the dancers stopped moving and languidly held their positions like anemic, degenerate department-store manikins, and a weird little guy came over to us as cheerful as a second cousin at a bar mitzvah. He hugged Kelli and introduced himself to me as Bongo, a dancer Kelli'd once worked with when she was doing a show in Las Vegas. He, apparently, was the one who'd gotten me into this nightmare and I wanted to beat him like a drum.

"What do you think?" he asked, all smiles as he gestured around the room at the dancers who now looked only slightly more substantial than the melting candles. The whole scene made you feel like you were living inside a depraved, human birthday cake. I'd've gotten the hell out of there but it didn't look like I was going to get to make a wish. I damn sure wasn't going to blow any candles.

"Great," said Kelli.

"Really something," I said.

"But that's not all," said Bongo. He ushered us over to where everyone was eagerly forming a rather unpleasant circle on the floor in the full-lotus position. I hadn't sat in the full-lotus position since I'd been a fetus.

After Kelli and I'd taken our places in the circle, Bongo introduced us to the group. Then, one at a time, each person shared his own intimate feelings, now that the magic of kundalini yoga had put all of them in touch with the energy in their spines.

"I feel utterly consumed by love for everyone," said one young man.

"I feel great anger at my parents for not letting me be myself," said another, who obviously held a black belt in Jewish whining.

The woman, for some unknown reason, began to sob. Her sobbing continued for some extended time so, thankfully, she missed her chance to share her experience.

"Next," I said quietly. Kelli elbowed me in the ribs and, before I knew it, a guy across the circle from me was orbing me rather heavily.

"I feel a great love for Kinky," he said.

31

Later, out on the street, I grabbed the first hack I saw, aimed it at Little Italy, and took Kelli to Luna's Restaurant on Mulberry Street where we finally ran down some real linguini. Luna's was the place Ratso and I'd had dinner with Mike Bloomfield several weeks before his death. Every time I went in there I thought I heard beautiful diminished guitar chords.

Luna's never changed. You had to walk by a loaded scullery sink just to get in the place. The waiter, a cheerful, obese, Italian version of a character from *Deliverance*, came up to the table singing "She'll Be Comin' Round the Mountain When She Comes" before he chucked the menus at us. Yola was the lady at the counter. She was Ratso's friend and was currently busy handling the Jewish piano and watching reruns of *Barnaby Jones*. The pasta was the best in the world.

The waiter had brought a large carafe of red wine and a loaf of Italian bread, and was onto the last chorus of "She'll Be Comin' Round the Mountain," when Kelli excused herself for the ladies' room. For a brief, shining moment there I'd had wine, woman, and song, if you counted "She'll Be Comin' Round the Mountain." Now, with Kelli and the waiter gone, I just had wine. I could make it.

I gazed across Mulberry Street at the little Franciscan monastery, The Church of His Precious Blood. I thought of the wine as Michael Bloomfield's blood. He was a Jew like Jesus. Skinny like Jesus. Died pretty young like Jesus. All Jesuses died young, I reflected, as the waiter brought two heaping orders of linguini with red clam sauce and a large pungent bowl of *zuppa di pesce* with everything but the scullery sink floating in it. It was hard to imagine what an old Jesus would've been like. A ragged, unemployed, homeless old fart in a frayed purple robe hanging out at domino parlors and bocci courts, irritating tourists with his eccentric antics. It was probably a good thing he died young, I thought. Like aging movie queens and aging homosexual queens, for an aging King of all mankind, the market just wasn't there. I poured another glass of wine and started in on the soup.

When Kelli returned to the table she sat down across from me and gave me a forced little smile. "Don't wait for me," I said. "Go right ahead."

"I found something in my purse," she said.

"That's fairly remarkable in itself."

Kelli smiled wearily. "Remember that ex-boyfriend I told you about? For some weeks he'd been calling me from Texas in the middle of the night. I told him not to call, I hung up on him repeatedly, but nothing worked. On his birthday he called me at four o'clock in the morning and, in a weird voice, sang 'Happy Birthday' to himself."

"My heart breaks for guys like that."

"Anyway, last week the calls suddenly stopped and I thought I was finally through with him. Now I go into the ladies' room, fumble around in my purse, and find *this*."

"So he's here in New York?"

"It looks like it," Kelli said with a hint of fear in her eyes.

"Let's see that note," I said. Kelli handed it over, and I unfolded and studied it on the table just to the left of my linguini. It was one of those sick things that serial killers and Son of Sam types often put together to maintain that deadly balance of fame and anonymity that they crave. The words were neatly cut from newspaper print and pasted on the page.

A very faint shudder went through me. I wasn't sure if it was the note or the *zuppa di pesce*. But there was something about people who wrote and sent notes like this. The crimes themselves, if and when they were ever committed, might be fairly routine. But the very act of cutting up words of newsprint and pasting them onto a page, unless you were a child or an old lady making a scrapbook, usually meant you were a creep.

I glanced at the note again. It read: "the EYES of Texas are UPON you. YOU cannot Get AWAY."

32

"T he problem," I said to the cat, "with being a country singer–turned–amateur detective is the clients you tend to attract. Even if I'm able to resolve the situation with Kelli's crazy ex-boyfriend from Texas, it'd be inappropriate, not to mention difficult, to collect a fee from a dancer. Of course, it'd be easier than collecting a fee from Tequila. You see the problem?"

It was a cold, dreary Tuesday afternoon and the cat, unfortunately, didn't see a damn thing except the large fly crawling up the side of my mug of hot chocolate. I did not wish the fly to attach itself to one of my melting minimarshmallows. Nor did I wish for the cat to take a swipe at the fly and spill hot chocolate on my scrotum. My only wish was that I wasn't wading Watson-less into a world of wickedness.

"I know you hate every living thing except yourself," I said to the cat, perhaps a bit harshly. "As far as you're concerned I could be a country singer–turned–homosexual, or worse, an accountant. Then I could carefully calibrate your meals and you'd never be without your beloved tuna for the rest of your life. You'd like that, wouldn't you?"

The cat said nothing, but a positively wistful look came into her eyes. I lit a cigar, took a sip of hot chocolate, and took stock of what I had. I wrote it down in rough form on my Big Chief tablet and looked it over for a while, maybe trying to read more into it than was there. The Big Chief tablet read:

Sunday, December 26th, Tequila croaked in rain room.

Friday, December 30th, Ratso zimmed in hallway. Windows of loft nailed shut.

Saturday, December 31st, Winnie's ex-husband, Bud, intrudes himself upon quiet domestic scene, burns a hole in the middle of Persian rug big enough for me to put the whole thing over my head and wear it as a serape.

The first two entries, I figured as I puffed the cigar and studied the Big Chief tablet, could very easily be seen as attempts on my life. Obviously, neither one had been successful. That was why I was smoking a cigar and studying a Big Chief tablet instead of whiling away eternity as worm bait in some suburban bone orchard.

The third entry on the Big Chief tablet, Bud's crashing of my little New Year's Eve party, seemed unrelated to the first two. I would've liked it to be related because Bud seemed a good perpetrator for just about anything, but his alibi was too tight. I still had almost nothing to go on in the riddle of the killer's identity. I was clearly going to need to recruit a new Watson, but there was a problem of a totally different nature that seemed to be nagging at the corners of my mind: Kelli's persistent, slightly deranged noodnik of an ex-boyfriend from Texas. I knew not to take him too lightly. After Charles Whitman, Richard Speck, and Charles "Tex" Watson, I wasn't going to be taking any chances with good ol' boys from Texas who liked to cut words out of newspapers, paste them into messages, and slip them into dance bags. No, Bubba.

If I had the chance, I certainly planned to find this guy and rearrange his bolo tie for him, but first there were other liver flukes to fry. I had to locate the five remaining former Texas Jewboys and the small handful of people who'd worked the closest with the original band. I had to talk to all of them. Try to flesh out some kind of background on Tequila. It wasn't going to be easy without my address book containing their telephone numbers. Tracking wandering Jews could shape up to be a formidable task under the best of circumstances, I thought. I empathized with the committee that had been given the job of writing the Old Testament.

I made a short list on another page of the Big Chief tablet of all the former Jewboys and road crew who'd been with the band from the start. I puffed on the cigar, took a few sips of hot chocolate, tongued a minimarshmallow, and looked over the list. It read as follows:

Band Members:
Snakebite Jacobs, Billy Swan, Willie Fong

Young, Little Jewford, Major Boles, Wichita,
Panama Red, Skycap Adams.

Others:
Cowboy Jack, Dylan, Big Jewford, Bo Byers,
and my brother, Roger. Deceased: Tequila,
Raymond Boatright.

Of course, Tequila and Boatright hadn't lived or died
in anything like the same manner, but dead is dead.
Once deceased, always deceased. It didn't matter who
you were or what you were. As Bum Phillips once said:
"The thing that's going to decide the size of your funeral is the weather."

I looked out the window and the late-afternoon
January sky seemed to be bleeding a frozen, semiviscous, gray-green ooze. Not a fortuitous day for a large
funeral.

I called Dylan first.

"So how was school today?"

" 'Don't know much about a science book. Don't
know much about the French I took.' "

Over the next few hours I spoke with a couple of
voices from the past and learned a number of things
including more than I ever wanted to know about the
effects of time on wandering Jewboys and other assorted Americans. I logged all information I gleaned,
trivial or inconsequential as it seemed, into the Big Chief
tablet. Many of the numbers I called had been discon-
nected. Some had taped referrals. Others had happy
Puerto Rican families residing at them. Most of the time
I had to leave messages on machines or with people I
didn't know.

Around seven I closed shop for the day, put on my
hat and coat, and grabbed a few cigars out of what was
left of Sherlock Holmes's head after a little reconstruc-
tive surgery with Elmer's glue. I left the cat in charge

104

and the answering machine to do the work. I had my lines out across the murky bayou of the years and the miles. Now all I had to do was wait for the fish.

Of course, by the time I caught them they'd probably smell worse than Winnie Katz's workout shorts.

33

"I just don't know," said McGovern, shaking his great head with an exaggerated sarcasm I felt was hardly warranted. "Moving up from your leg man to your Dr. Watson. I'm not sure I can handle all the responsibility. The enormous trust you're somehow willing to place in me. I'm thrilled, of course, beyond words, but I can only pray you find me worthy—"

"Put a sock on it, McGovern," I said irritably.

We both sat in silence for a while and watched a wooden chair burn in the fireplace of McGovern's quaint little newspaper-strewn apartment on Jane Street. We were drinking double shots from a giant bottle of Black Bush that I'd bought at great personal expense in an effort to soften McGovern's reticence toward actively helping me with the Tequila murder case. So far it looked like I was out fifty-eight bucks.

"The thing is," I said, "Ratso's out of commission for a while and Rambam's jumping with Los Cobras in Guatemala—"

"And you're here in my apartment jumping through your asshole for America." McGovern laughed loudly in the little room and knocked back a healthy jolt of the Irish whiskey. A sudden dignity came into his demeanor and, as the light from the crackling fire was reflected in his eyes, I thought I caught a glimpse for a moment of the part of him that was Indian.

"Of course I'll help you," he said. "Anybody who's in as deep shit as you are and doesn't even know it needs all the help he can get."

I stood up and grasped his hand firmly. "Welcome, Watson," I said.

Watson poured us both another double shot of Black Bush. He lifted his glass. "Here's to us, Holmes," he said. "We're all we've got."

My drink and I wandered over to McGovern's famous pink velvet couch, sat down, and loitered for a while as McGovern performed the final touches on the Chicken McGovern that had been obscenely bubbling in a pot for several hours now. Hopefully, it'd be ready before Elijah returned and discovered that he didn't have reservations.

Billie Holiday was on McGovern's old Victrola. The apartment had no television set or radio. In the time I'd known McGovern, since Christ was a cowboy, he'd never owned a television or a radio. I wasn't even sure he knew what they were. If giant ants from the third ring of Uranus attacked the world and you were staying at McGovern's apartment, you wouldn't know it until the invasion was pretty far along. You'd be sitting on a couch that'd been across the Atlantic twice, sipping a little Black Bush, listening to Billie Holliday, and reading a rather dog-eared copy of *The Great Gatsby*. Of course, if giant ants from the third ring of Uranus ever attacked the world, that wouldn't be a bad way to go.

"Chicken McGovern's ready," said McGovern finally.

"This place'd never make it as a fast-food joint," I said.

We both sat down at the little table against the wall to the left of the fireplace. The ancient Smith-Corona typewriter that had once belonged to McGovern's mother remained on the far side of the table like a short, rather quiet dinner companion.

"Who's going to say the prayer?" asked McGovern.

"How much prayer should a Chicken McGovern get?" I asked, somewhat rhetorically because a large drumstick was already on the way at a very rapid pace to my uvula.

"Prayer," said McGovern, pausing to take a large swill of the Bushmills, "is never out of place for a good Christian or a good Jew."

"I'm a pagan," I said. "Like Breaker Morant."

"Me too," said McGovern.

"That's obvious from your table manners."

McGovern laughed. "Me," he shouted. "You're the one eating like a young porker!" The Chicken McGovern was undeniably killer bee.

"Never say 'young porker' in front of a Jewish person," I said. "It causes us to have gas which leads to diarrhea and, quite often, simultaneous projectile vomiting. In layman's terms, squirtin' outa both ends. And, as you probably know, if you are experiencing diarrhea and projectile vomit and, at the same time, happen to belch, you will die."

"Yeah," said McGovern, "then who's going to say the prayer?"

Toward the end of the meal I reached into one of the inside pockets of my youth and pulled out the newspaper-print note from Kelli's Texas ex. I handed it to McGovern and explained a few of the circumstances of its coming into my possession.

"Of course, the main case we'll be working on is the matter of who lunched Tequila in my rain room," I said as I got up to pace off a little of the Chicken McGovern. "But we might be able to clear up this little item quite quickly, and it may prove to be diverting. Good way to get your feet wet, Watson."

McGovern nodded agreeably as he glanced at the note on the table. "Yes, boss," he said in what apparently was a rather weak, Irish-inflected Rochester impersonation. He studied the note more closely.

"Most dancers carry dance bags with them to classes and just about everywhere else they go. The dance bags are like portable attics. They keep their purses in them along with most of their worldly possessions. Everything from tampons to tap shoes. You with me so far?"

"No," said McGovern. "It's too hard to follow."

"Spare me your quaint Irish witticism," I said. "The guy who sent this is clearly deranged and certainly very potentially violent."

"In other words, your typical Texan." I ignored McGovern's remark.

"The guy could've slipped this note into Kelli's dance bag some time ago when she was back in Texas. She might've not known about it until she fumbled around and found it last night. So the good news is that while the guy's a strange bird, he very probably could be safely nesting somewhere back in Texas."

McGovern got up from the table, picked up the note, and held it up against the light. "That's the *good* news," he said.

I walked over to the kitchen and poured a little after-dinner drink. "Go on," I said.

"Many newspapers opt for distinctive makeup. Format, column size, typeface, and so on. The New York dailies fall into this category, as do, of course, the *International Herald Tribune, The St. Louis Post-Dispatch, The—*"

"So what the hell's the *bad* news?" I asked.

McGovern walked over to the table and took a

somewhat theatrical swallow from his tall glass. He set the glass down slowly, folded the note, and handed it back to me rather grimly.

"He's in New York," he said.

34

I hadn't spoken to Willie Fong Young, the original bass player for the Texas Jewboys, since I'd passed on an invitation to his wedding in order to attend the bas mitzvah of my cousin's daughter. Willie's wedding was in Nashville, and Steve and Loni Samet's daughter Erin was to be bas mitzvahed on the same day in San Antonio. Tough choice for the old social calendar. I figured I'd get sick drunk on champagne at either affair, but at the bas mitzvah I could wear my Yamaha on my head. With the Jews, you can wear a Yamaha or a tractor seat or a backyard satellite dish on your head and burp all you want as long as your head is covered. I wasn't so sure that the same rules applied for Willie's rather formal country-club affair.

I told Willie at the time that blood was thicker than water, that my whole family would be at the bas mitzvah, and that, as much as I'd like to go to his wedding, "In the eyes of God, when a young Jew is thirteen years old, the person becomes a man or a woman according to the Torah."

Willie's response, "Why don't you go fuck yourself," showed a certain lack of understanding of Judaism, Christianity, and several other religions, possibly even Islam. Now, as I dialed his number in Nashville, I hoped "The Singin' Chinaman," as I lightheartedly referred to him onstage, had softened his attitude toward me.

"Hey, Willie," I said. "How's the marriage holding up?"

"Just fine, bagel-nose." When a Chink from Arkansas calls a Hebe from Texas "bagel-nose," sometimes it's almost enough to get your Irish up. Remembering all the times I'd introduced him as "The Southern Slope," I let it pass. Besides, I needed Willie's help. The other Jewboys I'd contacted had mostly reacted positively to the notion of a Jewboy reunion tour, but when I came to information about Tequila it was like a missing chord in a faded melody. Of course, I hadn't heard back from Snakebite or Wichita yet, but it didn't seem as if anybody knew much more about Tequila's life since the band broke up than I did. All of them, however, seemed shocked to hear about his death.

Now, with Willie on the line, it was time to set aside the tension conventions of the past, stir-fry his brains, and maybe come away with a little take-out order of Tequila's movements, other than bowel. I made small talk for a while to steer the topic away from weddings and bas mitzvahs, then I dropped the news of Tequila's murder.

"Jesus Christ!" said Willie.

"I'll see that Jesus and raise you a Peter," I said. "Had you been in touch with Tequila at all over the years?" I held my breath. *Somebody* must've been in touch with Tequila since 1976.

"The last time I saw Tequila was in that godforsaken motel someplace in Colorado. The band had just broken up and nobody knew what the hell they were going to do. I walked into his room to say good-bye and he was arguing with Sharon." Sharon was a belly dancer,

110

a free spirit, and Tequila's wife, roughly in that order. She'd called herself by any number of names, including Fatimah, Sheena, and Madame La Tush. Not only did I not know where she was anymore, I wasn't even sure *who* she was.

"They were always arguing," I said.

"Yeah, but this one sounded especially vicious. Of course, she never argued with me. She was a pussycat, if you know what I mean."

"Cast your mind back," I said. "Can you remember anything they were saying when you came into the room?"

"Shit. It's been so long. I think—wait a minute—they were yelling about something that happened on a train."

"You sure it wasn't something that happened on *cocaine?*"

"On that tour, everything happened on cocaine. But it was something heavier than that. Tequila was livid with rage."

"Cocaine," I said rather wearily, "almost ruined my life."

"What do you mean 'almost,' " said Willie.

That was the trouble with having once lived in the fast lane. Every time you sniffled or cleared your throat people thought you were still on drugs. If you'd been known to take a drink in the past and then gotten a divorce, people blamed it on alcohol. Drugs and booze were always blamed for life's failures. My experience has been that drugs and booze tend to make dull people more interesting and interesting people more dull. Of course, if you're on drugs and booze at the time, it's often hard to tell the difference.

"Did Tequila say anything else?" I asked.

"Well, he was pretty bitter as I recall. He said he might just take a trip down to Mexico. And then he said something about you."

"Spit it," I said.

"You sure you want to hear it?"

"Look, Willie, Tequila's dead. This happened over thirteen years ago. What could he possibly have said that could hurt me now?"

"He said you were a burned-out star."

Later that evening I paced the loft, trailing cigar smoke and thinking about my conversation with Willie. What's past was past, I thought. Seine yesterday for clues but don't get caught in it. Life as trajectory, I said to myself. Life as trajectory.

I walked over to the kitchen window and looked up through the rusted fire escape into the narrow New York sky. No stars out tonight. But I knew they were there. Emily Dickinson wrote: "What are stars but Asterisks to point a human life."

It was a nice sentiment and one I could relate to, but maybe she should've gotten out of the house a little more.

35

Thursday morning, when Snakebite Jacobs called back, I was able to update my Big Chief tablet a little further. Snakebite had continued to play music in New Orleans since the band broke up. We talked about that a while, commiserated about Ray Boatright a bit, then I laid the news on him concerning Tequila. Snakebite, too, was shocked. I pushed for more on Tequila.

"Haven't seen him since the Jewboys," said Snakebite, "but Sharon was through here about three years ago."

"Through New Orleans?"

"Through my bedroom, actually. She'd cut her hair Egyptian style and called herself Cleopatra."

"And you were the asp, right, Snakebutt?"

"That's *bite*," said Snakebite. "Snake*bite*." This was an old stage routine that we'd used about eleven times every show. It became progressively more humorous to the audience but I never could tell whether Snakebite liked it or not.

"Cleo said she'd been divorced from Tequila for years. In fact, hadn't even seen him for years. She thought he'd gotten himself into some trouble in Mexico. We didn't talk about him all that much."

"I can understand that. What happened to—uh—Cleopatra?"

"When she left here she was heading for Vegas. Got a call from her a few weeks later in Miami."

"Belly dancers move around," I said.

"You know, one thing was kind of funny about her, though."

"What was that, Snakebutt?"

"*Bite*," he said. "Snake*bite*."

"What was it, Snakebite?"

"As far as she was away from Tequila and as long as it'd been since she'd seen him, she seemed almost *afraid* of him."

"If you hear from her again," I said, "you can tell her not to worry."

After I'd hung up with Snakebite, I looked over the notes I'd made on the Big Chief tablet. I'd talked to, or left messages for, everybody except Wichita who now lived in Tulsa. I'd given him more rings than Elizabeth Taylor but still hadn't gotten through to the boy.

Of course, there were other Jewboys I could've called, but they'd come into the band later down the

113

line and had known Tequila only in passing, pardon the expression.

I thought fondly of Van Dyke Parks, Country John Mankiewicz, Roscoe West, and Jimmie Don Smith, the brilliant blues guitarist who'd died of cancer in '86. I remembered our old bus that had broken down somewhere outside of Dolopolous, Mississippi. I smiled in spite of myself. Everything's funny if you wait long enough.

I decided not to contact these latter-day Jewboys just yet. They'd be great to fill out the band for some kind of imaginary childhood reunion tour, but they didn't know much about Tequila. Of course, nobody else seemed to, either. *Somebody* had to, I reflected. Otherwise I wouldn't've had to buy a new shower curtain.

At straight up Gary Cooper time I called Kelli.

"This is the Dancer," she said as she answered the phone.

"This is the Kinkster," I said.

"Oh, I was hoping it was you."

"Your wish has come true."

"Can I make another?"

"Well, it is my dime, but go ahead."

"Can we have lunch somewhere?" I could think of a few places I wouldn't've minded eating lunch with the Dancer. One of them was at the Y.

"You know, Dancer, I think you're going to be a piece of cake."

"You're wrong, darling. All good dancers are very tough. We only appear to be easy."

"That's what I was afraid of," I said.

Half an hour later I strolled up to Kelli's building on West Eleventh Street just half a step ahead of the mailman. We rang the buzzer together and I noticed he was carrying a package about the size of a shoe box.

"Too big for the box," he said.

"That's what she told me last night," I said. The

114

mailman scowled and said nothing. Reminded me of my cat.

"Hi, Mr. Mailman," said Kelli brightly as she came out onto the front step and kissed me on the cheek.

"Name's Gene," said the mailman sourly. He handed her the package and turned his attention to the mail-boxes on the wall.

"He doesn't like it when I call him Mr. Mailman," said Kelli as she led me down the little hall.

"How can you tell?" I asked.

She fumbled with the key in the lock for a moment and soon we were inside her first-floor apartment which, more than anything else, resembled a hall of mirrors. The mirrors almost completely covered the bottom third of three of the walls in the large front room. On the exposed brick wall, above the little fireplace, was a large framed photograph of a very familiar-looking ass and pair of legs, also exposed.

"Nice decor," I said.

Kelli set the box down on a small table and eyed it suspiciously. "That better not be from Travis," she said.

"Travis, is it?"

"Travis Parnell."

"What does this Travis Parnell look like?"

"He has blond hair. Very handsome. Comes from an extremely wealthy and prominent family . . ."

"Anything good about the guy?" I asked. I stood in the middle of the mirrored room and lit a cigar with my hot-pink Bic. I took a few reflective puffs.

"He has boots just like yours," said Kelli.

"Nobody has boots like these," I said a bit brusquely. "They're brontosaurus foreskin. They cost two or three hundred. What else about the guy?"

"He usually wears a bolo tie," said Kelli meekly.

"Every nerd in the world wears a bolo tie *now*," I said. "If he'd worn one thirty years ago I might've been

115

impressed with him. Of course, he probably wasn't born then. How old is he, anyway?"

"He was twenty-nine the night he sang me that spooky happy birthday song to himself."

"Oh," I said, "he's a kid." Kelli smiled indulgently and so did I.

"He's a cowboy," said Kelli.

"You mean he *thinks* he's a cowboy," I said. "There's only one real cowboy left in the world and that's Earl Buckelew who lives just outside of Medina, Texas. Of course, a lot of guys think they're cowboys. That's all right I guess unless they run into somebody who thinks he's an Indian."

I thought about it for a minute. I was jealous of Travis. I didn't like to admit it, but it was true. I also thought about the other person who'd come to me recently with a story about somebody being after him. I'd have to do a little better job watching Kelli than I'd done with Tequila.

"That's very funny," Kelli said, staring at the box again, "but he's scaring the shit out of me."

"I'm sorry," I said, and I took her in my arms. She felt very childlike and fragile and vulnerable. My eyes wandered up to the photograph above the fireplace. It was amazing, I thought, how many women a woman could be.

"Let's open the package," I said.

We went to the small table by the doorway and I picked up the box. There was no return address. It was postmarked New York. We opened it together.

Inside was a doll. A ballerina. She didn't look like she'd be doing any dancing soon. Her legs had been severed.

116

36

That night I decided to put the Tequila file on the back burner and turn my attention to Travis Parnell. Tequila's unfortunate croaking was almost two weeks old but it seemed like a lifetime, so to speak. I was tired of talking to long-distance voices from the past; the trail had grown old and cold.

I still had operatives working in the field. Captain Midnite in Nashville was poking around about the twenty-five thousand dollars and the Music Row–Sixteenth Avenue South connection. Billy Swan was in Los Angeles running down some drug rumors he'd heard about Tequila and his wife. Cleve was calling periodically with highly annoying "tour updates." And I'd contacted just about everyone I could think of with the exception of Wichita who, of course, lived in Tulsa.

I wasn't the FBI. I wasn't the NYPD. The only real manpower I had was me and McGovern and sometimes I wasn't so sure about McGovern.

I placed the Tequila file, which looked a lot like a Big Chief tablet, in the desk drawer with the book, lyrics, and music for *God's Other Son*, the Broadway show that Don Imus and I had been working on for about forty-nine years now. By this time, we'd both hoped to have some homosexuals tap dancing, but it just hadn't come to pass. These things take time, the lawyer said.

117

Lawyers, like cats and Moslem fundamentalists, have no notion of time. If you die, they know they'll be dealing with your estate. If your lawyer dies, you still have to get another lawyer, who, of course, looks happily forward to dealing with your estate. Where there's a will, there's a lawyer, I always say.

I closed the drawer, took a fresh cigar out of Sherlock's fractured skull, lit it with my pink Bic, and swung it around rapidly with my left arm in three complete arcs like I'd seen a guy in Austin do once. I figured this maneuver either produced an even burn or the guy was an outpatient trying to land imaginary Nazi aircraft onto the bridge of my nose.

I puffed peacefully for a while and thought about Travis Parnell. He'd grown up in Kerrville, Texas, according to Kelli, and his family still lived there. Kerrville is a beautiful little town, but, like all beautiful little towns, it has spawned a few rather ugly incidents over the years. One was the infamous slave-ranch situation that had occurred several years ago just outside of Kerrville near Mountain Home. Hitchhikers were picked up, forced to work on the ranch, at times at gunpoint, and at least one of them had been tortured, rather slowly, to death. The ranch was owned by people who could best be described as a sadistic, cedar-chopping *Bonanza* family gone bad.

The other unpleasant incident had happened even more recently and involved the horrific nurse Genene Jones, who'd made her rounds in San Antonio and Kerrville for several years, administering deadly injections to babies and then trying to save them. Not always successfully.

I wasn't going to sit around on my introspective Jewish buttocks and wait for Travis Parnell to create incident number three. I don't like waiting. And I know something about the waiting game. If you wait around long enough for your ship to come in, your harbor'll sink.

37

"It's no disgrace," I've often heard, "to come from Texas; It's just a disgrace to have to go back there." Whether or not I went back there now was beside the point, of course, because a little ray of Texas sunshine was apparently already here in New York. Its name was Travis Parnell.

But I was not without friends and connections in the Texas Hill Country. As luck would have it, the only two Jews the people down there knew were me and Jesus Christ, and I was the only one they knew personally.

I called my friend Max Swafford in Kerrville, Texas. Max worked as a counselor who officed in an institution called the Alternative School, which worked with emotionally troubled youngsters who couldn't get along within the educational mainstream. I'd thought about enrolling there several times myself.

Max was a very responsible and character-laden American who'd once served as my press secretary when I ran for justice of the peace in Kerr County. As I recalled, he'd done a fine job until he left in the middle of the campaign to search for a gold mine in southern Mexico.

Unfortunately, my fellow Kerrverts had returned me to the private sector. They hadn't responded too well to

119

my campaign slogan, "I'll keep us out of war with Fredericksburg." Fredericksburg was a little town about twenty miles down the road.

As I dialed Texas, I remembered that Max had grown up in West Texas close enough to Mexico to, rather annoyingly, pepper his speech patterns with Spanish. I don't understand Spanish and I don't much like the fact that, at bullfights, Spanish custom dictates they cut the tongues out of the horses so the people won't hear them scream when they get gored. Otherwise, I have nothing against Spanish-speaking peoples.

"*¡Hola! ¿Como está?*" said Max when he answered the phone.

"Yeah, Max," I said irritably. "This is Kinky."

"*¿Qué tal, Señor Friedman?*" It was maddening.

"I'm playing with my piñatas here in Nuevo Yorko," I replied to whatever the hell Max was asking me about. "Look, Max, I've got a little problem here."

I explained that I needed a brief thumbnail on Travis Parnell yesterday. I also needed him to try to pinpoint Parnell's present location. I puffed rather plaintively on the cigar and said: "I need your help, Max."

"The last time I helped you," he said, "*perdiste tu culo.*"

I took another patient puff and asked: "What the hell does that mean?"

"The last time I helped you," said Max, "you lost your ass."

It was creeping up on ten o'clock when I hung up with Max and snow was beginning to fall outside the kitchen window. I was getting that New York trapped-rat feeling that occasionally pervades the soul of all modern cliff dwellers, so I shut down operations, got inside my coat and hat, left the cat in charge, and began to walk up Vandam Street, threading my way through the crazy canopy of God's white geometry.

I was sure that Max would deliver the goods on

Travis Parnell. After all, he'd been a great press secretary in the justice of the peace race. Max had a theory that I was only good interpersonally for about five minutes. When people met me as a candidate, they invariably thought I was very charming and entertaining for the first two or three minutes. After that, they usually began to have their doubts about the wisdom of electing me judge. I'd often become rather nervous and defensive then, and start chain-bumming cigarettes and saying things like: "I'd be a fine judge if I'm any judge at all," or "When I get to be governor, I'll reduce the speed limits to 54.95."

Max would slip in at that point, take my arm, and say something like "The governor's on the phone for you, Mr. Friedman." Yeah, I thought, Max would deliver the goods on Parnell. When I got to Hudson I took a left and kept walking.

It's funny what you think about when you're walking in the snow alone. Though the case of Tequila was still firmly on the back burner, I could see his face very clearly, along with the others, in some long-ago middle distance between the flakes. The band was getting together to rehearse for our first big national tour. It must've been around '73 because everybody looked young, happy, and full of hope. Time and the road, like two sculptors, were just picking up their chisels.

I could see the place, too. It was an old house on a small isolated ranch out in the Texas Hill Country. My family'd owned it for a while, then sold it to some guy in Houston who'd used it only during hunting season. I didn't know who owned it now.

We called the place Rio Duckworth, after an elementary school teacher my brother Roger had once, Miss Duckworth. We all thought Rio Duckworth was a pretty funny name for a ranch, but, then again, it was 1973 and a lot of things were funny then that now seem almost kind of sad.

Like snowflakes.

I walked into the Cottonwood Cafe, a haven on Bleecker Street for transplanted Texans.

"I'll have a chicken-fried snake," I said to the girl in the Dallas Cowboys sweatshirt. "And give me the most esoteric Texas beer you've got."

"What's esoteric?" she asked.

"This restaurant," I said. I looked over to the picture of James Dean from the movie *Giant*. It was cool to be cool in the fifties, I thought. In the nineties, it was cool to be hot. Maybe somebody'd been screwing around with the thermostat.

"All we have is Lone Star," she said.

"That's a wide selection," I said. "Tough choice for an indecisive guy like me. Christ. Let me think about it for a minute. Okay, I got it. I'll have a Lone Star."

Her smile was paper-thin and very brief. Almost a tic. I never did too well with waitresses or stewardesses but I never let it bother me much.

When I'd finished putting my choppers around the chicken-fried snake, for $9.50 plus tax, and knocked off another bottle of Lone Star, I fished out of my pocket the photo of Travis Parnell I'd commandeered from Kelli and showed it to the waitress. Travis looked cute with his shy smile, his hunting rifle, and his military fatigues, but the serene face of the dead Angora goat he was holding up by the horns seemed to exude more humanity. Compared to Parnell, it glowed like the dead face of Christ.

"Know this guy?" I asked.

"No, but I'd like to," said the waitress.

I looked over at James Dean. He'd died two weeks after filming *Giant* and you could see it coming in his eyes.

"Maybe I can arrange it," I said.

38

It was still snowing Friday morning when I got up. Out on Vandam Street the garbage trucks seemed to shiver slightly under a thin blanket of off-white. Nothing stays clean very long in New York, not even the garbage trucks. But you get used to it. Like my friend Rambam said in teaching me one of the most important lessons in life: "Never eat pasta with a white shirt on."

The cat and I sat by the kitchen window and watched the little people running hither and thither like notes on a zither. Possibly it was the chicken-fried snake, but I felt like someone was taking zither lessons in my colon. For $9.50 plus tax, I hoped they were getting their money's worth.

It was a week into the New Year and it felt old already. Time flies when you're tracking psychos, I thought as I sipped a hot chocolate and wondered what to do next. I stood up to get a better view of the street, and the cat jumped off my lap and onto the windowsill. We watched the snow fall for a while in silence, each of us lost in our own whirling, ephemeral dreams.

"Where would you go," I said to the cat, "if you were a displaced Texan on your own in New York?" The cat just kept watching the snowflakes. She'd never been to Texas. In fact, like many other folks in the city,

123

she'd never been out of New York. To her, Texas might just as well have been the South Pole. Of course, the Texans might have something to say about that. So might the penguins.

"Put yourself in four of Travis Parnell's boots," I said to the cat. "Where would he be hanging out when he's not busy trying to terrorize Kelli?" The cat watched the snow.

"He could go anywhere, of course, but it's good odds that, being a Texas kind of guy, he'd've checked out a Texas kind of place. The girl at the Cottonwood said she's there every night and hadn't seen him. What does that leave us?"

I walked over to Sherlock's head and got a Romeo y Julieta Cedros de Luxe Number Three from Switzerland by way of Havana. A lady named Rocky'd sent me a box and the cigars had that old Cuban flavor that can't quite be described but is a cross between a hint of chocolate and a hint of vanilla. Gives you sort of a protein rush like you get from eating sushi after a bad night. The best Cuban cigars come from Switzerland and that's about all there is to say for Switzerland but it's usually enough. The only way to get cigars this good in America is if your favorite rich uncle gets run over by a bookmobile and leaves you his humidor.

When I got back to the window the cat was pacing back and forth on the sill. "Relax," I said. "I'll make you some breakfast." I reached under the counter and came up with a can of tuna. Nothing earth-shattering about that. Every can down there was tuna. Cats are creatures of narrow habit and so are most people and that's what keeps amateur detectives in business.

"There's always the Lone Star Roadhouse," I said. "Everyone from Texas makes a pilgrimage there." The cat jumped down from the windowsill and began hungrily attacking the tuna. I continued my relentless monologue. I'd worked harder rooms than this.

124

"Then there's the Cadillac Bar, Alamo, the Yellow Rose of Texas, and what's that new place on Hudson? It's just up the street from Pete Myers's place, Myers of Keswick, where they have those great pork pies. You ought to try them sometime. You ought to try anything sometime."

I puffed appreciatively on the Cuban cigar. The cat hadn't even looked up. Like a performer in front of an inattentive dinner-club crowd, I went staunchly on with my routine. Following Travis Parnell's mind around Manhattan.

"Cowgirl Hall of Fame," I said. "That's the new Texas place in the Village. I'll check it out, also. See if their chicken-fried snake costs more than nine-fifty plus tax. See if it tastes as good as tuna."

The cat had stopped wiping the tuna crumbs off her whiskers and was staring at me when the phones rang. I walked over to the desk and picked up the blower on the left. It was 11:47 A.M. by the alarm clock that had once belonged to Captain Midnite. He'd slept through five careers with it before he'd given it to me. I'd moved it recently from the bedroom to the desk. I didn't think I had that many careers left to sleep through.

"Señor Friedman," said the voice, "this is Max."

"Shalom," I said.

"You're dealing with a real bad *hombre* here, *amigo*. A girlfriend of mine used to date him some time ago until he got mad one night and broke her fingers."

"Okay, so he's not Alan Alda."

"There's another story about him pushing a girl over a cliff on a skiing vacation in Utah. Almost killed her."

"Well, there's not much to do in Utah."

"Believe me, he's a badass with men, women, and animals. If you're gonna tangle with him, be careful."

"So where the hell is he, Max?" I was starting to like Travis Parnell even less than I thought I would.

"Nobody seems to know for sure. But I did talk to

125

his family. All they know is that he left home a few weeks ago. He said he was going on a hunting trip. Said he wasn't coming back until he killed something."

"That's what I live for," I said.

39

I spent the rest of Friday afternoon cutting my nose hairs and listening to a Caruso tape I'd bought in a bargain bin on Canal Street for a lot less than I'd paid for the chicken-fried snake. It was still snowing outside and colder than Cooperman's eyes, so I figured I'd at least wait till the snow stopped before I continued my odyssey of Texas cultural oases in New York City. Unless I got very lucky indeed, the next move, unfortunately, seemed to be Travis Parnell's. Given his modus operandi—the late-night calls, the note culled from newspaper headlines, the ballerina with the severed legs—I did not think ol' Trav was the type to move in for the quick kill. He was more like a cat who liked to play rather extensively with the mouse before—well—before he killed it. That gave me, if nothing else, a little time.

I'd warned Kelli to be on the alert and to call me immediately upon the next sighting or contact with the out-of-state creature. She hadn't wanted to move out of her place, so the only other thing I could've done was to take a large bottle of Jameson's and a box of cigars and move into the hall of mirrors with her. It did have possibilities.

I called Ratso that afternoon just to check his pulse. His voice still sounded like the brakes on a subway train, but he said he was feeling better. He'd decided not to go to California until the spring. His jaw would be wired for about another month, and, after that, he looked forward to resuming his role as Watson if I hadn't already solved the case. I felt a small twinge of guilt for not telling him I'd hired McGovern as my new Watson, but there was nothing I could do about it. The dogs may bark, but the caravan rolls on.

Around four o'clock it stopped snowing. Up and down Vandam Street it looked like someone had laid a beautiful mantle of white over the pavement, the potholes, the garbage cans, the parked cars, the sidewalks, the rusted fire escapes, the pathetic big-city detritus that seemed like so many little children's toys left out in the snow. I toasted the view with a shot of Jameson's. It wouldn't last long, I thought. Nothing this nice ever did.

On my way out I passed Winnie on the stairs. We each said hello but the frosty look she gave me made it seem positively warm by the time I got outside. Too bad she was a lesbian. You couldn't just buy her a new pair of shoes and everything would be all right. I wasn't sure if that worked with anyone anymore. We live in a fucked-up, complex world where women are men and men are women, where JFK's an airport, RFK's a football stadium, and Martin Luther King's a street running through your town. Life's a magazine, love is pain, and death is waiting at the end of a needle or a prayer. Waiting like a rat in the gutter to snatch away the last crumbs of somebody's crumbling dream. One new pair of shoes, more or less, wasn't going to make a hell of a lot of difference anymore.

As I made my way through the snow, Tequila kept weaving his way into my consciousness. Sometimes in

127

life, I have found, it's hard to keep things on the back burner on the back burner. I took Parnell's picture out of my pocket and studied it deliberately to banish Tequila's face from my mind.

"Sorry, Tequila," I said. "I'll get around to you."

I walked a lot of snowy streets that evening and took four hacks, the drivers of which, incredibly, all were born in places that begin with an *I*. The first one was an Israeli, the second was from India, the third was an Iranian, and the fourth was an attractive dark-haired woman from Shenandoah, Iowa, with whom I was able to exchange phone numbers and hobbies.

I hit the Lone Star Roadhouse first and talked to Bill Dick, the owner, and Big Mike, the bartender. Neither had seen Parnell, but they helped me circulate the photo among the waitresses and busboys, an exercise which, unfortunately, came up empty. Bill launched into a massive clinical recall about his new 47-foot boat which had a 973 Slivovitz-Fuckhead engine in it or something like that.

"Sounds hot," I said.

"Is that a boat or is that a boat, Kinkster?" Bill asked, somewhat rhetorically.

"That's a boat," I said.

Before I left, Big Mike and I had a double shot of Jack Daniel's for the road. "Have you seen Cleve," he asked.

"Never could see Cleve," I said.

"But you've heard from him," Mike persisted.

"I'm afraid so," I said.

I blitzed the Cadillac Bar, the Alamo, and the Yellow Rose of Texas with similarly discouraging results. Travis Parnell was a spinning ghost. No one had seen him. But, then, New York, like Texas, was a big place. I knew he was here. I could hear his chains clanking in the dark, snowy side streets. I could feel strange, chilly gusts of air when everything around me seemed still.

128

Parnell had committed no crime and there was nothing I could go to Cooperman with, but, for some reason, the whole thing was becoming almost next door to scary. Not really frightening, in the true sense. But slightly spooky in spite of itself. Like staying up late alone and finding yourself suddenly being sucked spiritually into a Japanese monster movie.

40

"The chicken-fried *steak* is $10.95," said a somewhat effeminate-looking young man in a Roy Rogers suit at the Cowgirl Hall of Fame. It was beyond imagination that anyone could charge these prices for a product that in Texas was more mundane than the hamburger. Of course, in New York, who knew?

"Plus tax?" I asked.

"I'm afraid so," he said worriedly. "*Everything* today is plus tax except love."

"They've got a tax on love, too," I said. "It's called marriage."

He twirled a little gold tassel on his shirt. "What do you want to drink?" he said.

We went through the routine about esoteric Texas beers and he returned with something called Rattlesnake which, after the third bottle, was biting me in the ass so well I had to order a Wild Turkey chaser.

"That chicken-fried snake was killer bee," I told the waiter when I finished.

"Chicken-fried *steak*," he teased. If he could play the horn, and anything ever happened to Snakebite Jacobs, we could pop this guy into the reunion tour and put him out on the road. He was already wearing his high rodeo drag.

I showed him the photo and he shrugged his Roy Rogers suit. I paid the check, admired the Cowgirl's rather extensive barbed-wire collection, and, in what was becoming a fairly tedious routine, made the rounds of the waitresses and bartenders. Parnell's photo was becoming rather dog-eared and smudged with fingerprints, but somehow, vaguely suspecting the current state of his brain, I didn't think he'd mind.

I'd about decided that the boy either hated Texas culture or he'd blipped off the screen when my eye caught a cute blond cowgirl who worked sort of as a Joe Louis greeter in the place. I was leaving so there wasn't that much for her to greet, but I showed her the photo anyway.

Pay dirt.

"He came in here early last week," she said. "Monday or Tuesday night I think. It was late and it wasn't very crowded. I was working the bar. Are you a cop or something? You don't look like a cop."

It was important to keep this broad loose and flowing with the information. Keep everything lighthearted and easygoing. If she clammed up, I was going to have to crucify her on the barbed-wire collection. Upside down, like they did to St. Peter.

"Of course I'm not a cop," I said. "I work for Kodak. How'd you like your photo in the next issue of *Guns and Ammo*?"

She flashed me a country-cute smile.

"Did this guy say anything?" I asked.

"He said he'd just got to town a few days before.

130

Said he was here for a shoe show. Said he was tired of hanging around drinking with Dylan Thomas's ghost. Will that do?"

"Shoe salesmen are getting pretty literary these days."

"And Kodak representatives are getting kind of pushy."

Now she was really smiling. I may not do that well with waitresses or stewardesses, but give me a little time with Joe Louis–type greeters and I'm not without charm. I asked a few more questions and got a few more answers, none of which amounted to anything. Parnell hadn't told her where he was staying.

"Who are you, anyway?" she asked.

"My Christian name is Friedman," I said. Then I ankled it out of there before the saloon doors hit me in the ass.

41

Ten-thirty on a Friday night was not the time most people chose to take a power nap, but I'm not most people. As far as most people are concerned I just continue to follow my lifelong motto: "Fuck 'em and feed 'em Froot Loops."

"Most people, be damned," I said to the cat as we lay down together on the couch. I leafed through the little booklet that had come with the Caruso tape. I read a small portion of it to the cat. " 'Enrico Caruso,' " I began, " 'was the most celebrated and sought-after singer of his time, and possibly the greatest tenor of the century.' "

The cat was watching me intently. *"Possibly?"* I said. The cat blinked. I continued.

" 'Born in Naples in 1873, he was the fifteenth of twenty-one children.' " The cat was watching me now like a bird in the garden.

"That's quite a litter," I said.

The cat's eyes were perfect pinwheels, like a heroin addict's. "Have you been shooting up again?" I asked. The cat did not say a word, but her face took on an expression of haughty disgust. No sense of humor at all.

" 'His early musical and general education,' " I continued to read aloud, " 'was given by the church—' which also," I said, departing from the text, "gave us the Crusades, the Inquisition, and the Holocaust."

The cat began to make irritating kneading movements with her claws on my chest. I returned to the manuscript proper.

" '—where he sang as a choirboy in his beloved Naples. Finding a voice teacher proved almost impossible, as each teacher told him that he had neither voice nor talent!' "

"So much for most people," I said. The cat yawned. So did I.

Travis Parnell was stalking me with his hunting rifle. I was moving leaden-footedly, backward in time, through a tropical jungle of rambutan and durian trees that must've been somewhere in Borneo. I was heading desperately toward the long-ago safety of a childhood chinaberry tree that had stood in the front yard of our house in Houston. My mother was sitting beside the tree, and I knew as I saw her that I wasn't going to

132

make it. In dreams, you rarely win these kind of races. In life, you never do.

Parnell was getting closer and periodically taking aim with his rifle, which had a scope about the size of the Palomar telescope and flashed maddeningly in the sun. Suddenly, my friend John Morgan was there running beside me. " 'After the first death,' " he said, " 'there is no other.' " Then he was gone.

I was running as fast as I could but Parnell was moving relentlessly closer with a sickeningly engaging smile on his face. The leaves of the trees became familiar faces. I saw Tequila's and one that might've been Boatright's detach themselves, and, in slow motion, whirl hypnotically to the ground.

I had to run faster. There was kind of a fractured, country-western version of "Chariots of Fire" going on in the background, and I thought of the Christian runner Eric Liddell's words: "Where does the power come from? It comes from within." I ran faster.

I ran through the trees like Bambi's mother with Parnell moving as if on a track behind me. A full moon was rising and it seemed to have cross hairs on it. South American peasants began burning the trees as I moved past. Smoke got in my eyes and I ran blindly into the growing darkness. At one point, I saw a beautiful, delicate, nearly translucent butterfly whose wings seemed to embody the gentleness of my mother's hands. When I got to the chinaberry tree, my mother was gone.

I knew where she was, though. She was within.

I woke, at first, as a child. Then the reality of the years rushed back like a toxic Love Canal torrent of loneliness into the loft and I felt my heart ache for dreams that become true and truths that become dreams.

It was 2:15 A.M. I put on my cowboy hat and my hunting vest with the little stitched pockets for great white hunters to keep their bullets and shotgun shells

133

in. What wonderful sport, I thought, to send a tiny metal projectile crushing through the skull of a peaceful, harmless animal. I stuffed three cigars into three little stitched pockets and headed grimly for the door.

I figured I finally knew where I could find Travis Parnell.

"After the first death, there is no other," I said to myself in the back of the hack.

"Say what?" said the driver.

Dylan Thomas had been right, of course, spiritually speaking, but, in a practical sense, he might've been very wrong. Thomas had led an extremely funky, full-tilt, self-destructive life, but I didn't remember ever reading about anybody getting blown away in his rain room.

That quote, the one Morgan had recited to me in the dream, was a line from one of Thomas's poems that I first read because it had such a wiggy title. The title, "A Refusal to Mourn the Death, by Fire, of a Child in London," was a poem in itself. It showed that not only was Thomas a very angry man but he also had a pretty good sense of humor. Might've been a few of the reasons why a young songwriter from Minnesota named Bob Dylan had decided to borrow his name.

As I read it, there were only two possible places

Parnell could've been referring to when he told the broad at the Cowgirl that he was "tired of hanging around drinking with Dylan Thomas's ghost." I should've got it then and there, but sometimes things need to percolate through your dreams a little before you understand them.

The two places where Dylan Thomas's ghost might've been hanging around were the White Horse Tavern, where Thomas had reportedly drunk eighteen straight shots of Old Grand-dad, passed out at the bar, and been dumped out on the sidewalk, and the Chelsea Hotel, where he was taken and, apparently, did his dead-level best to "rage against the dying of the light" for the last time. His death certificate stated that Thomas had died of "acute insult to the brain," a phrase demonstrating that coroners have a sense of humor, too.

There was no reason for Parnell to be hanging around a bar and hamburger joint in the Village, even if Dylan Thomas had, unbeknownst to himself, put it on the map. Parnell more likely had become bored hanging around his hotel. And the Chelsea had a plaque out front commemorating the fact that Thomas had lived and died there.

Of course, Sid Vicious's girlfriend had lived and died there, too, but it doesn't have quite the same ring to it when you tell someone you're tired of hanging around drinking with Nancy Spungeon's ghost.

It was slightly after two-thirty when the driver let me off in front of the Chelsea Hotel. I'd been there before. It was the first hotel the Jewboys had stayed in when we played Max's Kansas City on our first New York gig in 1973. It was also the place where I'd first met Abbie Hoffman.

If you've ever stayed at the Chelsea for a while, a little bit of it rubs off on you and, though you may check out, you never quite leave. Then there are those, like Dylan Thomas, who checked out when they checked out. I wasn't eager to join that select group tonight if I could help it.

The lobby of the Chelsea looked like a cross between an art museum and a methadone clinic. A young girl was staring off into space. A man and a woman were arguing with each other. The paintings and the sculpture appeared to be done by Dalí, and might've been. The people in the lobby might've been the models he'd used.

It all came rushing back. How proud, seedy, and soulful the place seemed when you walked in the door. How perfectly the old, eccentric hotel seemed to suit the spirit of the band that cold winter night when we checked in there for the first time. Dalí could've painted us, too.

The night clerk at the desk, perpetually bored yet halfheartedly trying to seem busy, looked like an undertaker out of Charles Dickens. As I spoke to him, his eyes flickered with what could almost pass for interest. Was Travis Parnell staying at the Chelsea? The answer, apparently, was yes and no.

I pushed; he hedged. I cajoled; he wavered. The story, when I finally got it, was interesting and somewhat suggestive in terms of time frame. Parnell had checked in about twelve days ago, right about the time I'd been staring at salamis in the window of the Carnegie Deli. He'd paid for the week in advance. When the week was up, the hotel had tried to contact Parnell about leaving another deposit, but he hadn't responded to the phone messages they'd left or the notes they'd slipped under his door. A day later, the management moved Parnell's luggage down to the storeroom and rented the room to somebody else.

Ten minutes and forty dollars later, I was down in the dank Chelsea Hotel storeroom with the night security man, who had a buttocks about the size of the rear end of the squad car he'd once, no doubt, driven. The only thing more tedious to deal with than a cop is an ex-cop who still thinks he's one. That, however, was not my problem.

My problem was being in a small, dusty, poorly lit room at three o'clock in the morning, trying to navigate around countless trunks, boxes, and suitcases, racks of unclaimed fashionably forties clothing, one beautiful brown Borsalino hat that looked like it'd been there before the war, and one large, ubiquitous ex-cop's buttocks. A treasure map might've helped, or maybe my dad's World War II navigational bombing maps of Germany. These day's it'd be easier to find a needle in the Chelsea than Parnell's suitcase.

"Welcome to the Bermuda Triangle of all lost luggage, fella," said the security guy. I began checking the tags on suitcases while he stood just inside the door of the crowded little room. A look of disgusted impatience was on his face, like he was in a hurry to get back to sleep.

"Whatever happens to ferry-boat captains?" I said as I performed a slight variant of the Virginia reel, moving through all the crap in the storeroom.

It didn't take as long as it might've, but it took long enough. Travis Parnell's suitcase was an expensive-looking hand-tooled leather affair that had been shoved against a wall directly behind a steamer trunk that looked like it'd come over on the *Golden Hind.*

It wasn't locked.

Inside the suitcase were clothes, toilet articles, shaving cream, and a paperback of Robert B. Parker's *Looking for Rachel Wallace.* Underneath the first archaeological layer I found two cases of forty-five caliber bullets and a photo of Kelli Tuck.

"Judy Garland's luggage doesn't appear to be here," I said. Toward the end of her life, Judy'd been unable to pay her hotel bills, and several New York hotels had reportedly impounded her possessions. While this in-

137

formation was probably only of great interest to the homosexual community, it was more pleasant to think about than the implications of what I'd found in Travis Parnell's suitcase.

"Got what you wanted, fella?" asked the security guy as he moved to the door.

"Yeah," I said. "All that's missing is a man and a gun."

43

"Rectal realism," said Goat Carson as he stood in my loft smoking one of my cigars and drinking about five fingers' worth of my Wild Turkey, "is a school of art my brother Neke created here in New York in the early seventies."

It was Saturday afternoon and I was half listening to Goat, as I always did, and half watching the garbage trucks pull out of their staging area on Vandam Street. The city looked like a bomb had hit it. With the snow partially melting, you could see unpleasant-looking objects lying around everywhere, and the street itself looked like something that'd come out of Jimmy Buffett's blender.

"How interesting," I said.

"He wants you to have this," said Goat.

"Who wants me to have what?" I asked.

Goat unwrapped a large canvas on the kitchen table and leaned it against the counter. "This once hung in the National Gallery in Washington before it was stolen, but that's another story," he said. "Neke wants you to have it for catching that queer a few years back who was strangling the blond women in TriBeCa. Neke had a beautiful blonde then who lived down there and he feels you helped prolong his sex life."

"Ah, yes," I said. "The Bruce the Ripper Case, I believe." McGovern had called it that in the *Daily News* and somehow it'd stuck. That particular case had brought me just about as close to death as I'd ever come, but it had given Ratso a chance to explore his sexual identity.

"What do you think of it?" Goat was saying.

"What do I think of what?"

"The fucking painting," Goat shouted. He adjusted his little black-leather hat to a rather rakish angle and took another hearty shot of Wild Turkey.

I didn't know a hell of a lot about art. I wasn't sure I even knew what I liked. I figured I might as well walk over to the table and find out. I did.

It was a portrait of Andy Warhol.

"Andy videotaped Neke," said Goat, "as Neke was painting Andy."

"That Andy," I said.

"It's got a very primitive sort of Grandma Moses look to it, doesn't it?" Goat downed another shot of Turkey and cocked his head to one side, admiring the work.

"Very primitive," I said. I killed a shot myself. We both studied Warhol's bland countenance for a moment or two. The only thing Warhol had ever done that I liked was to put my friend Tom Baker in his movies. But there was something rather appealing about the painting. Warhol looked very colorful in his colorless sort of way.

"This may be a stupid question," I said, "but why is this called rectal realism?" If you don't ask, I thought, you'll never know.

Goat waxed professorial, like a deeply degenerate

graduate student hoping for tenure in the University of Life. He cleared his throat and repeated the phrase *rectal realism* several times. Then he began his little lecture.

"In the early seventies, when Neke was experimenting with rectal realism," Goat intoned, "he always favored a very short easel. When he was working, more than anything else, he probably resembled a center in football. Every now and then, he'd look between his legs at his subject. This work in oils of Andy Warhol is, I believe, one of his finest efforts, but he painted many other canvases in this fashion. Once he painted a very fine likeness of the audience from the stage of a Martin Mull show.

"During this period of his creative life, Neke employed specially rubberized tips on the ends of all his brushes. Then, placing the canvas either on the floor or on the very short easel, Neke would take the brush and . . ."

"You don't mean . . ."

"Yes, I do," said Goat, nodding appreciatively at the student's sudden grasp of the subject matter. He poured us both another shot of Wild Turkey. "Yes, I do."

"You're not really saying . . ."

Goat put a hand up to stop me. He made a rather obscene gesture with the other hand.

"I'm telling you," said Goat, "that Neke painted this portrait with his ass."

"My God," I said. "It's a masterpiece."

Later, after Goat had taken his departure, I threw out an empty bottle of Wild Turkey and wondered where to hang my new art acquisition. The dumper was certainly a possibility, but somehow, it just didn't seem right. On the other hand, if you're going to have somebody watching you take a Nixon, Andy Warhol's about

140

as good a choice as any. Out of respect for the artist, however, I finally jetted the idea.

Eventually, I chose an aesthetically pleasing, high-profile locus on the wall above my desk where many Americans would see it when they walked in the door and realize I had a little more refinement than they'd suspected. The downside of this particular portrait placement was that people who live alone never seem to be able to hang pictures straight because they've got nobody to stand by the door and say, "A little to the right."

Now anybody coming in the loft would immediately suspect I was a highly refined, pathetically lonely bastard, and it wouldn't even be true. I'm not that refined.

As Saturday evening cradled the city in a muffled, moth-eaten blanket of horns and darkness and sirens, I found myself still silently staring into Andy Warhol's Evian water eyes. For the first time in my life, I looked upon Warhol with something almost akin to empathy. I was the one who was supposed to come up with the answers. I was the one who was supposed to seek out the truth. Yet I felt like a befuddled participant-observer of life. With all the many dark and deep and blue currents swirling about my head and eddying into my life within the past two weeks, I still had done little, and knew even less.

I thought, with a grim smile, of the phrase Truman Capote had once used to describe Warhol: "A sphinx without a secret."

44

On Sunday morning, with a cup of steaming espresso in one hand and the first cigar of the day in the other, it did not take me long at all to realize that Andy Warhol's eyes were inspiring me even less than they had the night before. Taking nothing away from the unique, dexterous talents of Neke Carson, I was beginning to feel very strongly that either me or Andy had to go.

If the portrait had been of, say, Ernie Kovacs, Hank Williams, or Anne Frank, it would've been a very different matter. They were my three patron saints; I admired these people, and privately believed they were all Jewish and all born in Texas. I believed the same about Gandhi, Emily Dickinson, and Tony Curtis, and admired them greatly, too, though I wasn't sure about Tony Curtis being born in Texas. I admired Ira Hayes, the American Indian who was one of the four men who raised the flag at Iwo Jima. I also admired Isaac Hayes, Gabby Hayes, Helen Hayes, and Woody Hays. And "Purple Haze."

I did not particularly admire Andy Warhol, and judging from his rather limpid, Aryan, pastel expression, he did not particularly admire me. It was nothing personal. Tom Baker had introduced us once at the Lone Star Cafe and we'd gotten along fine. It was just that his demeanor always seemed to evoke the essence of a Campbell's soup can. I needed the lost recipe for that Jewish Hungarian goulash that Ehrich Weiss's mother used to make for him before he grew up and changed his name to Harry Houdini.

These were the Sunday morning thoughts that were going through my head as most of my fellow Americans were in church praying to Jesus to help them make the payments on their latest four-wheeled penis. Jesus, of course, was Jewish also, though he, quite obviously, had not come from Texas. He was still batting .500.

I turned the chair away from the desk so it faced the window. The view was fairly weak but it beat gazing at Andy Warhol's lips. I made another cup of espresso and gave the blower a little workout just to keep my left ear warm.

I called Kelli and got her playing the blues harmonica on her answering machine. I called Cooperman, got put on hold three different times by three different cop-shop functionaries, and then got cut off before I could leave a message. I called Winnie but she slammed down the phone as soon as she heard my voice. Reaching out and touching someone was not what it used to be.

I decided to take a break from the blower for a while, got my pliers and Phillips screwdriver off the shelf, and located a rerun of *Quincy* on my old knobless black and white television set in the living room. I'd seen this show before, but I liked Quincy and Quincy liked me and I needed to talk to someone. The first adult I ever saw carry on a conversation with a television set was my old friend Slim back in Texas. Slim used to talk to *Bonanza*.

After the vignette that runs at the end of each *Quincy* had reached its final poignant freeze-frame, I turned off the set with the pliers, took a large blob of Lone Star Roadhouse five-alarm chili out of the freezer, served the cat some tuna, and we both had Sunday brunch to-

143

gether. When the brunch was over, the cat curled up in her rocking chair and I put on the Caruso tape and schlafed out on the couch for a little power nap. Now that I knew he had no voice and no talent, I had a new and greater respect for Caruso.

Around four that afternoon I was able to reach McGovern at the National Desk of the *Daily News.* "McGovern World Headquarters," he said.

"Watson," I said, "I need you."

"I didn't know you cared," said McGovern, sending small tidal waves of chuckles crashing deep into my inner ear. At least Ratso had laughed more infrequently.

"We need to get together," I said with some urgency. "We need to have a Watson Transitional Power Caucus as soon as possible."

I quickly brought McGovern up to speed on the fact that Travis Parnell was lurking around somewhere with a gun and a bad attitude, and gave him my considered opinion that all hell might break loose at any time and possibly from several directions at once. It was imperative that our relationship be functionally operative in case the unforeseen occurs, as it almost invariably does.

McGovern informed me that he was wrapping up a story about the very large and terribly overweight visiting Russian female downhill bobsled team, and would be ready to assist me in my crime-solving efforts a little later that evening.

As fate would have it, things came to a boil a little sooner than that. I was standing on the chair, reaching high above the desk, in the midst of a little spontaneous Andy Warhol relocation project, when the phones rang. Without personal injury, I was able to collar the blower on the left after the fourth ring.

"Start talkin'," I said.

She did.

I didn't recognize the voice, but as she talked, I did

144

recognize that something terrifyingly, timelessly evil was taking place. By the time I hung up, I'd also recognized something else.

The back burner was on fire.

45

"Wichita was killed in Tulsa?" McGovern said incredulously as he eyed the tall Vodka McGovern on the little table. We were sitting in a dark booth at the back of the Corner Bistro, about as far away from Portugal as you could get.

"Hunting accident," I said. "That's what his sister told me when she called." I knocked back about half of a healthy shot of Jameson's.

McGovern's intelligent eyes met my own. Then he shrugged and picked up the Vodka McGovern. "Hunting accident," he said.

"Wichita had a little cabin on some land outside of Tulsa. They got a severe cold spell last week and the plumbing froze up. He went out in the woods with a roll of toilet paper and . . ."

"Somebody blew his shit away," said McGovern.

"That's a rather coarse way of phrasing it, but it's essentially correct." We drank for a moment in silence.

"In 1980," said McGovern, "Tulsa was the number-one city in the country with over two hundred thousand population in terms of accidental fatalities per capita."

"Watson," I said, "you always cease to amaze me. What other enlightening spiritual trivia do you have filed away in your large head?"

"I'm on the National Desk," said McGovern a bit defensively. "That's what they pay me for. But since we're on the subject of accidents, who was the pilot in the first fatal plane crash?"

"Let me think," I said as I signaled Dave for another round of drinks. "Pontius Pilate?"

"That's a good guess, Sherlock, but it's incorrect. The pilot in the first fatal plane crash was Orville Wright. It occurred on September 17, 1908. Orville survived but his passenger died."

"Oh, the humanity!"

McGovern looked at me. "You're not really so sure Wichita's death was an accident, are you, Sherlock?"

"Well," I said, "Wichita and Boatright appear to have died accidentally, and Tequila's manner of croaking was quite obviously murder."

"Quite," said McGovern as Dave brought the drinks to the table.

"But that makes three former Texas Jewboys who've all made the one-way trip to Hillbilly Heaven within the space of two weeks. It *could* be coincidence, but I doubt if even a Brooklyn bookie would give odds on that."

McGovern was silent for a moment. Possibly he was considering placing a bet.

"And there's something else that's rather suggestive," I said. "Wichita's sister told me—these are not her words—but before Wichita went outside to take the last Nixon of his life, he'd been playing the guitar. That's what he did about twenty-four hours a day, which is one reason why so many musicians tend to get up your sleeve after a while."

146

"Present company excluded, of course."

"Of course. But near Wichita's guitar, the state police found the musical charts for 'Ride 'em Jewboy,' a song off my first album. That didn't mean much to them, but it tells something to me."

"Maybe he was just indulging in a bit of nostalgia," said McGovern.

"Unlikely, my dear Watson, unlikely. You only use charts when you're unfamiliar with a song. Wichita'd played that tune thousands of times on the road. Why would he need charts?" I killed the shot of Jameson's and went about initial preparations for lighting a cigar.

McGovern seemed to be lost in thought. Still in somewhat of a semitrance, he got up and walked over to the jukebox. I knew he was onto something because he'd left his Vodka McGovern on the table. Soon Billie Holiday was singing in the Corner Bistro. It was the kind of place she would've liked.

When McGovern returned to the table, his eyes were shining with triumph. "I've got it," he said.

"Watson, don't tell me you've cracked the case?"

"No, but I've got the headline." I winced slightly and lit the cigar.

"Christ," I said rather irritably. "Lay it on me."

McGovern took a long drink from the tall glass. He leaned back in his chair and stared intently at me across the little table.

"SOMEBODY'S KILLING THE JEWBOYS OF TEXAS," he said.

46

One of the most frightening aspects of childhood ghost stories is that some of them tend to haunt us for the rest of our lives. When I was a kid at summer camp, just outside of Kerrville, Texas, our counselor, Vern Rathkamp, told us one particular late-night tale that I've never forgotten. It was called "The Last of the Thirteen."

Vern was very big and very tall, and though I was ten years old at the time, I still think of him that way today. I can see the sleeve of his T-shirt rolled up to hold his packet of cigarettes. I can see all of us, staring with the ingenuous eyes of the early fifties over the edges of our bunk beds as Vern told his story, occasionally pacing back and forth like a tiger in the semidarkness. And no matter how nonsensical, disjointed, and downright ludicrous they may appear today, when you're ten years old every story is true.

It was Sunday night and I wasn't sleeping anyway. So I sat at the kitchen table in my purple robe, drank black coffee, smoked Cuban cigars, and let my mind wander back to Echo Hill Ranch, a little green valley full of smoky campfires and dusty dreams. Through the ears of a child, I heard Vern again telling "The Last of the Thirteen."

When Vern was very young he'd met a man on a

148

train about half an hour before midnight. The man was not an old man, but the striking feature about him was that his hair was pure white. Every few minutes or so the man would ask Vern, "What time is it, son?" and Vern would tell him. As it grew closer to midnight, the man became increasingly nervous in the service, and finally unburdened himself of what had been, for many years, his own private hell.

Some time ago, when he'd been a freshman in college, the man with the white hair had joined a fraternity. During that first year, as part of the hazing process, he and his twelve pledge brothers were blindfolded and taken out into the country by the upperclassmen. When the upperclassmen had dropped them off and driven away, the pledges took off their blindfolds and realized that they were lost in the middle of a dark forest.

"What time it is, son?"

"It's a quarter to twelve, sir."

They wandered through the forest and stumbled eventually upon an old abandoned house. It was very dark and they had no flashlights or camping gear and they were exhausted, so all thirteen of them slept in the living room of the creepy old house. At dawn, they left and found their way back to the city.

In the next four years, they finished college, graduated, and went their separate ways. Several years after graduation, the tragic word arrived that one of the young men in that freshman pledge class had fallen down the stairs in the basement of his home and died. The only unusual thing about the unfortunate accident was that, when they'd found the body, the young man's hair had turned white.

"What time is it now, son?"

"Ten minutes till midnight, sir."

The following year it was learned that another member of the group had been killed in a one-car accident on a lonely road around midnight. His car had run into a tree, killing him instantly. His hair was white as driven snow.

During the next five years, five more from the freshmen fraternity class died. One fell off the roof of a tall building. Another jumped off a diving board into a pool without any water. Another choked to death in a fancy restaurant where no one felt it was appropriate to give him the Heimlich maneuver. Still another died when his Honda Civic was T-boned by a shuttle bus. Yet another died of mysterious causes, possibly brought on by the ennui engendered by his hearing about the deaths of all the others. In every case, the hair of the victim was white as a suburb.

"What time is it now, son?"

"It's five minutes to midnight, sir."

The remaining six men decided it was about time they got together for a little power caucus. They met in the same city where they'd attended college. They discussed the deaths of their friends and surmised that some strange kind of curse must have been responsible. They thought back over their years at college. The only thing they could recall that all thirteen of them had done together was spend the night in that old house in the middle of the forest.

So they went back to the house. They went back on a dark, stormy winter night, but this time they brought flashlights, weapons, and overnight gear. The place looked a lot spookier than they'd remembered. Tall spruce trees grew in front and shrieked in the wind. Inside the living room, all the furniture was covered with sheets, and cobwebs and dust were everywhere. The old house creaked and shuddered from the storm outside and the devil knew what inside. They looked around with their flashlights but found nothing of interest until they saw a picture over the fireplace. It was a painting of a very old and wrinkled woman. A witch to the superstitious mind.

"What time is it, son?"

"It's almost midnight, sir."

The man with the white hair on the train told Vern that nothing had been resolved. They each returned to their separate lives, and every year or so he'd hear of another strange and tragic accident. At this point the man became very highly agitato. Vern, of course, asked him what was the matter. He said he was going to tell Vern something that he'd never told anyone, but Vern must promise never to tell a soul. Vern promised a promise he had broken only now, many, many years after meeting the man on the train.

Vern's voice was like a hushed whisper as he told us the words the white-haired man had told him. "Son," he'd said, "*I am the last of the thirteen.*"

Then Vern screamed so loudly that it scared the shit out of every single one of us.

I poured myself a fresh cup of black coffee and sipped it with a large Jack Daniel's chaser. I paced the loft a little and smiled to myself. But at the same time I was smiling, I felt the hair on my forearms rising involuntarily. It was amazing how much that story had frightened me when I was a kid.

What was even more amazing was how much the story frightened me now.

47

Monday morning I'd fed the cat and had my first cup of espresso almost to my lips when Cleve called from the Pilgrim State Mental Hospital. It wasn't the way I would've chosen to start the week, but maybe things would pick up.

"Hey, dude," said Cleve shrilly. "The responses are rollin' in!" I've acclimated myself to the younger generation referring to me as "dude." In fact, I think I like it a little better than "mister" because it means they think I'm hip, with it, now, today, or mod, as my father calls it. But when a man in his forties who lives in a mental hospital calls you "dude," it's a rather saddening experience for more reasons than I wish to go into here.

"What responses, Cleve?" I asked.

"What responses? To the questionnaire, of course."

"What questionnaire, Cleve?" It's an unsettling feeling on a Monday morning to realize that every sentence of conversation you conduct is brick and mortar binding you irrevocably closer in a relationship with someone who is criminally insane. But you can't hang up on a monstro-wig. They take it personally.

"The questionnaire I sent to all the Jewboys."

"And what did you ask in the questionnaire?"

"I asked would they be able to come to New York by the end of the month to rehearse for the tour?"

I paused for my first sip of espresso. I didn't say anything. There wasn't a hell of a lot to say.

"Oh, I asked them other things, too," said Cleve in a frighteningly toneless voice.

"Like what?" I asked.

"Like any changes in addresses or phone numbers. Any picking they'd been doing in the past few years. I've got to be sure they're keeping their chops up. Whether they've seen *Ghostbusters II*." Cleve's voice trailed off.

"Had they?"

"Had they *what*?" shouted Cleve.

"Seen *Ghostbusters II*."

"No."

Cleve didn't enlarge upon his answer and I didn't deem it wise to inquire further into the matter. I sipped my espresso, lit my first cigar of the morning, and looked reassuringly toward the cat, my companion in relative sanity.

"The responses about doing the tour have been very positive," said Cleve a bit petulantly. "I've heard from everyone but Tequila, Wichita, Raymond Boatright, and Willie Fong Young." Not hearing from three out of the four was pretty understandable, I thought.

"Willie's probably just miffed because I went to the bas mitzvah instead of his wedding."

"Those bar mitzvahs'll get you every time."

"*Bas* mitzvah," I said. "Bar mitzvahs are for boys and bas mitzvahs are for girls." I was sure this information would do Cleve a lot of good.

"What's a Botswana for?" he asked. I puffed the cigar patiently and looked at the cat.

I took a deep breath and made a decision. Either Cleve was crazy or the whole world was crazy and Cleve was sane, and either way I couldn't see that it really

153

made a hell of a lot of difference. So I told him about Tequila, Boatright, and Wichita.

Cleve didn't say anything for a moment. Then I heard a strange, flat whistling in my left earlobe. Cleve was whistling a little tune. It sounded kind of familiar. Then he supplied the words.

"This old man, he played three./ He played knick-knack on my knee."

"Yes," I said, "you could say that." Most people wouldn't, of course, but there was a reason Cleve was where he was.

There was a long and uncomfortable silence. I looked up and met the cool gaze of Andy Warhol. That picture had to come down. Suddenly, I had a sperm-of-the-moment idea.

"Cleve," I said, "tell me about that interview you mentioned last time we talked. Who was the reporter? What was the newspaper? What'd he ask you?"

"Sir?"

Now Cleve seemed to have a nice little multiple-personality thing going for him. "Come on, Cleve," I said. "Try to remember."

The voice on the line was a strangled, whiny affair that came out of nowhere and disturbed me greatly. It sang: "Try to remember the kind of September/And follll . . . oooowwwwww . . ."

In what I hoped was a calm, rational voice, I tried to get Cleve back in the remote vicinity of the target. He maintained he could remember long-ago things like they were yesterday, but he had a hell of a time remembering yesterday. That sounded so normal it scared me.

About all I was able to get out of Cleve finally was that the interview was a lengthy one with the reporter asking a lot of questions about the band. He couldn't remember the reporter's name, but he thought the paper had been the *Daily News*. I thanked him and told him he'd been very helpful.

There was a rather lengthy silence, and then Cleve said: "So *they* probably didn't see *Ghostbusters II* either."

"Cleve," I said wearily, "that's something we'll never know."

48

That evening the Dancer and I had a little dinner date in Chinatown. Big Wong's was, of course, closed on Monday's. Even on the days when Big Wong's was open, if you got there after eight o'clock at night, they started running out of things. One of them was charm.

Kelli and I walked leisurely down Mott Street, drinking in the sights and smells and sounds of people living their lives in a manner that is raw and beautiful and close to the ground. Maybe it was my years in Borneo that kept the East always close to my heart. Maybe it was a Chinese girlfriend of mine who went on to marry a Kraut. I don't recall being heartbroken at the time, but they say once your heart's been broken it's not always so easy to tell when it happens again. I wouldn't know. I do know that if I ever get married the first thing I'm going to do is hire a nanny and adopt a couple of little Oriental kids. I have no plans, at the moment, however, to adopt an adult Korean.

We picked a restaurant on Mott Street a few blocks

down from Big Wong's and took a booth by the front window fairly close to a large squid hanging on a hook. We sat across from each other in the booth.

"You can always tell rednecks from normal Americans," I said to Kelli, "because the man and the woman tend to sit together on the same side of the booth, leaving the other side, possibly, for Elijah."

"I've noticed that," said Kelli, looking over the menu.

"You're a bright kid," I said. "You don't miss much."

Kelli continued happily studying the menu's vegetarian section and didn't seem too put off by my yammering on so I continued. Maybe she was in some advanced state of kundalini yoga that normal Americans didn't know about.

"The reason the rednecks like to sit on the same side with each other is because they're more visceral than the rest of us. They're kind of raw and beautiful and close to the ground, very much like the Chinese. Of course, never tell a redneck that."

"I'll have the Chinese vegetables over pan-fried noodles," said Kelli.

"Sensible order," I said.

After I'd chosen a few dishes from the nonvegetarian portion of the menu, the waiter took our orders and buzzed off into the bowels of the kitchen. Kelli and I sipped hot tea and discussed Travis Parnell a bit.

"That rather unpleasant package he sent you was postmarked just before Christmas, you know. Packages take forever to arrive this time of year."

"Hmm," said Kelli. "I'll have to mention that to Mr. Mailman."

"There wasn't much luggage of his at the Chelsea. He might've just got tired and fed up with hanging around New York and buggered off somewhere else. Almost everybody in New York feels that way. They just don't leave. That's why it's such a friendly place."

"It's been five days since I got that horrible doll. I

156

haven't received any more late-night calls. Maybe he *is* gone."

"Let's hope. Of course, you do have probably the best country singer–turned–amateur detective in the city on the case. Just be sure to stay on your toes."

"A dancer," said Kelli, "always stays on her toes."

Turning the subject deftly away from Travis Parnell, I talked for a while about some of the cases I'd worked on in the past. Then, just to keep it light, I launched into my views of the art scene in New York.

I hadn't gotten too far along into explaining rectal realism when I realized it wasn't really going to fly. Dancers are often nonverbal childlike creatures and they don't always like to put into words the things that they feel. They don't like to hear anybody else do it either. I steered the subject delicately away from rectal realism.

"Let's redirect the conversation back to myself," I said.

Kelli sipped her tea. It's hard to tell with dancers whether they're happy or pissed off or just content to sit there across from you sipping their tea with their lips resembling the beak of a cute, sexy, little bird. And you never know when that bird may turn into a giant, angry cassowary and try to kick your balls off under the table. That's probably another reason why rednecks always have the women sit on the same side with them.

Since Kelli was in a fairly inscrutable, nonverbal mood, possibly quite understandably because of the strain she'd been under lately, I left her alone at the table for a moment and went into the little hallway to call McGovern on the pay blower. It was broken, so I went outside to find another one on the street. Just up the block I found a phone booth with a pagoda on top of it. I put a quarter in and, sure enough, the voice on the other end sounded farther away than usual. It wasn't even McGovern's.

"Kinky! My hero!" said Tony Burton, the feisty Brit

157

who'd worked with McGovern at the *Daily News* from the days of pencils to typewriters to supercomputers. He'd met McGovern working on the Richard Speck case in Chicago and was responsible for McGovern's coming to New York twenty years ago. If it hadn't been for Tony, I'd probably be tackling two very dangerous cases totally Watson-less right now. Tony did have, however, one rather tedious habit. Almost everything he said could be taken as either high praise or low ridicule, and Tony wasn't going to help you figure out which it was. That was your job.

"It's a rare privilege to hear your voice," said Tony. Possibly it had something to do with his British background.

"Yeah," I said. "Is McGovern in?"

"No," said Burton, "but I've been graced to have seen a bit of the piece he's working on. The 'Somebody's Killing the Jewboys of Texas' piece. I must say McGovern has certainly again risen to the high plain of journalism we've all come to expect of him. And I've every confidence, Kinkster, you'll soon be wrapping this one up and adding it to your growing list of triumphs."

"Thanks," I said. "And Tony, will you ask McGovern to call me as soon as possible."

"About the case?"

"Affirmative."

"Roger. You're my hero, Kinkster."

"I'll try not to let you down."

"Pip pip, old chap."

I hung up the phone wanting to believe that Burton was coming from a sincere place. For some reason, I didn't want to let him down. It was as good a rationale as any for toiling on this planet: so I wouldn't let Tony Burton down. What else was there to life? But there was the distinct possibility, I thought, that in a very abstract, twentieth-century sense, I was a hero to Tony Burton. Adults had been known to have some pretty weird heroes.

With a little more pride in my step, I walked back up Mott Street and into the restaurant. By the time I got to the table, Kelli was about halfway through eating the Chinese vegetables over pan-fried noodles.

"Don't wait for me," I said. "Go right ahead."

Kelli gave me a nice smile and continued eating. I could start to like these nonverbal types. Of course, it's hard to be very verbal with a mouth full of Chinese vegetables over pan-fried noodles.

I could be nonverbal, too, I thought. She could be the Dancer and I could be the Strong Silent Type. We could sit forever eating Chinese food and occasionally smiling at each other in a little frenzy of autism. At the moment, with New York City hurriedly clanging by in all directions around us, it didn't sound too bad.

I was starting in on my spare ribs with black bean sauce, and the waiter was just approaching us with a very handsome-looking steamed flounder, when I heard the shot out in the street and saw blood suddenly spurt across the table.

49

Most of the customers in the place were Chinese and they hit the decks probably thinking it was a tong war. Kelli was sitting quite still across the booth from me, still holding a bloody set of chopsticks. I reached low across the table and pushed her down against the seat almost like a rag doll. Then I hit the decks myself. I knew it wasn't a tong war.

We all studied the gum under the tables for a frozen moment or two, and then the place came slowly back to life. Cautiously, I stood up and looked past the ugly little hole in the front window out into the street. No one out there except the usual crowd of onlookers on the near sidewalk staring at us in expectation, waiting to see if there was going to be a second act.

I looked over at Kelli. She seemed to be fairly fossilized but unhurt. I asked her if she was all right and she nodded her head. Then I looked over at the waiter. Blood was spurting at regular intervals from somewhere near the top of his left bicep. I grabbed a linen napkin, stepped over the flounder on the floor, and took a closer look.

There was a small hole going into the man's arm and a much larger one going out. From the way the blood was continuing to spurt, an artery had apparently been hit. I quickly found several more linen napkins and wrapped them all tightly around the wound to cut down the loss of blood. Miraculously, it seemed to work for the moment. Kinky Nightingale.

We sat the waiter down in a chair to wait for the paramedics. I was standing by the table talking to Kelli when a customer from one of the other tables came rushing over.

"I saw man with a gun," he said excitedly, pointing to a spot somewhere on the far sidewalk. "Wore big hat just like yours. Cowboy! Just like *Dallas.*"

"Remember," I said, taking Kelli's hand, "he only *thinks* he's a cowboy."

50

The following afternoon, a Tuesday, it was raining cats and dogs in New York. My cat was safe and relatively warm in the loft. She was sitting on the windowsill watching McGovern's large form cursing and chasing around a little puppet head on the rain-wept sidewalk.

"See the funny man," I said to the cat.

The cat said nothing.

The night before, I'd taken Kelli back to her place, watched her throw about half her apartment into a big red suitcase, hustled her down to Grand Central Station, and put her on a fast train for my nation's capital. Not that Washington, D.C., was a particularly safe place to be, but under the circumstances, it beat New York with a tire iron.

My kid sister, Marcie, who lives in Washington and works for the Red Cross, had just moved into a large, new apartment. One dancer more or less wasn't going to make that much difference for a week.

"What kind of person is Kelli?" Marcie had asked when I'd called to let her know about her imminent housepest.

"Well, when she was a child, she used to talk to the old Christmas tree ornaments before her mother hung

161

them on the back of the tree. Kelli'd tell them that the back of the tree was a very important place to be."

"That's sweet," said Marcie. "I hope she doesn't hang herself."

"No problem. However, she does have a slightly arrested case of social development. Most of her friends today are Christmas tree ornaments."

"She'll fit right in," said Marcie.

Presently there came a loud knocking on the door of the loft. The cat and I both looked up. I went over and unbolted the door. There was a time when I didn't usually keep the door bolted but this wasn't it.

A large McGovern head and a little puppet head came in the door together. Both were soaking wet. "Ah, Watson," I said, "good of you to drop by."

"I've been standing outside in the rain for the past fifteen minutes," said McGovern, taking off his drenched trenchcoat. His hair was pasted down over his eyes. McGovern didn't own a hat because men didn't make hats as big as God had made McGovern's head. In spite of his travails, he laughed good-naturedly, a very Watsonlike temperament, I noted with approval.

"The whole time I was in the street shouting for you, that fucking cat was sitting on the windowsill watching me with a smile on her face."

The cat stared at McGovern and blinked several times rather rapidly, a sure sign of displeasure. I turned to the cat.

"Why didn't you tell me McGovern was out there, darling? Why didn't you let me know?"

The cat did not respond.

"Why don't you ask her to pour me a drink?" said McGovern.

Later, with McGovern and myself sitting at the kitchen table, and the cat and a bottle of Jameson's sitting on the kitchen table, we discussed the two current cases that suddenly seemed to have risen up like evil

162

twin trade towers to dominate the landscape of my soul.

After a few shots of Jameson's, I recounted to McGovern the specific details of the previous evening's events in Chinatown. "Travis Parnell," I theorized, "being a hunter and probably a crack shot, could've easily spliced Kelli if he'd wanted to. But he seems to still be playing his twisted little game of making her life a living nightmare. So he shoots the waiter in the arm instead."

"Charming fellow," said McGovern.

"Nothing worse than a good old boy turned bad," I said. I lit a cigar, McGovern poured us both another round, and we sat in silence for a moment or two, watching the rain slant down onto Vandam Street.

"Tony Burton said you wanted to talk to me. What do you want me to do? Round up a posse?" I looked at McGovern.

"You're big enough to be a posse yourself," I said.

"Yeah," said McGovern, "but who'd lead?"

I killed half the shot and thought about it. It wasn't a bad question. Being a perennial unemployed youth, I'd sat at my desk for some time now, opening the occasional bill or bar mitzvah invitation with my Smith & Wesson knife. The cigar smoke at times had grown stale. The medicinal shot had aged for the better perhaps while settling into the old bull's horn. Cobwebs, at times, had extended from my cigar to my nose to my two red telephones, and, no doubt, into the little gray cells of my atrophying brain as well.

Those were the fun times.

Now, suddenly, a vortex of hatred was swirling around me. A maniac with a gun and a mission was on the loose, bent, apparently, upon the gradual emotional and physical destruction of a young lady who looked to me for wisdom and advice and protection. And if that wasn't enough to keep me busy, a horrific childhood ghost story appeared to be coming true right before what

Emily Dickinson had called my "unfurnished eyes."

Coming up against these seemingly inexorable twin terrors were myself and the large, friendly, intelligent Irishman sitting across the little table from me. We were the forces of good, I thought, rather wryly. If there were ten good men in the world, which at the moment I wasn't at all certain of, McGovern and I were surely two of them. On the other hand, if there were ten good men in the world, that left a hell of a lot of bad guys running around out there. I suddenly felt colder and more evanescent than the rain outside the window.

"Watson," I said with a quiet determination, "from now on we shall handle these two cases simultaneously. We shall take up both the Travis case and the Tequila case, and we shall crack them both or die trying."

"Here, here!" said McGovern as he poured another round into my already-full shotglass. The Jameson's flowed into a clear little puddle and dripped off the edge of the table like rain falling inside a distant, half-remembered dream. It wasn't going to be pleasant, I thought.

Since it was a rainy, thundery day, I took the opportunity to briefly recount the story of "The Last of the Thirteen" for McGovern, who at least had the courtesy not to rush to the phone and try to commit me to the Pilgrim State Mental Hospital. Reflecting upon the Pilgrim State Mental Hospital brought me back to Cleve and that brought me back to what I'd needed from McGovern in the first place.

"Sometime in the past couple of months," I said, "Cleve gave an interview to a reporter about the Texas Jewboys. Cleve doesn't seem to remember much about it anymore. Cleve goes in and out of lucid periods like some guys change their underwear. Except me, of course. I don't wear any underwear. It's a little hygiene trick I learned in the tropics."

"How clever of you," said McGovern.

164

"Anyway, Cleve thinks he gave the story to a guy from the *Daily News*." McGovern's interest perked up noticeably.

"You want me to find the article? You think it's connected to this 'Last of the Thirteen' business?"

"I won't know until I see it, but I'll tell you this," I said, pausing to puff the cigar rather dramatically. "It's the only lead we've got."

"If it can be found, I'll find it."

"Good man, Watson!"

"Let's take these cattle north," he said.

As McGovern was rather laboriously putting on his coat to leave, I reflected grimly that it was already too late for Tequila, Boatright, and Wichita. Some diabolical curse was definitively operative here. There had to be a way to push aside this curtain of Transylvanian mist to reveal the mind and hand of a modern-day murderer. And time, I thought, was doing a pretty good job of running out.

At the door, McGovern turned and looked at me. "It's too bad," he said, "that Big Wong's was closed yesterday."

"Why is that, McGovern?" I asked.

"WAITER WINGED AT WONG'S has kind of a nice ring to it," he said.

51

The next few days passed rather uneventfully. For all the excitement they were fraught with, I might as well have been a witty, young CPA or a born-again proctologist. I knew what brand of cigars I smoked. I knew the cat ate only tuna. About the only difficult decision I had to make was one morning when I couldn't decide whether I wanted to drink hot chocolate, coffee, or espresso. I imagined that the loft was a large, wide-bodied airplane and that there was a lithe, blond stewardess standing next to me saying "Hot chocolate, coffee, or espresso?" with a rather stern yet whimsical expression on her intelligent, sulky, languorous lips. It didn't help me decide what I wanted to drink, but it did make me want to ask the stewardess if she had a layover in Dallas.

The weather was as gray, somber, and monotonous as my mood. If I was going to get in a brighter, more positive mood, I was going to have to do it without the help of January. I took a certain cold comfort in Sherlock Holmes's assertion that all great artists are very highly influenced by environmental conditions. If I was such a great artist, how come I didn't understand the violent abstract of life that was hanging in the corner of my mind's eye and nudging the elbow of my soul like a bottle imp? As a child, I never really understood the nature of the curse of "The Last of the Thirteen." As an adult, for something like this to occur in real life was yet further beyond my ken. Hell, I didn't even understand rectal realism.

At night, visions of Kelli would dance intermittently through my dreams. By day, other visions, darker and bloodier and more foreboding, seemed to gnaw their way, like a Blakeian worm in a rosebud, through the pupil of my left eyeball and ejaculate evil onto my brain. If these visions were sugarplums, the date on their carton had expired.

Kelli and Marcie had called to let me know that all was okay in my nation's capital, but just to be sure, I assigned Washington Ratso, a Lebanese rock 'n' roll guitar player with a band called Switchblade, to look after them. His real name was Jimmie Silman but he'd been called Ratso longer than Ratso had been called Ratso, although Ratso had met me before Ratso had, or was it the other way around. At any rate, I called him Washington Ratso to differentiate him from New York Ratso. Life can be complex when you're a two-Ratso man.

Washington Ratso had once helped me locate a rather unpleasant Nazi who was trying to kill me. I figured if he could help find a Nazi, he could entertain and keep an eye on a dancer and my little sister. Don't hose 'em, just show them the town and keep a mild surveillance on them, I'd told Washington Ratso. Not to worry, he'd replied in some kind of unpleasant-sounding, exaggerated Arabic accent.

I'd felt better after talking to Washington Ratso. If you couldn't trust a Lebanese Druse Christian who'd once played with the Texas Jewboys, who could you trust? There were a number of people who'd played with the Texas Jewboys, I reflected. But there weren't that many of what we liked to call original Texas Jewboys. And from that small handful of chosen people, you could now subtract three, I thought grimly.

Friday afternoon looked like it was going to roll uncomfortably along pretty much like Wednesday and Thursday had. No progress. No sunshine. No joy. No phone calls that promised to change my life.

Around three o'clock, the cat vomited. That was always something to be on the planet for. There was a little scurry of action as I rushed to get an old towel to clean it up and the cat rushed into the bedroom, I suppose to hide her Cheshire chagrin. Eventually, she came back into the living room and I poured a tall shot of Jameson's to relax after all the activity.

I killed the shot.

I seemed to be spending an inordinate amount of time glaring up at Andy Warhol, and he seemed to be spending a commensurately inordinate amount of time glaring down his rather fragile nostrils at me. Of course, neither of us had that much going on.

"What the hell am I going to do with that thing?" I shouted to the cat as I gestured disgustedly toward the wall above the desk.

The cat said nothing.

Warhol said nothing.

I poured another shot of Jameson's and walked it around the loft with me. I certainly couldn't move the picture to the far wall. That wall was entirely filled with the huge Patton-like American flag Vaughn Meader had once given me. In the early sixties, Vaughn had created the enormously popular "First Family Album," in which he'd done a brilliant impersonation of JFK. Vaughn had traveled around the country doing his JFK act and making a fortune until one day in 1963 when he'd gotten into a cab at the airport in Milwaukee and the driver had said: "Did you hear about the President getting shot in Dallas?"

"No," Vaughn had answered. "How does it go?"

From that moment on, Vaughn's record sales and appearances had declined so drastically that later that week it had prompted Lenny Bruce to mention it in his act. "There'll be two graves at Arlington tonight," Bruce had said. "One for President Kennedy, and the other for Vaughn Meader."

Some years after that, Vaughn had gone fishing up in Maine and never bothered to come back. Couldn't blame him really. I'd rather be fishing myself. I looked up at the giant flag and thought of Vaughn and myself and Tequila, and Raymond, and Wichita, and I was suddenly filled with some kind of strong emotion that I couldn't quite identify. It was too deep and close to the heart to be patriotism and too lonely to be love.

Later that day, as the evening shadows fell gently across the gray afternoon like an Indian blanket from your childhood, I found myself standing at the kitchen window talking to the cat about McGovern.

"He's the kindest, most decent person I know," I said. "He's smart enough to know how very useless and futile life is, and yet he lives it to the fullest. He's one of my dearest friends and I would trust him with my life. He's smart, he's sincere, he's impeccably slovenly, he's unworldly, he's a mensch—all important Watson-like qualities—yet I sometimes wonder what put it into my head that I could ever be a Sherlock."

The cat lowered her head, intently studying a cockroach as it slowly moved along the windowsill.

"But that large head of his is filled with pubescent headlines. He cares more about covering the case than he does about solving it. And when Ratso finds out that McGovern's working with me, he'll be so miffed he'll never want to help me again. I need Watson! I must have Watson!"

The cat looked up at me for a moment and then went back to the cockroach. I lit a cigar and stared out at the blue-black densely populated emptiness. My heart was out there somewhere alone. Alone like my old friend Slim used to be back at the ranch, adjusting his little paper Rainbow Bread hat and leaning back on an old wooden Coca-Cola carton against his ancient green trailer that was never going anywhere again.

Slim used to say: "You's born alone. You dies alone. You might as well get used to it."

The phones rang.

I walked over to the desk, picked up the blower on the left, and listened for a while. I puffed with satisfaction on the cigar. At one point, I looked over to wink at the cat, but she was already curled up asleep on the rocking chair.

"Excellent work, Watson," I said to the blower. "Excellent work."

52

He looked like a slightly confused Moses. An old man with long gray hair and beard with his palms outstretched. As I got closer I saw the sign around his neck. It read: I'M 69 YEARS OLD, HOMELESS, AND DYING OF CANCER. I took a few bucks out of my pocket and started to hand them to him when he began screaming like a maniac. You can meet some interesting people on the way to McGovern's house.

"Get away!" the old man shouted. "Don't come near me with that cigar! I'm anemic!"

Feeling somewhat shaken, I put the money back in my pocket and kept walking. Another aristocratic freak, I said to myself. He's not only anemic, he's crazy as a bedbug. It'd take a social worker driving a Zamboni to straighten out this guy's attic.

"Basically, I feel rejected," I said to McGovern, after I'd told him of the encounter over shots of Black Bush. "When a sixty-nine-year-old homeless man who's dying of cancer turns you down, you've got problems."

"You forgot anemic," said McGovern. He laughed and I did too. I laughed what I imagined to be hearty Jewish laughter, which is kind of nice because you don't hear it all that often. I killed the shot and McGovern poured me another.

"So you found the interview Cleve couldn't remember giving?"

"It wasn't easy," said McGovern, getting up and pacing around the little room. Looked like he'd been taking Kinky lessons. I lit a cigar and waited.

"Newspaper morgues are filled today with people who have master's degrees in journalism but have been reduced to clipping articles from back issues because of the heartbreak of what journalism has become. These people are understandably difficult to deal with and you've got to work to try to keep them sober," said McGovern as he walked around the room with his drink in his hand. He crossed over to the mantel and started fishing around in a large mess of papers under a framed photograph of Carole Lombard.

"Don't tell me you've *lost* the son of a bitch?"

"Not hardly," laughed McGovern as he continued to shuffle stacks of aging newsprint. "It's here."

"So's the Magna Carta," I said.

"It turned out," said McGovern, "that it wasn't a *Daily News* piece after all. It was in *Newsday* sometime in late November. And get this. It was written by Dennis Duggan." Duggan was a star columnist for *Newsday* and a friend of both mine and McGovern's.

"Jesus," I said. "Not only is it a rather tedious world, it's a small one, too."

"Not when you're looking for something that isn't

where you left it," said McGovern as he moved farther down the mantel, past Carole Lombard and over to a large campaign poster from my ill-fated race for justice of the peace. It was slightly unnerving that I didn't remember autographing the poster. I looked at the inscription now as if reading it for the first time. It read:

To McGovern—

A good American,
A good Christian?
A good friend.
Fuck yourself,
Kinky

I chuckled as I read the inscription. Sometimes I really slayed myself. But it wasn't all that humorous watching McGovern, now searching with what I thought was a touch of desperation, around and behind the poster. I knocked back the shot of Black Bush and puffed impatiently on the cigar.

"Look at this," said McGovern. I glanced up hopefully. McGovern carefully extracted a piece of yellowed journalism from a pile.

"It's from back when I was covering the Charles Manson trial out in Los Angeles."

"This is exactly what I didn't want to happen," I said to myself, shaking my head disgustedly.

"Certain court officials took money from spectators," said McGovern, "to let them watch on monitors as Manson was being strip-searched. Charles Manson had a rather legendary *schlong*, you know."

"That's a piece of information you don't learn at vacation Bible school," I said.

"Not only that," said McGovern, "but according to the British tabloids, Roman Polanski, whose pregnant wife was murdered by the Manson Family, made films of his wife being hosed by Yul Brynner, Peter Sellers, and Warren Beatty, among others. Those films, apparently, were what Manson was really looking for that night."

"What about Bob Hope?" I asked. "Was he one of the guys Polanski filmed hosing his wife? That'd be a good piece of information to add to the Bob Hope obituary you've been writing for the past ten years."

"I haven't *been writing* the Bob Hope obit," said McGovern indignantly. "I *wrote* it ten years ago. I've been *refining* it."

I was thinking of going into the bathroom and looking for a shower rod to hang myself on when McGovern suddenly rushed into the bedroom and emerged moments later clutching a fluttering clipping in his large hands. "Here it is," he shouted jubilantly. "The Dennis Duggan story!"

"Have you ever thought," I asked, waving my hand around casually at the piles of old newspapers, clippings, and magazines squirreled all over the little apartment, "about computerizing this setup?"

"Why would I want to do that?" McGovern asked, his face shining with an almost childlike candor. "The system works."

Dennis Duggan's article was a retrospective on the Texas Jewboys, including a rather lurid account of the crimes Cleve had committed in order to get where he was today. The piece also made note of the fact that, while Cleve seemed somewhat disoriented about the present, he remembered yesterday with an almost uncanny lucidity.

As I continued to read the piece on McGovern's little kitchen table, I felt fingers of ice moving along the base of my spine. At first I attributed it to the ungodly draft that moved through McGovern's apartment like a Texas blue norther. It was a small apartment but it had a big draft. McGovern poured us both another round of Black Bush and that warmed me up a bit.

Cleve had provided Duggan with several colorful anecdotes from the road, involving people and situations I'd long ago forgotten, that now came rushing back in a surge of nostalgia. I said as much to McGovern.

"There's a lot of that going around these days," he said as he refilled our glasses again.

"Abbie Hoffman said: 'Nostalgia is a symptom of illness in an individual or a society.'"

"That's too bad," said McGovern, looming over my shoulder like the Chrysler Building, "because sometimes I think nostalgia's all I've got to look forward to."

"It's all anybody's got to look forward to," I said, "after five rounds of Black Bush."

I tried to concentrate on Duggan's article but my eyes were beginning to wander. Then something got ahold of my optic nerves and riveted my vision to the page. It was the last portion of the story. Duggan had written a "Where are they now?" closer, and it listed the names of all the original Texas Jewboys, what instrument they played, where they were living, and what they were currently doing or not doing.

"McGovern," I said, "read this 'Where are they now?' section." McGovern picked the article up from the table and scanned it for a while.

"Well," said McGovern, "I don't want to bruise your ego, Holmes, but this is what our modern culture calls trivia. It's almost as popular as nostalgia."

"You mean it's almost the same as nostalgia."

"That's what I mean, but I was too sensitive to say it."

"This is no time for sensitivity, Watson. Listen to what Duggan says about the first three names on the list: 'Tequila—guitar. Still true to the gypsy spirit of the road, Tequila has no known address today. Says Cleve: "We get a postcard from him once every ten years whether we want to or not." Last heard from in Mexico.

" 'Raymond Boatright—keyboards. Lives in Dallas, Texas. Works as piano tuner.

" 'Wichita—guitar and fiddle. Lives in cabin with no indoor plumbing twenty miles outside of Tulsa, Oklahoma. Still plays local gigs whenever he can.' "

"Jesus, Mary, and Joseph," said McGovern.

"I'll see your Jesus, Mary, and Joseph," I said grimly, "and raise you an Abraham, Isaac, and Jacob."

"The first three names on this list—"

"That's correct, Watson," I said. "This may look like an interview with a guy who needs a checkup from the neck up. It may appear to be a 'Where are they now?' trivia piece. But it's also something else."

Suddenly the icy fingers made themselves felt again on my spine. I killed the final round and puffed almost paranoically on my cigar. The little apartment seemed colder than it had any right to be.

"What I believe we have here, Watson," I said, "is a road map for a killer."

53

"Well, you've got to admit," I said to the blower on the left, "that three Jewboys in a row dying in the same sequence they were listed in a *Newsday* story is a bit suggestive."

It was a little after ten o'clock, Duggan's article was spread out before me on the desk in my loft, and Cooperman's voice was growling into my left ear like a pneumatic bulldog.

"Okay, Tex, Tequila was iced, I'll give you that. But these other two birds you're telling me about sound clearly like accidental deaths. Maybe your band was accident-prone."

"I've got this 'Where are they now?' story right here in front of me. Suppose somebody else is looking at it, too. Suppose somebody's checking his list and killing people."

"Were they naughty or nice?" Cooperman asked.

Before our intercourse was terminated, I was able to give Cooperman the details of the two out-of-state deaths, and he was able to tell me that since things were sailing along so smoothly in the city and there was nothing much for cops to do, he'd try to check it out and try to get back to me. I told him I'd try to hold my breath.

I fished an old, half-smoked cigar out of the wastebasket and fired it up. Sometimes when you resurrect one after a few weeks or so it gives you a little buzz. The way things were going I was going to need a little buzz. Also, the Black Bush was beginning to have a rather undulating effect on my medulla oblongata. I had to think clearly. A little alcohol will help you think clearly. A little more will usually have an undulating effect on your medulla oblongata.

I walked over to the espresso machine, performed the necessary ablutions upon it, and kicked it into gear. Soon it sounded like Orville Wright coming in pretty low. I poured a healthy steaming portion into my old "Save the Males" coffee mug. Not a bad choice of receptacles, I thought, all things considered.

Duggan's list was still waiting for me when I got back to the desk. I puffed the remains of the rather elderly cigar and took a few tentative sips of espresso. Then I focused my orbs on the fourth name on the list.

It read: "Major Boles—drums. Lives in St. Louis but still does regular session work in Nashville and performs with his own band."

This brief account, I felt, failed to capture the Major. Like all drummers I'd known over the years, the Major was, of course, clinically ill. You have to be to want to be a drummer. He was also a very colorful American who often could be heard to complain that his "sperm count was redlining."

That was another problem with drummers. They were always horny. Drummers were horny, bass players were Austrians who wished they were Germans, horn players all thought they were black unless they were black, in which case they thought they were white, and lead-guitar players thought they were Jesus Christ. Once you understood this you could lead a band right into the Valley of Death, which, unfortunately, looked to be a fairly close approximation of exactly where the Texas Jewboys were headed.

A little after Cinderella time, I called Dennis Duggan. It wasn't that easy to call Duggan. You had to dial his number, let it ring twice, then hang up and call again. Obviously, there was somebody Duggan didn't want to hear from. All of us have somebody we don't want to hear from and all of us have somebody we do want to hear from. The problem is getting them to realize who they are.

"Kinkster, my lad," said Duggan after I'd identified myself, "what can I do for you?" Aside from already providing what I increasingly believed to be a guidebook for a murderer, there wasn't a hell of a lot Dennis could do for me. Still, it never hurts to check your sources.

"Dennis," I said, "that story you wrote about the Texas Jewboys was aces."

"Thanks, Kinkster. That friend of yours, Cleve, is really—uh—"

177

"He certainly is."

"Are you really considering getting the old band together for a reunion tour?"

"You never know, Dennis. We may get our aluminum walkers all shined up and head out for the road again any day now. I wanted to ask you about that list of Texas Jewboys you ran in your article."

"The old 'Where are they now?' list. We'll all be on that roll one of these days, Kinkster."

"Some of us already are," I said. I paused to take a few puffs on what was left of the old cigar. "Dennis, I'm interested in the sequencing of that list. Was the sequencing of the names your idea? Was it all done in a random and haphazard order?"

"Neither," said Duggan. "The names were listed in precisely the order they came to me out of Cleve's head."

"And that," I said, "is no order at all."

When I hung up with Dennis Duggan, I scanned the list again. Tequila, Boatright, Wichita, Major Boles, Bryan "Skycap" Adams, Billy Swan, Little Jewford, Willie Fong Young, Panama Red, Snakebite Jacobs, and tour manager Dylan Ferrero. They had all been there in the early days of the band. There were others who came to mind, but most of them joined the band a little later down the road. And these were the ones who came out of Cleve's head.

The list by now had taken on a rather foreboding quality. I could see all the names in some frightful roll call of the dead. It seemed certainly appropriate to inform these people of the danger they were in, even if I turned out to be wrong and nothing ever came of it. Yet a still, small voice that wasn't quite my conscience kept nagging at me. It didn't want me to tell them yet.

A few things were beginning to add up but many seemed to make even less sense than ever. I still didn't understand why the puppet had been hiding its head behind the refrigerator or why somebody'd bothered to nail my windows shut and not wait inside to finish me off. Why wait out in the hallway where some innocent lesbian or troublesome Ratso might wander along? Especially once you'd picked the lock.

Given Duggan's piece in *Newsday*, the stolen address book seemed to fit into the picture a little better. But the specter of Travis Parnell loomed as foggy and fearsome as ever. Of course, he didn't really have anything to do with the Jewboy situation, but, for some reason, he kept popping into my thoughts like a smiling, inflatable good-ol'-boy doll.

Eventually, all the Black Bush, the cigars, the stress of doing battle with enemies you couldn't see, and the wretched weight of the world began to lower my lids like a merchant shuttering his shop in Chinatown. I killed the lights in the living room, wandered into the bedroom, got undressed, put on my old batik sarong from Borneo and my Canadian Wildlife sweatshirt with a picture of a cuddly little baby seal, and got into bed. I was just beginning to count Young Republicans when the phones rang. I could've picked up the phone by the bed, but it sounded like the kind of call that ought to be taken on the blower to the left. I got up and stumbled out to the desk. In the tired, refracted New York moonlight, Warhol looked positively evil.

"Start talkin'," I said.

"Tex," said Cooperman, "you're on what we at the Sixth Precinct like to refer to as a wild fucking goose chase. I checked with the boys in Dallas and in Tulsa. They've both conducted thorough investigations and they've both resulted in findings of accidental death. Not the slightest sign of foul play. The files have been closed. They're convinced, and so am I, that you're wasting your time. You're also wasting *my* time. Why don't you wait a few weeks before you bother me again."

Cooperman hung up. I held on to the blower for a moment as if there were more to say, then I hung up,

179

too. There was always more to say, I thought. That was probably why so few people ever did anything.

Regardless of what Cooperman thought, I could feel an almost palpable presence irradiating my existence with a jagged, eternal evil. Somewhere, I believed, there was a mystery man, and in his head and in his hand he kept the bombing maps of his own private Germany. For whatever rhyme or whatever reason, I knew, beyond the shadow of the grave, something horrific was stirring. And it was out to get the Jewboys again.

54

It was Saturday morning and it was time to gather in the Texas Jewboys from their musical Diaspora. I felt it was essential to get as many members of the original band as possible to New York, if for no other reason than to get them the hell away from wherever they were. At least in New York, I could keep an eye on them and not be gradually informed by long-distance phone calls that life, indeed, was imitating some fantastic childhood ghost story.

The band could rehearse in New York and, if things went well, maybe we really *could* go out on a big reunion tour, make it all into a financial pleasure, leave the curse of the Texas Jewboys far behind us, and, of course, retire again. We could all look forward to living in little pink houses by the airport, with white picket fences protecting us from the past. We could spend our weekends washing our lox-colored '59 Cadillacs and watching our kids grow up to be lawyers and fagolas and BMW distributors.

Anything but a road musician.

The object of this protection plan was, of course, to make it harder for someone to know "Where are they now?" And, as the large tribes of Philistines attacking ragged little bands of long-ago Jewboys always used to remind each other: "There's safety in numbers."

That's why they called them Philistines.

Of course, if you're going to go on a big road tour with a band you might as well get the best pickers possible. I thought of some of the hottest musicians I'd played with in recent years. Larry Campbell, an all-around virtuoso and great producer as well, was in New York, but how interested he'd be in a road tour I didn't know. Lee Roy Parnell (no relation to Travis) was a very hot original new songwriter and guitar player. But he'd just recorded an album and was getting his own band together in Nashville. Neil Kulhanek was one of the greatest steel-guitar players in the world but he was currently with a band in Austin and it might be hard to get him away.

There was one thing lacking, however, in all three of these world-class performers. None of them had been an original Texas Jewboy. Under the circumstances, that certainly appeared to be their good fortune.

The first action I took was to ring up Dylan Ferrero in San Antonio. He didn't have to go to school today and I didn't either. He was also the one guy who could pull this little temporary relocation project together and keep it rolling long enough for me to nail the killer before he decided to get busy again.

"Dylan," I said, "how'd you like to have your old job back for a little while? Take a few weeks sick leave.

Road-manage the Jewboys on a little reunion tour. What do you say?"

Dylan said: " 'Left a good job in the city./Workin' for the man every night and day—' "

"So you like the idea," I said.

Dylan did not respond immediately. When he did, it was with a rather marked reticence.

"What's the matter," I said. "You're afraid to try something new?"

" 'What's new, pussycat?' " said Dylan. I waited.

"I don't know, hoss," he said. "I've got a suit and a tie and a job and a wife and a house and a dog."

"You mean you traded that swell python jacket you got in Singapore for *that*?"

" 'That ol' rockin' chair's got me,' " said Dylan.

"Why do I always feel like a middle-aged Peter Pan trying to get Tinkerbell off of standby?"

Dylan said "I don't know, hoss" a few more times and I realized I was going to have to show him a couple of cards.

"Look, Dylan," I said, "I told you about Tequila and you told me about Raymond Boatright. Now Wichita's dead, too. A story about the band ran in *Newsday* a couple of months ago. It listed the original Jewboys by name and gave information about where they were currently living. I think somebody's using that article to find and kill the members of the band. You may not play an instrument besides the Jewish mouth bow but you were part of us and you still are. That's why your name's on that list."

I let my last words sink in for a bit of effect. Dylan remained silent. He had the right. After all, this wasn't the best-dressed list or the employees of the month. This could easily be the most unpopular list to be included in since the group called up some years ago before the House Un-American Activities Committee.

"If anything should mysteriously happen to you," I

said, "then you won't have to worry about your dog and your house and your wife and your job and your suit. Did I forget anything?"

"Tie," said Dylan. "I always kind of liked that tie."

In the end, Dylan took the new job I'd offered, which was really an old job, dealing efficiently and sensitively with people and music and the road. Few had Dylan's smooth, magical, part flimflam man, part Pattonlike aptitude for this highly unspecialized line of work. The only two Americans I knew who could touch Dylan with a barge pole when he was on the road were Gary Shafner, who'd worked with Bob Dylan, and Sandy Castle, who'd worked with the Band. But they weren't really Americans; they were Californians.

" 'Give me weed, whites, and wine,' " said Dylan. " 'Show me a sign, and I'll be willin' to be movin'.' "

Before we hung up, Dylan and I agreed to try like hell to get the band to New York in two weeks time, without alerting them to the reason behind our urgency. We would lure them up instead with the promise of a big, glorious, profitable, fun, nostalgic reunion tour. And we would keep our fingers crossed that nothing unpleasant would happen before they got there. I was also keeping my fingers crossed that the concert promoters wouldn't find out that my booking agent was operating out of wig city.

I felt a certain sense of relief mixed with a sidecar of fatalism after hanging up with Dylan. The reunion tour would help protect the band and might just be fairly lucrative as well. But I had another reason for wanting to bring the Jewboys to New York, one I didn't wish to reveal to Dylan, McGovern, the cat, or anyone. It was looking more and more to me like the killer was one of the original Texas Jewboys.

183

55

Ten tedious days later on a brisk Tuesday afternoon I walked up Fifty-second Street with a strong case of déjà Jew. Now that the band had arrived in the city and I'd be seeing them again in a matter of moments, the years since we'd been together seemed to telescope down to almost nothing at all. Like a boxer whose adrenaline starts flowing on the way to the ring or a thoroughbred kicking up as he walks to the starting gate, I could feel the road humming in my blood. Already bits and pieces of music, lyrics, and stage patter were running through my head. It would be easier this time. Much easier. I could almost hear the applause of the crowd as we hit the stage.

Fleetingly, another train of thought seemed to move through my mind. It was not a very pleasant train. Its freight was human doubt and uncertainty. Car after car roared across rusty lifelines from the past, over high, rattling trestles of terror that made me wonder at the wisdom of what I was embarking upon. Could I protect the band from an unknown enemy any better in New York than if I'd just let them be? What would happen when we got out on the road? Was it wise to keep them in ignorance of the pattern of danger that I foresaw in the days ahead? This train of thought was still a distance away but it was getting closer. And it looked like it was coming toward me on the same track.

I lit a cigar, put all negative thoughts from my mind, and took a sharp right into Gallagher's Steak House. Dylan had called the night before to inform me that everyone was checked into the Chelsea Hotel—might as well dance with who brung you—and our first band meeting would be over lunch at two o'clock at Gallagher's. I was running fashionably late like Marilyn Monroe. The band had waited thirteen years for this; twenty minutes more or less wasn't going to make any difference now. I wasn't sure that anything was going to make any difference now if I didn't find out pretty fast who was snuffing semiretired rock 'n' rollers.

It wasn't hard to pick out the Jewboy table at Gallagher's. It looked like a group of fallen disciples assembled at a rather licentious, middle-aged Last Supper. James Clare, the charming, dapper Irishman who runs the place, had given me special dispensation from the Pope to wear my cowboy hat in Gallagher's. He understood that Jewboys and cowboys both like to wear their hats indoors and attach a certain amount of importance to it. The fact that he understood this rather stubborn, arcane notion, and created a spiritual loophole in the policy of the restaurant, defines fairly well the difference between the Irish and the British.

Shouts, greetings, and embraces were exchanged and the years all but melted away. When James Clare sent over a couple of bottles of champagne, it seemed almost like old times. I was happy to note that our little group did not bear much similarity to the gross caricatures you usually see at high school reunions. Maybe the road had served us all well. It certainly wasn't the result of clean living, I thought, as I sipped a champagne toast Snakebite Jacobs was making. The waiter filled the glasses again and I looked carefully at Snakebite.

A gray hair here and there, but he looked great. In

my mind I could see him playing two saxophones at once in front of a wild crowd in San Francisco. I remembered how I used to introduce Snakebite, telling the audience that I'd found him in an alley playing his saxophone with a coat hanger around his neck. Suddenly, I had an image of Snakebite's dead blue face with a coat hanger tightly twisted around his neck. I shook off the macabre picture and thought of my brother Roger's line that I'd often used onstage: "If you want to wake up in the mornin' smilin' go to bed with a coat hanger in your mouth." It was a slightly nicer image.

Billy Swan looked almost distinguished now, a far cry from the wild child I'd known in Nashville. He'd played in Kris Kristofferson's band both before and after the Texas Jewboys, so his chops, I knew, were always up. When Billy Swan smiled, in his eyes you could still see a twinkle of the road. Swan could play any instrument known to man and some that weren't. Dylan and I'd moved him to keyboards for this tour because Little Jewford had had to stay in Houston. That made Jewford the only living original member of the band not making the reunion tour. The thought gave me pause. I drank another toast someone was making. Champagne was not my drink of preference but if you drank enough of it, you forgot which one you preferred.

I scanned the rest of the table. Willie Fong Young looked as if marriage had been good for him. Also, I noticed with some relief, he didn't seem to be bearing any further grudge about my boycotting his wedding in favor of the bas mitzvah. Some people could carry grudges for a long time, I reflected, as James Clare sent over another two bottles of champagne.

Panama Red's mouth still resembled Mick Jagger's more than I would've liked, but there was nothing I could do about it except hire a rabid kangaroo to jump up and pluck his lips off. Panama was wearing his Panama in January in New York in Gallagher's Steak House.

He wasn't Jewish or a cowboy, but if his sky-piece was good enough for James Clare, it was good enough for me. I could see Panama under the lights, wailing away on his electric, metallic cocaine bebop guitar. Panama liked to think he played rock 'n' roll with a country sensitivity and I liked to think that I played country with a social conscience, but basically, I made their eyes wet and he made their crotches wet. That was the real difference between country and rock 'n' roll.

Bryan "Skycap" Adams got his name when the band was passing through the airport in Kansas City and we heard them paging Skycap Adams. He dressed in sort of a mod, Negro style with flashy suits and droopy, velour skycaps. I could hear Skycap snartin' and fartin' on the Tennessee walkin' bass. He still looked like a kid.

Major Boles was bitching already about the first rehearsal, which Dylan had announced would be at the midtown studio he'd rented at two o'clock the next afternoon.

"Two o'clock's too early," said the Major. I used to say that I'd found him in the Congo beatin' on his bongo, and he pretty much looked the part. Sometimes, when the mood hit him, the Major would play the drums with little American flags waving from his sticks.

Dylan looked like Dylan. He'd taken his python jacket out of mothballs and replaced his squares with an old pair of sky-shooters from the seventies. I didn't even remember if Dylan had eyes. But he'd been in contact with Cleve, with McGovern, even with Duggan, with Bill Dick at the Lone Star Roadhouse just down the street, and with about forty other people. If anybody could get this large, awkward, very-endangered bird into the air, it was Dylan.

Somewhere during my revery, eight steaks had been ordered and eaten along with about seventeen different kinds of Gallagher's potatoes. Everything was killer bee, including James Clare's personally guided tour of Gallagher's meat locker—one of the few peaceful places in New York.

A few people ordered dessert and a few ordered coffee. The waiter came over to Willie's end of the table and stood next to him.

"How would you like your coffee, sir?" he asked.

"Black," said Willie, "like my men."

Swan was keeping his eyeball in his head and everybody appeared to be in a pretty good, confident mood. There isn't a murderer in the crowd, I thought. There couldn't be. Musicians were gentle people. They just weren't cut out to be premeditated murderers. Maybe Cooperman was right. Maybe Wichita and Raymond Boatright had gone to Jesus by accidental death.

James Clare had sent over still more château de cat piss and I was half-buzzed and lifting my glass to make a toast, when I remembered something McGovern had told me recently. "Charles Manson," he'd said, "was a musician."

"Charles Manson was a musician. Charles Manson was a musician," kept playing over and over in my head—like a bad champagne trip.

I got to my feet, struggling slightly to keep my balance, and lifted the glass higher. Somehow, "Charles Manson was a musician" didn't seem like it'd make a very good toast. But as I looked around the table, I couldn't honestly say for sure whether these people were murder suspects, innocent victims, or just old friends getting together again.

"The future," I said.

If I could've seen the future, I never would've made the toast.

188

56

I don't remember getting home that night or going to bed but I do remember waking up early Wednesday morning with one of the worst hangovers in my life, picking up a jangling telephone, and finding Cleve on the other end of the line.

"I'll see you at the rehearsal this afternoon," Cleve seemed to be saying. My head was pounding like I'd taken up residence inside Major Boles's bass drum.

"You will?" I said, in disbelief I didn't even try to hide.

"It's cool," said Cleve. "It's cool."

It was cool, all right, I thought. With Travis Parnell biding his time somewhere in the underbrush, and an unidentified madman out there who was express-mailing Texas Jewboys to Hillbilly Heaven at fairly regular intervals, all I needed was a criminally insane idiot savant booking agent loitering around the band rehearsals. Of course, it was extremely doubtful that Cleve was going anywhere, I figured, as I managed to coax him off the phone. He only thought he was going to the band rehearsal. A lot of people in this world thought things that weren't true. Possibly, even myself.

I drank about a gallon of espresso that morning, and, when the hangover finally went away, the weight of my responsibility for the lives of the band members began to reassert itself. It'd been about three weeks since Wichita'd gotten himself croaked ostensibly by a stray shot from a hunter. Travis Parnell was a hunter, I thought, as I lit my first cigar of the morning. But I just didn't see where he fit into this picture. Tormenting Kelli was one thing, but what could he possibly have against the Texas Jewboys? A lot of people hadn't liked our music, of course, but why wait thirteen years to start doing us in?

The killer, I figured, was someone other than Travis Parnell. Someone who hadn't made a move since whacking Wichita more than three weeks ago. If I was right about Wichita and Boatright not dying of accidental causes, it was about time for the other cowboy boot to drop. Not for a New York minute did I believe that bringing the band up here would make them all invulnerable. I just felt I would be able to keep a closer eye on things. Show business, like politics, is a very open, public casino of endeavor. The biggest, most powerful people in the business, with all their bodyguards and security fences and disguises and bulletproof limousines, can't stop some lightly salted assorted nut from abruptly terminating their careers if his parakeet continues to send him coded messages. Sometimes this manifests itself in nasty letters to Michael J. Fox. Sometimes it results in the death of John Lennon. It depends on the parakeet.

I puffed the cigar, sipped a little espresso, and thought about it for a while. Even with someone who was out where the buses don't run, there had to be a motive. The motive, usually, was out where the buses don't run as well. So, in order to understand the motive, you had to get out there yourself. You had to walk a long, tortuous journey far into your own mind and your own memories. Once you get there, of course, and you understand the motive, the truly frightening thing is that it doesn't really seem so crazy after all. You've probably had the same thoughts yourself at one time or another. Something very deep and essential within the mind of man has always wanted to impress Jody Foster and kill Ronald Reagan.

I sipped some more espresso. Voltaire, I remembered reading somewhere, had drunk more than seventy cups of coffee a day, and, though the doctors said it would kill him, he figured it must be a pretty slow poison because he lived to be one of the oldest and smartest frogs in the pond. I sipped some more espresso.

If some kind of "Last of the Thirteen"–type curse was in effect upon the Texas Jewboys, something was going to happen pretty soon and it wasn't going to be something very nice. Though Vern's ancient ghost story, like so many aspects of life on this planet, never resolved itself, the bunch of white-haired guys did rack their brains to discover what it was that they all had in common that could've engendered such a curse. In the story, the only shared experience they could remember was the night they'd all stayed in the old haunted house in the middle of the forest.

I sipped some more espresso.

What would be the modern, nonfictional equivalent to the guys with the white hair spending the night together in the old haunted house? What act or experience did all the band have in common that could now be causing someone to wreak some kind of crazy vengeance upon us? I thought about it for a long while, but, in the end, nothing was delivered. We'd done a hell of a lot of things together on the road and off. None of them seemed serious enough to have invoked this kind of hatred upon the band.

I would have to warn Major Boles, of course. He was the fourth name on Duggan's list, and, if things ran true to form, the killer being a methodical, compulsive type, the fourth place on the list was not a healthy place

191

to be. I, as fate would have it, was not on the list, but I'd been dealt with by Duggan earlier in the article. I wondered now about the time shortly after Tequila's death when someone had nailed my windows shut for obviously more nefarious purposes than keeping out the draft. Maybe I'd been the first intended victim. But why hadn't the bastard, once he'd already picked the lock, waited inside to finish me off? Instead, he'd waited out in the hallway, bopped Ratso when he'd come along, got spooked and fled, and then continued his way, apparently, down Duggan's list, giving me a temporary reprieve.

He'd iced Tequila, then gone to Dallas to croak Boatright, then traveled to Tulsa to splice Wichita. Armed with Duggan's information, my telephone book, and the insight and focus that only a murderous mind possesses, he seemed to move pretty much at will. He seemed to enjoy traveling. I wondered if he flew business class.

I looked up and observed that Andy Warhol seemed to be gazing down upon me with a rather thin, slightly condescending smile. He had white hair, too, I noticed. I glanced over at my old guitar leaning against the wall. It was about two hours until the rehearsal. Why not rehearse? I thought. If we were all going to die soon, we might as well give the folks their money's worth.

I sipped some more espresso.

"The monkey ain't dead and the show ain't over," I said to the cat.

57

Divorces and IRS audits are the only things in the world, I'm told, that are more tedious than rehearsing a band. I've never been divorced mainly because I've never been married, and I've never been audited because I've got a black accountant and the feds always leave him alone. But I have been to a lot of band rehearsals and they are roughly up there, in terms of tedium, with four hours of root-canal work by a glib, heavy-handed, possibly suicidal dentist.

I won't bore you with a detailed description of a band rehearsal, but you should know that the first hour and a half is usually eaten alive by the drummer hitting his drums repeatedly as loud as he possibly can and the bass player striving valiantly to match him in both volume and monotony. The rest of the band often takes this opportunity to urinate, go out for a drink, do drugs, or hang themselves from a shower rod. Finally, the whole band takes the stage and then the bickering starts.

There are also beautiful, private moments, without press, onlookers, or audience, when a handful of musicians who've known each other for years become something bigger than themselves, and fly on the majestic wings of music played well together. It was into one of these moments that a startling and disconcerting thought came into my head. I thought about it for a good while

as I sang and played the guitar with the band. Sometimes when you're performing, your thoughts can travel
elsewhere with an almost brilliant clarity. In fact, if the
audience ever found out what most entertainers are
thinking while emoting from the stage, they'd demand
their money back.

What I was thinking about was that the original
Texas Jewboys had existed as a viable entity only for
about three years, from 1973 to 1975. After that, I'd
toured with Bob Dylan, played the Lone Star on a regular basis, and, later, made the rounds again with res-
surected versions of the band. At one time I had a group
of Texas Jewboys in New York, one in L.A., and one in
Texas. After all, I wasn't Chuck Berry. I couldn't just
pick up a house band anywhere I played and expect
them to know "They Ain't Makin' Jews Like Jesus Anymore."

From 1973 to 1975, I thought. That had to be it. If
there'd been a "Last of the Thirteen" incident, it had
to've happened during that time. And it must've happened on the road because that was the only time we
were all together during those three years. That did
narrow things down.

As the band plowed painlessly through the set, I
did some more reflecting upon things past, but nothing
earth-shattering came to mind. That had always been a
problem with me. I never remembered things until
somebody reminded me about them. Then I never forgot. It was either burned synapses or the Baby Jesus
was protecting me from my past. It was kind of like the
chorus from a song of mine, "Silver Eagle Express":
"And I'll ride the Silver Eagle to the last town on the
line. There's nothing to remember if there's nothing to
remind."

But Dylan remembered yesterday. And, God help
us all, Cleve remembered yesterday. I'd have to have a
serious power caucus with those two. Of course, other
guys in the band no doubt remembered yesterday, too.

The problem was that one of them, I was very much afraid, remembered something about it too damn well.

When the band took a break for dinner, I noticed that the rehearsal studio was beginning to develop a little traffic of well-wishers and kibitzers, most of whom I knew. It was nice to see that Ratso had come down, though he seemed a bit quiet, tight-lipped, and almost thin, very un-Ratsolike qualities. McGovern had come around, too, and was listening to Major Boles and Panama Red swap tales of conquest on the road.

". . . the redhead with the giant zubers in Denver," the Major was saying.

"I hosed her, too," said Panama. "The next night in Boulder."

"They *were* boulders," said the Major.

"You hold her, I'll milk her," said Willie Fong Young as he walked by.

"She was a newcomer to my cucumber," said Snakebite.

"I should've been a musician," said McGovern.

"You're not kiddin'," said the Major. "In Chicago on that first tour there was a knock on my door about four o'clock in the morning. Tequila's wife. I porked her till her nose bled."

Panama smiled knowingly. Then he said: "Too bad about Tequila."

"Life's a bitch and then you die," said the Major.

"Let me write that down," I said.

"I hosed these two sisters in San Antonio once," Panama said. McGovern was listening in rapt attention. The Major gave me a broad wink. "One was named Trixie and one was named Dixie."

I felt a tap on my shoulder and turned to see an attractive, well-dressed, dark-haired woman wearing those large, black glasses that women sometimes wear to show that they're not there to have fun.

"I'm Dr. Allison Klitsberg," she said.

Next to her stood Cleve, humming some song in his

head, a sick, little smile on his face, and looking, generally, like he belonged on the third ring of Saturn.

"Cleve is here with me," said Dr. Klitsberg, "as part of our resocialization program."

I took another look at Cleve. He didn't even recognize me. I turned back to Dr. Klitsberg, who was now drawing approving nods from Panama and Major Boles.

"Good luck," I said.

On the way to the men's room I was accosted by Dylan and a tall, thin Charles Manson look-alike who hugged me and picked me up off my feet. When he set me down I realized it was Bo Byers, who'd done the sound for the band and was with the road crew on the first tour. Bo and I exchanged a few somewhat more subdued greetings, then he drifted over to say hello to the other guys.

"Might as well make the reunion tour as authentic as possible, hoss," said Dylan. "Bo's been knocking around for a while and he said he needed the work, so I took him aboard. He came in last week from Tulsa."

"Why does that ring a bell?" I said.

58

"**I** know it sounds a little far-fetched," I said.

"No, it doesn't sound far-fetched," said Major Boles. "It sounds abso-motherfuckin'-lutely crazy. Of course, people are gonna die in thirteen years. They'll also get married, get divorced, go to bar mitzvahs—"

"Don't say 'bar mitzvah' in front of Willie."

The two of us were sitting in a little Irish bar on Forty-third Street a few blocks over from the rehearsal studio. The rehearsal had been brutal but the band sounded a lot tighter than I'd ever have believed after all that time off the road. It was almost eleven o'clock. On the jukebox the Irish Rovers were singing "The Unicorn" in a thick Irish brogue. The song was written by Shel Silverstein, who no one ever mistook for being Irish.

"I'll admit," said Major Boles, "that the three of them checked out in a pretty short period of time, but sometimes things happen in threes. Like airplane crashes."

"They weren't on airplanes," I said as I signaled the bartender for another round of Jameson's. "They were murdered."

"You say that. What do the police say?"

I killed the shot and chased it with a little Guinness. I looked out the window into the street. "They say people go to bar mitzvahs," I said.

"Ah ha!" said the Major. I looked at him for a moment. His face still seemed to have the disbelief and recklessness of youth about it. You had to look closely to see the fine lines of time and worry that had etched themselves around his eyes like side roads and minor tributaries on an old map of Kansas before Dorothy left. The Major was not that much younger than myself, but he was young enough to make it still rather hard to convince him that his life might be in danger.

I took the clipping of Dennis Duggan's article out of the pocket of my hunting vest and spread it on the mahogany in front of the Major. "You'll notice," I said, "that the three names directly above your own are all recently deceased. They were croaked in the order they appear."

I let the Major study the crumpled little hit list while I studied my empty glass and motioned the bartender for another round of drinks. "What do you think?" I asked, finally.

"Where are they now?" said the Major facetiously. "I'll tell you where they are. They're right exactly just in the same goddamn place they've always been. Nobody really changes much, you know."

I looked at the minor tributaries again. "That's what I'm counting on," I said.

The bartender poured another round. "Humor me," I said to the Major. "Just assume someone's behind these deaths, methodically trying to kill off the band."

The Major belched.

"Can you remember anything the whole band did that could've provoked someone into seeking this kind of vengeance? Can you remember anything at all?"

"I can't even remember the Alamo," said Major Boles.

If he hadn't been a drummer I probably could've made him see the light. But you can't warn anybody about anything today. Half the world's a bunch of paranoid nerds who are afraid of life, and the other half just don't give a damn. The latter group is usually more fun to drink with.

Nothing ever happens when you expect it, even if you're ready for it. But there is an uncanny timing to certain events on this planet that leads one, if not to believe in the Baby Jesus, at least to realize that somebody's building a lot of time-share condos in hell.

It was almost midnight, the time the white-haired man on the train was waiting for, when we finished the last round. Major Boles had folded Duggan's article into a paper airplane and headed for the door. I refolded the clipping, put it back in my pocket, and paid the bill. I took out a cigar and started to light it in the doorway.

The Major was standing in the street yelling something when a pair of headlights swam by me like a laser shark. A speeding taxi cab with its radio blaring hit him with that deep, sickening "WHUMP" sound that, once you've heard it, resonates forever in your fondest nightmares, like a horrible human bell.

59

"**W**ell," said Sergeant Cooperman, "I asked you not to bother me for a couple weeks and that's about how long it's been."

It seemed like Cooperman and I'd been out on Forty-third Street long enough to start asking people for spare change for a sex change. The guys from the stiff casino, with the demeanor and emotional range of workers fixing a pothole, had finally taken Major Boles's body away. My heart felt like it'd lost its rhythm section.

"You didn't get the license number or the number on the cab?"

"It happened too fast," I said. "I don't think there was a license plate. Just the headlights. The loud music. It seemed like it all occurred in the time it took to strike a match and set fire to a cigar."

"Maybe you shouldn't smoke," said Sergeant Cooperman as he took a Gauloises out of a crumpled pack and, narrowing his eyes like a street cat, lit it with a Zippo. We both stood under a streetlight looking at the place where Boles's broken body had lain. There'd been a shoe and a smashed pair of shades there too for a while, but they'd taken them downtown, too. He'd been killed instantly, the medical examiner had said, but I'd known that already.

Traffic was rolling on the street again. The excitement was over. I looked away for a moment and then back to the place where he'd died. I wasn't exactly sure where the place was anymore. Places change, they say. I put my hands into the pockets of my coat to keep warm.

My fingers fumbled onto something in my left pocket and my hand came out with Dennis Duggan's story. I gave it to Cooperman. He unfolded it and I pointed out the top four names on the list.

"Christ," he said. "Too bad we're not at the racetrack." He'd read the story, he said. He knew the list. "Describe the driver again."

"I told you. All I saw was a brief impression of a blur going by with a hat pulled down over its face."

"Maybe it was James Cagney."

Cooperman was hot tonight, I thought. Death seemed to sharpen his wit. He asked a few more questions. I gave him Dylan's room number at the Chelsea and the names of the guys in the band that were staying there. Finally, he put his little notebook away. He lit up another Gauloises and I began the spiritual foreplay that is occasionally required of lighting a cigar at certain measured moments of your life.

Cinderella's coach had retro-metamorphosed rather unpleasantly to a leering jack-o'-lantern several hours ago. Cooperman and I still stood there, almost friends, watching cars go by and vagrants peer into garbage cans, looking for the world. The brash loneliness was achingly vibrant; it seemed to belong to another place and another time. Casablanca. The Paris of the twenties. New York did not feel like my home anymore. Maybe it never had. Maybe I belonged in Texas. The Texas of the nineties, I knew, was not the Paris of the twenties, but how many kinds of sauces can you put on a chicken-fried steak?

At last, Cooperman shook his head and began walking toward his generic squad car. I turned and started to head for Seventh Avenue.

"Hey, Tex," he said. I stopped and turned around.

"You said the driver of the vehicle was playing loud music as he drove past?"

"Yeah," I said.

"What kind of music was he playing, Tex?"

Something made me stop for a moment. Auditory and visual images seemed to be slowly sorting themselves out in some jumbled federal office building of my mind.

"Country music," I said.

"Figures," said Cooperman as he got into the car.

60

When I got back to the loft it was two-forty in the morning and I hit the blower running. Most people, for reasons I've never understood, don't like to receive phone calls at two-forty in the morning. As my friend Marvin Brener always tells me: "People have their lives." They do, indeed. They have their tragic little lives and a horrible thing like a late-night phone call from New York is just too much

201

for them to handle gracefully. It's foreign to their sub-urban souls to have a voice from the past intrude itself across a wire into the shipwreck they've made of their lives. Oh, there were people I used to be able to call late at night but they are almost all dead. Now I can still call them anytime I want, only they never answer. All the circuits in hell are busy. Of course, many so-called living people are dead and in hell, too, they just don't know it yet.

I think late-night phone calls can be spiritually im-portant and the absence of them is a significant index of the advance of middle age. When you've truly reached middle age, the only late-night phone calls you get are wrong numbers or news that somebody died. Well, somebody had died. Four somebodys had died.

"Why did you call me?" asked Little Jewford.

"To see if you were there," I said.

"Where the hell else would I be?" he wanted to know. "It's two o'clock in the morning."

"It's an hour later here," I said. "Should we cir-cumcise our watches?"

The conversation was fairly brief and it wasn't too pleasant, but it did prove that Little Jewford was in Houston, and it's hard to commandeer a hack in New York if you're in bed in Houston.

I called Max in Kerrville. He wasn't ecstatic either. He had to work in the morning.

"I don't know what you're bitching about, Max," I said. "It's an hour later here."

Max said something in Spanish that didn't sound nice.

"Listen, Max," I said, "we've got to pull out all the stops on Parnell. There's a guy in a cowboy hat killing people up here and every time I mentally round up the suspects, he's always up there at the top of the list. He doesn't seem to have a motive, but he does have a cow-boy hat."

"So does Gabby Hayes," said Max.

I got Max to promise to call Parnell's family again in the morning and to press them on his whereabouts. He would call me as soon as he talked with them.

"*Buenas noches,*" said Max sleepily.

"*Salamat mimpi,*" I said. It was about all the residual Malay I remembered from Borneo, unless, of course, I was drunk. Then I remembered a lot of Malay and a lot of phone numbers that were no longer working in Los Angeles. *Salamat mimpi* meant "safe dreams." That was about the nicest thing you could wish anybody, I figured.

When I hung up with Max I called Dylan at the Chelsea Hotel but his line was busy. I left a message with the night clerk, and, in honor of Dylan Thomas's last residence on this particular planet, I located a bottle of Old Grand-dad hiding behind a bag of cat litter. It was covered with cobwebs and dust and looked like it'd come with the loft. I poured a shot into the bull's horn to settle my nerves. I raised the bull's horn in a toast to Major Boles. The cat sat on the counter looking bored.

" 'After the first death there is no other,' " I quoted. I was beginning to wonder if Dylan Thomas knew what the hell he was talking about. I downed the shot.

The Old Grand-dad was funkier than Jack Daniel's and gave the certain impression of being capable of inducing degeneracy faster than Jameson's. But it cut the phlegm.

"You know," I said to the cat, "that time at the Chinese restaurant when Parnell winged the waiter?"

The cat looked at me. She blinked several times.

"Suppose it wasn't Travis Parnell."

I had a few more Old Grand-dads just to unwind a little bit and think things over. I was sitting at the kitchen table with the cat when the phones rang. It was almost four o'clock in the morning. I might be a lot of things but at least I wasn't middle-aged. I walked over to the desk and lifted the blower on the left. It was Washington Ratso telling me that the girls were safe and having a great time and why didn't I tell him that Kelli had very well-shaped buttocks and my sister had terrific breasts. He didn't say it all in precisely those words, but that was the gist.

"It's nice to know you're looking after them," I said.

"They're pretty hard to miss," said Ratso. "I've really enjoyed working with you on this one."

I lighted a cigar and listened as Ratso went into a little more anatomical detail than I would have liked. Finally, he said: "Hey, I read in the paper that you're getting the Jewboys together again for a big reunion tour."

"We've run into a few problems," I said. "Or rather, they've run into us."

"Well, if you need a Lebanese Jewboy who plays a mean butane guitar, I'd love to come."

"Sexually?" I asked.

"No," said Ratso. "I mean join the tour. Sure you don't need a guitar player?"

"Too bad you don't play the drums," I said.

It was a quarter after four by the time I killed the lights, said good night to the cat, and got into bed, with images of Major Boles still very vivid in my mind. I'd almost gotten into the fitful-tossing-and-turning stage when the phones rang again. Maybe I was younger than I thought.

I collared the pink princess phone by the bedside that the Greek woman I was subletting from had left along with her green plants and ballet poster. It was Dylan.

He said: " 'I Fought the Law and the Law Won.' "

"Ah, so Sergeant Cooperman's been to see you."

"They came through here like the 'City of New Orleans.' "

I talked to Dylan for some time, and as we talked, the sense of personal loss we both felt became evident. My friend Dr. Jim Bone says that everyone has two families: the one you're born into and the one you make for yourself. The Texas Jewboys, with all our strife and separation, were a family, and this latest loss diminished us all.

Cooperman and his boys had interviewed everyone in the band about Major Boles's death, getting background, establishing alibis. The only two people whom they still hadn't located were Snakebite Jacobs and Panama Red.

"Not unusual for musicians not to be in a hotel at four in the morning," I said. "Or anywhere else."

" 'Four o'clock rock,' " said Dylan.

After I cradled the princess I lay back in bed and stared for a long time at the paint peeling off the ceiling. A few more lesbian dance classes, I figured, and there'd be nothing left to stare at. A numbing hard-edged guilt was beginning to settle somewhere deep in my soul. I'd brought the band to New York. It was my brilliant theory that they'd be safer here. I was the leader of the band. I was responsible in a large way for what had happened to the Major.

I did my dead-level best to push the guilt out of my mind. Catholic and Jewish people, as well as practically everybody else, seem to enjoy engendering guilt in others, but it serves no one well to experience an undue amount of guilt yourself. Even if you deserve it.

I thought about Snakebite and Panama Red. I didn't lamp Snakebite as a killer. I couldn't really see Panama murdering anyone either. Maybe he could flog somebody to death with his lips. And he did wear a hat all the time. But it just didn't make sense. It was impossible. Or was it? Charles Manson was a musician, I said to myself. It was almost becoming a mantra.

I finally got to sleep and, sure enough, I had a

205

hideous, slow-motion, Technicolor dream about Major Boles.

But first there were a few short trailers. I got a Mr. Pibb and some Milk Duds and hurried to my seat just as the lights went down.

61

Dale Haufrect, the kid who lived across the street, reached his hand into the goldfish bowl. I must've been very young because I regarded my three goldfish as my secret friends. An adult, of course, can look upon goldfish as secret friends, too, but it's usually not considered all that healthy a relationship. Dale Haufrect took the goldfish out of the bowl one by one and slit their sides with his thumbnail before dropping them on the floor. I watched in that state of suspended animation that only a four-year-old or an adult New Yorker who doesn't want to get involved can obtain.

But the goldfish never came back to life like Dale Haufrect said they would. Instead, little drops of cotton-candy–colored blood fell from the fish to the floor and my own eyes of ancient childhood filled with tears.

All my youth, I suppose, I've waited for those three goldfish to come back to life, but they never have. Maybe they moved up to the next incarnation. Maybe God sent them back as Goodman, Schwerner, and Chaney. Sounds like a law firm, but it isn't.

I did a few bed turns and vaguely, sadly, semiconsciously realized that one of the things that God probably couldn't do was bring dead goldfish back to life. Not even Dale Haufrect could do that.

I spun a few more times in the shallow grave of Morpheus and the dream fast-forwarded about twenty-four years or so to a large, dank basement of some club in the Village. Several hundred people were crowded around staring at a screen upon which appeared to be a home movie of a fairly large goldfish. The goldfish seemed to have a wound in its side out of which periodically would seep cotton-candy–colored blood. In the dream, I couldn't understand why several hundred people would be standing in a room at rapt attention staring at the rather gory spectacle of a dying goldfish. I was older now and it wasn't quite that traumatic an experience. You could see a dying goldfish on your way to work.

I scanned the room for a familiar face and finally orbed Ratso waving to me with one hand and holding a large, heaping plate of food in the other. The hand he was waving had what looked like a corned beef sandwich in it. I walked over. Next to Ratso stood Allen Ginsberg wearing little Tibetan finger cymbals.

I heard Ginsberg say to Ratso in a soothing, almost hypnotic voice: "Why don't you try on these finger cymbals?"

Ratso replied: "I can't. I'm eating a sandwich. They could give me lead poisoning."

Ginsberg then offered the cymbals to me but I, too, declined. Then Ginsberg smiled beatifically and began playing the little cymbals himself, dancing around, and chanting, as near as I can remember, the following poem:

Live when you live
Die when you die
Laugh when you laugh
Cry when you cry
Fuck when you fuck
Shit when you shit
Pee when you pee—

"Excuse me," I said, "but why is everybody watching that goldfish die?"

Ginsberg and Ratso both started laughing, and Ratso laughed so hard I was glad I hadn't accepted Ginsberg's offer. It's hard to give the Heimlich maneuver when you're wearing Tibetan finger cymbals.

Ginsberg started to play the finger cymbals and jump around again. This time he chanted gleefully: "It's Abbie's dick, it's Abbie's prick, it's Abbie's dong, it's Abbie's *schlang*, it's Abbie's thing, it's his *I Ching*, it's Abbie's dork, it's in New York."

"Come again?" I said.

"It's a movie," Ratso said, "that Abbie Hoffman had made of his recent vasectomy."

"Hell of a cinematographer," I said.

"It's Abbie's penis, gonna send it to Venus," said Ginsberg.

I walked over to the doorway and was trying to light a blue bubble-gum cigar when a hack high-beamed me from the left wing and slowly moved past like a yellow fog of death. In horripilating slow motion I watched the hellish hack reduce Major Boles to eleven different herbs and spices. I heard the loud, familiar country music again as it ricocheted off the buildings and Dopplered down to me in the dream. It was the same snatch of music I'd heard earlier in the evening when Major Boles had been killed on Forty-third Street. But this time, in the dream, I clearly heard the words *Ronnie Reagan.*

* * *

When I woke up it was still dark, but I'd seen the light. At least I'd seen enough of it to know I was on the right track. I still didn't know where the hell I was going, of course, but, I could decide that when I got there. For starters I'd have to talk to Captain Midnite, Willie Fong Young, Skycap Adams because he was next on the list, and Dylan, because he remembered yesterday. So did Cleve, of course, but it was chancy because he might forget it by tomorrow.

I programmed the espresso machine, chased some cockroaches out of the frying pan, and made some scrambled eggs with a heavy dollop of frozen Lone Star five-alarm chili, throwing in some red Vietnamese peppers a little friend had sent me recently from Arkansas. As dawn broke over the warehouses I had breakfast and thought about my dreams.

All of them stemmed from real incidents, of course. Dale Haufrect had killed my goldfish when I was a little kid. I'd performed some songs at a party for Abbie Hoffman where he'd shown a movie of his recent vasectomy. I'd opened for the vasectomy. Two weeks later, Abbie'd jumped bail and gone underground. Now he was underground for good, I thought sadly. Well, at least he'd feel at home there.

As far as "Ronnie Reagan" went, I was now sure I'd heard the same music at the actual time of the hit-and-run accident. "Ronnie Reagan" was part of a line of a song, the whole verse of which went like this:

It's retro-rocket time inside my attic
I'm all wrapped up in the flag to keep me warm
I've got my brain locked in to cruise-o-matic
Rollin' Ronnie Reagan in suppository form.

The song was called "Flyin' Down the Freeway" and it was written by a young songwriter in 1973 in Nashville. I remembered it well. I ought to.
I was that songwriter.

209

62

Later that Thursday morning I called Captain Midnite in Nashville. He had that certain renaissance in his voice that you hear only from very soulful former disc jockeys.

"Little Jimmie Dickens International Fan Club," he said. I identified myself.

"I was going to make a big donation this month to the United Jewish Appeal," said Midnite, "but I'm a little short."

"Yeah. Midnite, have you got anything for me?"

"I gave you that alarm clock seventeen years ago."

"You'll be gratified to know it still works," I said. "Otherwise I might've slept through this conversation."

"I do have some news for you. Tompall Glaser injured himself trying to sing as high as his brothers. Now he walks with a lisp."

"I was looking for something unusual or unpleasant that might've happened to Willie Fong Young."

"Well, he went up to New York to do that reunion tour with you. That's unusual and unpleasant."

"Midnite, you know how Willie is. It'd take me days to get anything out of him and I don't have the time. Has he been in any accidents or near misses that you know about?"

"Come to think of it, his car was totaled about three weeks ago. Brakes went out."

"Willie didn't mention it."

"That's because he wasn't in it. He'd loaned it to his smother-in-law."

"How is she?"

"Sexually?"

"Walked into my own trap, didn't I? You've been taking Kinky lessons. What's her condition?"

"Willie's smother-in-law? Broke her leg is all. Cast was a bit unwieldy. It was made of chopsticks."

"I picked right up on that."

"Since the accident she's been a shell of herself. When Willie visited her in the hospital he lifted her up and held her to his ear to see if he could hear the ocean."

It was getting interesting. After terminating social intercourse with Midnite, I paced the loft a bit, puffing on a Punch Rothschild Maduro. If I was right there were four victims. There were certainly four stiffs, and I didn't have to extrapolate things too far to see that they were all victims of the same maniacal, methodical mind. You could add to that the failed attempt to eighty-six Willie Fong Young, resulting in the injury to his smother-in-law. You could also add two attempts on my own life, for I now thought it more likely that a poor marksman had been gunning for me rather than Travis Parnell deliberately winging the waiter to send a message of terror to Kelli. Hadn't heard much about Travis Parnell lately. I wondered who his agent was.

Images of the Major kept intruding themselves into my mind's bloodshot eye. Try as I might, I just couldn't quite see the whole picture. The style was obvious. The method. The pattern. But the work remained unsigned, unfinished, insidious, foreboding. You couldn't really tell what it was going to be when the artist was through. It seemed as if an insane Impressionist were carefully creating an abstract painting, splashing fresh bright blood

211

onto the beckoning canvas, cocking a grinning, almost apologetic face to one side, not quite entirely happy with his macabre, death-wreaking work. Rectal realism was never like this, I thought.

Through the blue haze of cigar smoke I saw the Major standing in the street calling me. I just couldn't hear his words. It tore at my heart and at my conscience. I paced a little more rapidly and the cat followed my movements back and forth across the loft from her perch on the counter. She looked like a slightly bored spectator watching a rather slow tennis match, except that she flicked her tail occasionally in irritation, to be sure that I knew she didn't give a damn who won or lost.

Gradually, it became clear to me what I had to do. This was no time for grief. It was no time for guilt. The reunion tour must proceed as scheduled, fraught as it was with danger and death. I was convinced it was the only way to catch the killer in the act. The only other option would be for the band to scatter itself to the winds, and then to learn at fairly regular intervals, like the white-haired man on the train, of the demise of every single member of the original Texas Jewboys.

Around noon I called Dylan. He told me that Snakebite and Panama had gotten in early that morning and Cooperman planned to talk to them. I did, too, I said. I told Dylan to go ahead with all rehearsal and tour plans as scheduled. He wasn't surprised and allowed that he'd come to the same conclusion himself. For some reason, I felt better when I heard that. If we were both wrong, we'd soon find out.

"I'll get a new drummer for the tour," I said. "Corky Laing may have enough of a death wish to want to do it."

" 'Drums keep poundin' rhythm to the brain,' " said Dylan.

"I'll also be checking with Cleve today about the

itinerary. I'm going to get him to try to add a date sometime next week at the Lone Star to sort of kick things
off. Maybe we'll be able to resolve this madness before
the actual road tour starts. I hope Cleve's mental hygiene's in a little better shape than it was at the
rehearsal."

" 'Here comes your nineteenth nervous break-
down,' " Dylan said.

"Anybody in the band who wants to bug out for the
dugout has my blessing. I know a lot of guys who would
love to be in this band."

There was a brief silence on the line. Then I heard
the high, Brenda Lee–like, unmistakable sound of the
expulsion of gas occurring fairly close to the receiver of
the phone.

"I'm telling you, Dylan, this reunion idea is going
to prove triumphant yet."

" 'The magical mystery tour,' " said Dylan, " 'is
coming to take you away.' "

63

"Of course I'm staying,"
said Skycap Adams, "but it's going to be kind of hard to
rehearse the band without a drummer, don't you think?"

"We could go on the road with one of those drum
machines they use in lounges at Holiday Inns."

I'd just returned from the Monkey's Paw where I'd

had a liquid lunch with McGovern and brought him up to date on the situation. In tune with the new freedoms in Eastern Europe and the easement of apartheid in South Africa, the management of the Monkey's Paw had decided to lift the ban on McGovern for peeing on the leg of a lady standing at the bar in 1974. "Free at last," McGovern had said to me as he'd sipped a tall Vodka McGovern.

"We could give Wayne Newton a Hebrew natural and a cowboy hat," Skycap Adams was saying, "and maybe he could take *your* place."

"He'd probably want an entourage of forty-nine buttboys."

"You got to get a drummer, Kinkster."

"I was thinking," I said. "You remember Cubby? Used to play drums for the Mouseketeers? I wonder what he's doing?"

"Probably wishing he was still staring at Annette Funicello's tits."

I told Skycap to be on the alert. I warned him again that his life was in grave danger whether he stayed with the band or not. I told him I was sorry about Major Boles, very sorry. I knew Skycap had been close to him.

"When you play with somebody that long," said Skycap, but he didn't finish the sentence.

"All I can tell you," I said, "is what the great producer Huey P. Meaux once told me: 'All musicians are brothers in music.'"

When I hung up the phone with Skycap I walked over to the window and stared silently at the unfocused street.

"All but one," I said to the cat. "All but one."

Snakebite Jacobs, Billy Swan, Panama Red, Willie Fong Young (possible), Skycap Adams (possible), and Bo Byers (looks like Charles Manson and just came in from Tulsa).

That was the list of suspects I was perusing in my

Big Chief tablet late Thursday afternoon as frightening February shadows reached their tendrils across Vandam Street and into the little loft. The only other possibilities I could think of—Dylan, my brother Roger, Little Jewford, and his brother Big Jewford—were so thoroughly alibied by virtue of their teaching, professional, and family structuring that I now ruled them totally out. As a rule of thumb, I always permitted the accusatory finger to point at every conceivable individual connected with a case, regardless of my subjective feelings for them. Of course, if things continued at the current killing pace, all my potential suspects would soon become victims and there'd be no one to blame at all. It's always been my personal policy to leave the blame for God and small children but, unfortunately, in a murder investigation, somebody's got to be "it."

Another distant possibility crossed my desk. Could the killer be someone outside the band who was nonetheless close enough to the band to have motive, method, and means? If there was such a person, I wished he would please step forward. Country bands on the road are like small nuclear families, and outsiders can usually get only as close to them as the one-night-stand permits. A lot could occur on a one-night-stand, but nothing I could think of that might carry such a long-smoldering vengeance across so many years. Hatred, very much like love, is a thing that must be nurtured.

My mind went back to the idea of some kind of curse upon the band. It was far-fetched, fantastic, next door to ridiculous. Yet four methodical murders of people with nothing in common except their membership in the Texas Jewboys was enough to give even a non-superstitious person a measure of pause. And even something as melodramatic and medieval as a curse, if it occurs in what we like to think of as real life, must have a motive.

I wished fervently that my old camp counselor Vern would suddenly spring up in the loft and scream, and the story would be over. But I knew that he wouldn't and it wouldn't. It was remarkable, I thought. Here I was, an adult, looking out the window for something between the faltering light and the insidious shadows of the February of the soul. And yet I felt like a small child in a summer cabin, peering frightfully over the edge of my bunk into the inexplicable, ever-darkening darkness.

64

I was having shredded wheat and rambutans for breakfast Friday morning when Cleve called from wig city. He sounded very lucid, almost businesslike.

"You're going to the wake for the Major?" he asked.

"Yeah," I said. "They called me about it last night. It's at the Lone Star at ten o'clock."

"I'm not sure I can go. Dr. Klitsberg's concerned about the ambience there reawakening certain anxieties of mine."

"Well, the doctor knows best."

"She's got some nice nay-nays on her, too, doesn't she?"

I ate some shredded wheat. Cleve hummed to himself a little.

"Cleve," I said, "can you get us a warm-up gig at the Lone Star? Say, sometime next week? It'd be good to have one show under our belt before we hit the road."

"Done, dude," said Cleve.

"Also, can you make a little list for me of any incidents or unusual experiences you remember that everyone in the band was involved in?"

"Done, dude."

This was really reaching, I thought. Asking a criminally insane mental patient if he could remember anything that might help me find the origin of a supernatural curse. It wasn't standard detection procedure, I was sure. Neither was pissing up a rope.

"Thanks, Cleve. Give Dr. Klitsberg my best."

"Done, dude."

Rambutans are hard to find in the States. So are durians. They're both native fruits of Borneo. If you eat a durian and drink alcohol, they say it'll kill you. There haven't been too many studies done on rambutans and shredded wheat, but sometimes you've got to take chances. If you want to try rambutans or durians, you can find them, occasionally, in Chinatown. They'll usually be tucked away somewhere between the octopus beaks and the Michael Jackson posters.

When I finished breakfast I fed the cat some tuna, took a cup of coffee over to the desk, sat down, lit a cigar, took a few puffs, and tried to make sense of a situation that made no sense at all. We couldn't afford to lose any more Jewboys. There weren't that many of us to begin with.

I was not looking forward to attending Major Boles's wake. Going to a wake was like going to a bar mitzvah without the bar mitzvah boy. Going to a wedding without the bride and groom. People wandered around saying how much he would've liked this and how much he would've appreciated that, and the stiff was already worm bait spinning in limbo. Wakes were for the living, not, as advertised, for the dead. Like my friend Tim Mayer once told me: "We mourn for ourselves, Kinkster."

The Timster himself, a great American, went to Jesus a few years back. I didn't go to his wake. I know he wouldn't have minded.

I used up what was left of the afternoon calling Westport, Connecticut; Montreal; and several less glamorous places in an effort to locate Corky Laing and offer him a gig with the Jewboys. I left a spate of messages scattered around for him and then tried Max in Kerrville and Kelli in Washington, neither of whom were home.

By the time the Corkster got back to me I was in the dead middle of a power nap and I had a minor problem identifying who he was and why he was calling me. Then I had the little problem of making the offer sound attractive.

"We've had a few, uh, accidents occur to band members recently."

"So I've heard," said Corky. "Just between us girls, you guys are being talked about kind of like the Average White Band."

The Average White Band was the average white band until one of its members brodied on drugs. Then they suddenly became media darlings and their price went through the roof.

"We could do worse," I said.

"And you have," said Corky, somewhat insensitively.

The Corkster was now a big-time record executive in Montreal and he was a long way from throwing his drumsticks up in the air at the Lone Star and catching them without missing a beat.

"So you don't want the gig," I said.

"I didn't say that."

"Corkster, I knew you'd come through. You're still

running on rock 'n' roll time, baby. All musicians are brothers in music."

"How much are you paying?" said Corky.

We haggled like Turks in an alley for a while. The Corkster insisted upon ridiculously exorbitant "hazard pay." I did my best to Christian him down. Eventually, a compromise was hammered out.

"We need you for rehearsals this weekend, Corkster."

"I'll get down there if it kills me," he said.

When I got off with Corky I thought about the "accidents" that had befallen the Jewboys. Only three of them had been made to appear as accidents. Of course, it's pretty hard to blow a guy away with a riot gun in a rain room and make it look like death by misadventure.

I was struck fully for the first time by this radical departure of MO. That's *modus operandi*, if you never took Latin. Most cops never took Latin either, but they know that it's strange for the same killer to alter his work methods drastically. Why would the same person cap Tequila and then take such great pains to make the other three murders look accidental? That was the question. I had the answer right on the tip of my Smith & Wesson knife but I just couldn't see it. If I could've, more tragedy might've been averted.

I had a few shots of Jameson's, thought about the problem from a few rather oblique angles, then threw in the towel. But something was nagging me about this convoluted case. There was a very simple explanation, I figured. All things that appear complex are actually very simple. And all things that appear very simple are actually quite complex. It was a variation on a theme my father had developed about relating well to people. He said: "Always treat children like adults and adults like children and you'll never go wrong." He didn't say anything about lesbians, bass players, or murderers, but some things you've got to find out for yourself.

I had to get ready for a wake. Whether you like them or not, I suppose it's always a good idea to attend wakes when you get the chance. One thing's for sure: You'll never get to go to your own.

65

The Major would have liked the wake. Almost nobody else did, but what did he care? He didn't have to listen to a pretentious, posturing, heavy-metal band called No MSG for three and a half hours. The Major didn't have to do anything but look down (or up, as I suspected) upon us, shake his head, and say: "I'm glad I didn't have to sit through *that* shit."

There was a quantity of alcohol consumed, possibly because, by this time, the band had put two and two together and come up with something approximating "The Last of the Thirteen." They did not, for the most part, seem to suspect murder in the three deaths that appeared to be accidental. They felt the deaths were strange, unlucky, an omen, but they spoke with the same sense of fatalism as the Major had when he told me about plane crashes coming in threes. Nonetheless, I found myself attempting to answer as many questions as I felt myself wanting to ask. At a wake, after you've gone through the drill of what a wonderful guy the honoree of the function was, the topic swiftly moves to other areas. To spend the whole time talking about the dear departed stiff would be morbid.

So it was that what conversation was possible with No MSG cacophonating all around us drifted to the past eventually, to memorable events and incidents on the road. That topic suited me fine.

We sat in a big corner booth by the bar: Dylan, Billy Swan, Willie Fong Young, Snakebite Jacobs, Skycap Adams, Panama Red, and Bo Byers, the latest addition to the reunion-tour road crew. It was a small wake, but it was a small world. I noticed, with some relief, that Dr. Allison Klitsberg had not seen fit to allow Cleve to attend the wake. The doctor knows best, I thought.

It was a strange feeling to sit at a wake, even a hip, little informal job like this, and realize that somewhere among us very probably was a murderer moonlighting as a mourner. I figured I'd leave the alibi department to Cooperman. A killer as clever as the one I was looking for was clever enough to be somewhere else when he was supposed to be. As I saw it, my job was to encourage everybody to take a little walk down memory lane, an easy task at any wake, and see what joint experiences emerged. Not that I believed for a moment in the notion of a curse upon the House of Jewboy. I just had a feeling that somebody might slip, that something germane to the recurring nightmare we were all experiencing might be said.

Billy Swan remembered the time in 1974 when the entire band got stuck in an elevator between floors at the Sunset Marquis hotel in L.A. "It was the show at the Troubadour," said Swan, "our big debut on the West Coast. We were supposed to open for Tony Joe White. We were in the elevator, about ten of us, but it felt like a cast of thousands. Four and a half hours in that elevator and Kinky had to smoke his fucking cigar. Some of the guys really wanted to kill you, Kinkster."

Maybe somebody hadn't gotten over it, I thought. I

downed a shot of Jameson's and asked Swan quietly about his researches into Tequila and his wife's drug-dealing habits.

"Oh, I was going to tell you," said Swan, "it was mostly Sheila. She was pretty big time in L.A. back then apparently. I don't think Tequila knew how big."

"Sheila?"

"Sharon," said Billy. "Her West Coast drug alias was Sheila."

A drug dealer by any other name, I thought. But it was interesting. Maybe there was a drug angle in this that the OCCB hadn't uncovered. One matter I decided was long overdue. Finding Sharon.

Skycap Adams recalled the infamous gig on the campus at Buffalo. It was just when women's lib was becoming a hot issue. "We'd just launched into 'Get Your Biscuits in the Oven and Your Buns in the Bed,'" he said, "when these cranked-up diesel-dykes started attacking the stage in waves. Looked like a Kraut's-eye view of Normandy. Then they started smashing the amps and pulling the cords out of the walls. The cops carried them out as the broads wept hysterically. We needed a goddamn police escort to get off the campus. Remember that?"

We all remembered. I killed another shot of Jameson's. Could a woman be behind these killings, I wondered? Driving a speeding hack with a hat pulled low over her face?

"Remember that slit," said Panama Red, "that terrorized the band up in Denver? Crazy Helen, I think they called her. She followed us everywhere we went for a while. One night she went into Kinky's room, stayed there for a time, then went into Dylan's. After she left, I asked them both if they'd hosed her. They each said, 'No. We just gave her money. We felt sorry for her.'"

"And I remember what you called both of us," said Dylan.

"Homos?" said Panama.

"Worse," said Dylan. "You said Kinky and I were 'a couple of Peace Corps nerds.'"

Everybody laughed. I killed another shot of Jameson's. Crazy Helen had been too crazy to pull something like this off, I thought. But women were better than men at carrying grudges for long periods of time. At least that's been my experience.

"That San Francisco gig at the Old Warehouse was the scariest," said Willie Fong Young. "We were co-billed with Buffy Sainte-Marie and the audience was about half Kinky cowboy types and half American Indian Movement braves on the warpath."

"That was the show," said Panama, "where Kinky had that ugly gold costume bracelet in the shape of a snake. He showed it to the audience there in San Francisco and told them: 'Janis gave me this.' The crowd all went 'Ahhhhhh.' Then Kinky says: 'Janis Bormaster. From Houston, Texas.' And the crowd started booing."

"There were a lot of gays in the crowd, too," said Bo Byers. "Half the audience looked like it was trollin' for colon."

Everybody laughed. Billy Swan said: "Back to your story, Willie."

"Anyway," said Willie, "we had that song 'Kind of Like an Indian,' and Kinky had a big Indian headdress. Whatever happened to that headdress?"

"It's down at Duckworth," said Dylan, "with everything else."

"Too bad," said Willie. "We could've used it on the tour. We're not doing any shows with Buffy Sainte-Marie, are we?"

"Get on with the story," somebody said.

"Well, Kinky's headdress had feathers hanging all over it and everything and the song featured a repeating chorus of 'Hi-a-wath-a Ooo-guh-chuk-aas.' After Kinky'd worn his headdress for a while, Snakebite and

Jewford both donned these little dime-store Indian headdresses that kids wear. They looked very unhealthy on the heads of adults and really funny contrasted with Kinky's big headdress. We were about halfway through the song when I saw somebody coming onto the stage through the backstage curtain. It was Buffy Sainte-Marie and she stalked right between me and the Major toward Kinky. If looks could've killed, we'd all have been dead."

We may still get our chance, I thought. I killed another Jameson's. Willie continued the interminable tale.

"Then Buffy, who was such an authentic Indian that she had her hair in braids and had on a leather miniskirt, comes right at Kinky, who wisely tries to stay out of her way. She's grabbing viciously for the headdress, trying to pull it off of Kinky's head. The crowd now, of course, has taken sides and fistfights are breaking out in the front row. Half are cheering for Buffy and half are cheering for Kinky and diehard A.I.M. followers are moving menacingly towards the stage."

"How'd we get out of that one?" asked Snakebite. "I forgot."

"Buffy got the headdress," said Bo, "and ran offstage with it. Kinky launched into 'I'm Proud to Be an Asshole from El Paso' and then, during Buffy's set, I liberated the headdress from her dressing room and put it back in the U-haul."

"That was a pretty ugly show, all right," said Snakebite, "but it wasn't as bad as the one at the Bluebonnet Club in Temple, Texas. Now, that one was almost mortal combat."

"I think I missed that show," said Swan.

"You were already back with Kris by that time," said Dylan, "but, believe me, you didn't miss a thing. Except maybe Van Dyke Parks. He was on keyboards then. He was brilliant. Wore a white aviator jumpsuit with little American flags sticking out all over it. He was afraid of Texans, he said."

"Turned out he was right," said Skycap.

"Anyway," said Snakebite, "back to the Bluebonnet. Van Dyke was with us and Roscoe West and Jimmie Don Smith. Van Dyke had this great intro, a combination of 'Exodus' and 'I've got Spurs That Jingle Jangle Jingle.' The show was one of the best. We were rockin' along and then we noticed a real surly looking Texas highway patrolman standing by the door. You couldn't tell if he hated the show, or the song 'They Ain't Makin' Jews Like Jesus Anymore,' or if he just had hemorrhoids."

" 'You never know what the monkey eat until the monkey shit,' " said Dylan, quoting our old friend Slim. "I get twenty years to the gallon on that one."

"Well," said Snakebite, "it didn't take long for the monkey to shit. Before we knew it there were two deputies there. Then four. Then pretty soon there were ten of them. And they all looked like their guppies just died."

"Sounds like a nice house to work," said Swan.

"The crowd wasn't that big to begin with," Snakebite continued, "and soon there were almost as many Texas state troopers and sheriff's department deputies in the place as there were patrons. Van Dyke, among others, was not pleased.

"The next thing we know, the troopers and sheriff's deputies are grabbing guys out of the crowd and dragging them out of the place, kicking and struggling. Some of the guys' wives and girlfriends were crying. And Dylan kept shouting: 'Keep playing. Keep playing.' "

I thought back to the grim scene which now seemed quite funny. When violence broke out in a place, the best thing to do was to keep playing. This usually, though not always, tended to place you above the fray and discourage all hell from breaking loose.

"We kept playing," said Snakebite. "And the fuzz kept dragging people off in handcuffs. Finally, there were about twenty people left in the crowd, if you wanted to call it that, and the sheriff's deputies were right at the lip of the stage, showing no sign of slowing their forward progress. Dylan yells: 'Everybody backstage!'

"We didn't have to be told twice. With Van Dyke in the lead—I think this was his first trip to Texas—we got out of there quick. It turned out the owner hadn't paid his liquor license or something, but we didn't know that until much later. That was the first time I've ever seen an audience get arrested."

"I went in later," said Bo, "to take a farewell dump in the men's room and there was the Major who'd just finished dumping and wanted to show me something he'd written on the men's room wall. I didn't want to go in the stall, but he was so insistent that I put on my hydrogen mask and went in and took a look. This is what he'd written on the wall."

Bo cleared his throat a few times and downed a shot of Wild Turkey. Then he recited the following verse:

"Here I sit, strainin' my pooper
Tryin' to give birth to a Texas state trooper."

Everybody cheered. Panama stood up. "Here's to the Major," he said, lifting his glass. I looked around the table as everyone stood up and raised his glass in a toast. If there was a killer in the group, he could've fooled me.

We all toasted the Major for a last time. There wasn't a hell of a lot else we could do for him. Except find his killer.

66

As Blane Borgelt, a white lawyer who wants to be a black preacher when he grows up, often says: "Life knows you better than you knows yourself." Life knew me well enough to know that this case was bringing me alarmingly close to squirtin' out of both ends. It was Saturday morning, the day after the wake, and there seemed nothing to look forward to but a week of rehearsals for what was almost certain to be a disaster.

It was exceedingly frustrating to be dealing with a killer who left only tracks, it appeared, that were intended to be seen. Not only did I not seem to be making much progress on the Jewboy case, but Travis Parnell apparently had pulled off the best disappearing act since Ehrich Weiss. These could be the first two cases, I thought with chagrin, that might have to be lamped into the Kinky Open File. So much for my vaunted reputation, such as it was.

There were things to do, of course, other than just staying home and playing hide the helmet. I could try to find Sharon, which wouldn't be easy because her name frequently wasn't Sharon. Quite frankly, she seemed to be just about the last lead I had in the case. Everybody in the band knew her, most of them, it appeared, in the Old Testament sense of the word.

It was also just faintly within the realm of conceivability that Sharon was keeping such a low profile currently for a very good reason. Suppose Sharon was the killer. Suppose she'd had some reason to splice Tequila, brooded over it for thirteen years while she hosed various members of the band, then tracked her ex-husband down and blew his gray-matter department all over my soap dish. The spouse or the ex-spouse is usually the one behind most unsolved violent murders. Somehow, though, this case seemed too complex, too intricately interwoven, to be resolved by finding a woman whacking her long-ago ex. The scenario didn't take into account, either, what this rather far-fetched virago might have to gain by continuing to knock off Jewboys after eighty-sixing Tequila. Was she trying to cover her tracks in the first killing? Was she overcome by a fiendish lust for blood? Was she still rankling over the band's performance of "Get Your Biscuits in the Oven and Your Buns in the Bed"? Somehow, as a murder suspect, Sharon left a great deal to be desired.

Not wanting, however, to appear a male chauvinist pig in my now almost desperate search for the killer, I decided to try to get an update on any Sharon sightings from the boys in the band. Swan's last news of her drug deals in L.A. using the name Sheila was almost ancient history. Snakebite's account of his fling with "Cleopatra" was over three years old. Willie hadn't seen her since the original band had broken up thirteen years ago and she and Tequila had been arguing in their hotel room about a train, or a boat, or a plane, none of which would quite explain Tequila's brain going down my drain. The Major, of course, had said he'd hosed her in Chicago, but, unfortunately, he was no longer around to provide me with the color commentary.

I called the remaining personnel: Skycap, Panama, Dylan, and Bo. Bo said he was too busy screwing with all the equipment and sound to have time for somebody's wife. Dylan allowed as the opportunity had presented itself once a long time ago, but he had not permitted himself to succumb to the flesh.

"You *are* a Peace Corps nerd," I said.

" 'Lay, lady, lay,' " said Dylan.

Panama and Skycap, however, came forth, so to speak, with tales of a slightly more sordid nature. Panama had hosed her "and everything else that moved" in 1974.

"When you're on the road," he said, "you let the little head think for the big head."

"Maybe that's what I need to do to solve this case," I told him.

Skycap, it emerged, had had the most recent encounter with Sharon. It'd been two and a half years ago in Knoxville, Tennessee, and she'd called herself Regina.

"Nice name," I said.

"I remember leaving her at some little motel by the highway," said Skycap. "She was standing there in the parking lot and she picked up this stray cat and held it in her arms and said: How do you like my nice little pussy?"

"Thank you for sharing that poignant, rather personal moment with me, Skycap. I think I've heard enough."

In truth, I'd heard more than enough. I felt vaguely ashamed for looking into the pathetic details of a dead friend's unhappy love life. But this was just one of the seedier avenues I needed to explore in thoroughly looking into the case. It was a commentary on husbands and wives, men and women, the loneliness of the road. It made me sad and lonely. And looking back over an achingly empty expanse of time and geography, mournful music seemed to carry across the years, making the endless highway seem like the ribbon in the hair of the girl I used to know.

67

Sunday was the Lord's day of rest, but, for the Jewboys, it was another day of relentless rehearsal. The first gig at the Lone Star, according to Cleve, was now set for Thursday night. Corky Laing, hopefully, would be arriving in time for the rehearsal in the afternoon. If not, I thought, we might *have* to get one of those automatic drumming machines from the Holiday Inn lounge.

It was 11 A.M. and I was already up and about. I'd fed the cat and had my own breakfast, which consisted of a cup of semiviscous espresso and a rather sad-looking banana with liver spots that probably wished it was back in Guatemala and I was a tarantula.

I called Max again in Kerrville and got some not entirely unexpected, but, nonetheless, unsettling news. Travis Parnell's parents were now very worried about him. They'd notified the local authorities and were wondering openly if their boy had gone off the deep end. "Hunting season is over and he's still not back," his mother had told Max. She probably didn't know, I thought grimly, that hunting season in Manhattan is year-round.

I wondered about Travis Parnell, Texas's version of the elusive butterfly of love, all the way over to the espresso machine. It was not always easy to keep the two

230

current cases separate and distinct in my mind. Sometimes it seemed like I was schlepping around a rather unpleasant pair of Siamese albatrosses. The only thing the two cases appeared to have in common was that they were both going nowhere at a fairly tedious clip. Yet somehow, for no reason I could name, I felt there was an overlappage between the two. Maybe it was because the time frames of the cases were fairly similar; both had managed to cut severely into my cocktail hour over the past month or two. Maybe it was only in my mind that the two cases seemed to embrace each other like the Pacific Ocean and the nighttime California shoreline. Maybe I needed a checkup from the neck up.

It was pushing Gary Cooper time when I raised Kelli on the blower in our nation's capital. She wasn't as restless to come back to New York as I'd hoped. As well as being a dancer, Kelli was an interpreter for the deaf, and she'd become involved in a new project in Washington. She'd been commissioned to choreograph a number for the dance troupe at Gallaudet University. The subject matter was to deal with saving the rain forests, and the troupe was slated to perform the number at the Kennedy Center and the White House. Kelli and Marcie had become good friends and Kelli hadn't been thinking about Travis Parnell at all. It didn't sound, from the conversation, as if she'd been thinking too much about the Kinkster either. Hell, I was endangered, too. I didn't even have a support group.

When I was through talking to Kelli I'd learned more about Gallaudet University than I needed to know, though some of it was quite interesting. Gallaudet is an old school. Abraham Lincoln, Marilyn Monroe's favorite president, was the one who signed the proclamation making Gallaudet into a university. Daniel French, the sculptor, created a statue for the campus, a young girl learning to sign. During the time he was building the statue, French became interested in sign language and learned it himself. I asked Kelli if French had also looked into rectal realism at the time, but she didn't find it all that amusing.

When Lincoln was assassinated, French was the man they tapped to design the Lincoln Memorial. And that is why, if you look closely at Lincoln's hands as they rest on the arms of the chair, you'll notice that Lincoln is signing "A.L.," the initials to his name.

This bit of spiritual trivia I found fascinating as I lighted a cigar and sipped my third cup of espresso. Daniel French had made a timeless, poignant statement that was so subtle, even the tour guides probably didn't know about it. It was a little thing representative of a big thing.

I thought about who might be killing the Jewboys of Texas. The fact that most of them weren't Jewish and many of them weren't even from Texas was beside the point. They were Jews by inspiration. They were Texans by inspiration. That was all I needed, I thought. A little bit of inspiration.

Later that afternoon, as I was getting ready for the rehearsal, I felt more than ever convinced that the whole case would turn on some little thing. Some little thing that millions of tourists to Washington every year would never notice. I felt like one of those tourists myself. The little thing, I knew somehow, was already there. I just couldn't see it.

68

The next three or four days, filled as they were with rounds of rehearsals and press interviews, flew by like an angry Texas turkey buzzard, on occasion pausing very briefly to take a little peck out of my heart. By Thursday afternoon, the day of the gig at the Lone Star, the Average White Band Syndrome had kicked into high gear. Dylan and Cleve were sharing the responsibility of fielding the press and, between the two of them, had their hands full. Cleve had heard from almost all of the New York press establishment, other than McGovern and Duggan, who were both keeping close tabs on me and seemed to be enjoying my life a lot more at the moment than I was. Andrea Stevens from *The New York Times* planned to cover the Lone Star gig. Jann Wenner of *Rolling Stone* was sending somebody to stay with the tour as long as it lasted.

"He may have to get his story in pretty quick," I said.

"We've also got a call from *Feeble* magazine," said Cleve.

"You're sure that's not *People* magazine?"

"It sounded like *Feeble*."

"Maybe it was," I said.

"We've also heard from Dave Dawson and Jim Oram

233

in Australia. Maybe we could do a tour there sometime. Call it the 'Come Home in My Pouch Tour.' "

"I'll jump right on it," I said.

Dylan, similarly, was swamped with morbid fascination on the part of the press. People who had never cared whether I lived or died now wanted to know if I had any pet peeves. I did. I wanted to know why the press and Hollywood had ignored Ava Gardner and her career for almost forty years, then, when she died, alone and broken-spirited, slapped her on the cover of *Feeble* magazine next to the words "The Last Goddess." I had a few other pet peeves, too, but I figured they'd keep.

According to Dylan, almost every newspaper in Texas was chomping at the bit for an exclusive interview with anyone in the band down to and including the auxiliary buttboy. Ratso was off his sickbed, covering the tour for *National Lampoon*. Boyd Matson had a camera crew ready to drive the band around for the syndicated show he did from his 1958 fire-engine-red Cadillac.

"The Jewboys in the Jew canoe," said Dylan. "That's the angle Boyd's looking for."

"The old Jewish Cadillac," I said. "Stops on a dime and it picks it up."

"There's twenty years to the gallon in that one," said Dylan. "Did I mention that Jay Maeder wants us for his next cover of the *Daily News Magazine*?"

"It may have taken Major Boles to put us over the top," I said grimly, "but obviously we're hot. Piers Akerman called from Adelaide. He's the editor now and he's planning to come here to cover the tour himself."

" 'Tie me kangaroo down, mate,' " said Dylan.

"Look, Dylan," I said, "we can't let all this attention, pleasant as it is, go to our heads. Nor can we allow the possibility of tragedy interfere with doing a fine performance on every gig. We need to keep our eyes open, yet still follow our lifelong watchword: 'Another show in our hip pocket.' "

" 'Money doesn't talk; it swears,' " said Dylan.

"Assume," I said, "that the threat of death does not hang over us like the sword of Damocles. Assume that this is just another tour, full of all the innocence and exuberance of the old days."

"Assume this," said Dylan. There was a slight pause. Then there was the unmistakable sound of a large amount of gas escaping through a rather small orifice.

69

From the stage of the Lone Star Roadhouse that Thursday night, the crowd looked pretty much like any other crowd I'd ever played to. There was a familiar face here and there and, every once in a while, a friendly, encouraging smile from someone you don't know who really seems to be enjoying himself. As my friend Will Hoover once wrote in a great country song: "Sometimes that's all that keeps you goin'."

Looking out over a crowd of people from a stage, along with evoking many other emotions, never fails to remind you that you're alone. A Judy Garland–like rapport with an audience can carry you so far, but it never quite carries you all the way to the shelter of the warm applause and the easy laughter on the other side of the microphone.

One reason I felt alone, of course, was because I was. I was closing the first set with a solo version of Woody Guthrie's classic, "Pretty Boy Floyd." The band had already performed one encore with "Waitret, Please Waitret, Come Sit on My Face," a barroom ballad written by Major Boles, Roscoe West, and myself. Because of being passed along in the oral tradition, it was well on its way to becoming a minor American classic. As we'd sung the rather raunchy song, the crowd had all joined in, and for some reason I'd found myself thinking about the Major and realizing that, eventually, the song becomes the singer. But that moment of performance insight was brief.

With "Pretty Boy Floyd" I was flying pretty much on Jewish radar, just thankful that, musically and physically, we'd all survived the first set. Shucking all modesty, the crowd really seemed to love everything we did. Of course, people don't come to a reunion show prepared to sit on their hands. They're there because they want to sift the ashes of their misspent youth, re-create the ambience of a happier, simpler time. For the band's part, we were all veteran applause junkies by this stage of our lives; when the crowd cheered, we'd pick up our little umbrellas and go right back up on the high wire.

In a semidream state, like a fairly ethereal Texas politician working the house, weaving my way through the crowd, I accepted the praise and adoration gracefully. I used to have trouble accepting praise. When somebody'd say it was the greatest show they'd ever seen, I'd say "Well, the monitors weren't working very well," or "The drummer was getting a little carried away." I always liked to scapegoat the drummer. But the older you get, the easier it is to accept praise. Just remember you probably deserve it as much as anybody. Don't make excuses where you don't need any; just nod your head a few times, and smile. Remember, they came to see you. You're merely there to re-create the ambience of your billfold.

About halfway to the dressing room, I realized that I was following Dylan and Dylan was following Cleve.

Cleve, I noticed, was following Dr. Allison Klitsberg who, apparently, had decided that a little ambience wouldn't do him any harm either. What the hell, I thought, as I wormed my way through the final fringes of the crowd. It was a resocialization experience for all of us.

To get up to the dressing rooms at the Lone Star Roadhouse, Bill Dick has thoughtfully provided about half a dozen very long, very steep staircases, an aerobic experience not particularly appreciated by middle-aged musicians. Most of the band was already at the top of the building in the dressing room, probably the shabbiest penthouse in New York, as our little entourage started the steep climb. We were halfway up the second set of stairs, Dr. Allison Klitsberg still in the lead, when we observed a cop and a small knot of people on the second-floor landing. Two bodies lay sprawled out on the small, cold, concrete landing, as if they'd been hurled down the steep stairs to their deaths.

"Oh, my God," said Dr. Klitsberg. "Isn't that your bass player, what's-his-name?"

"Skycap," I said. Skycap lay very still, his head turned at an impossible angle.

"This is horrible," said Dr. Klitsberg. "Who's the big one?"

The other body, lying equally still, was indeed a large one. The face had a startlingly serene appearance, not dissimilar to what the big man might've looked like when he'd been a small boy.

"That's Mike McGovern," I said. "My favorite Irish poet."

70

We stared at the two still bodies from the limbo of the second staircase for what seemed like an eternity, then a uniform took us down to a small office on the first floor. Panama Red was sitting at a desk smoking a Kent cigarette.

"I was just coming down from the top of the stairs," said Panama. "I heard a shout and then it sounded like Samson was bringing the temple down."

I lit a cigar and noticed that my hands were shaking. The only one in the room who looked completely at ease was Cleve, who'd picked up a menu off the desk and was studying it with a little Tweety Bird smile on his face.

"Can I have a cheeseburger?" he asked Dr. Klitsberg.

"Cleve," she said as one might reproach a five-year-old.

"Can I? Can I? Can I?" said Cleve.

This was not the most conducive environment, but I knew I had to do some serious thinking. The way the steep stairways were constructed, anyone could lurk just below a landing and hurl someone down below with a very good chance of doing them grievous bodily harm. There was virtually no security along the stairwells until you got to the fifth floor and the dressing room. Very

238

few people ever went up that far anyway unless they were working on their Royal Canadian Air Force exercises.

I was sick at heart about McGovern. I'd asked him earlier in the day to shadow Skycap, and obviously he had. The killer had flung them both down the stairs, apparently, one after the other, like a crazed jai alai player. The killer still could've been anyone in the band, or anyone in the house for that matter. Skycap had known the risks and had elected to stay with the band. He was a helpless victim of this monster and he would be sorely missed. The tour was going to be over almost before it had begun. Jumbled thoughts were running through my head, but the one thing I didn't think I could accept was a McGovernless world.

"You didn't see anybody going up or down the stairs?" I asked Panama.

"Not a soul," said Panama as he chained another Kent. "Everybody else was in the dressing room."

"Where were you going?" asked Dylan.

"Just out to get some air."

"And you didn't catch a glimpse of *anyone* on the stairs?" I asked.

Panama stood up. "What the hell's the matter with you guys?" he shouted. "You think I killed them?"

"Double cheese," said Cleve, still looking at the menu and smiling. "Drag it through the garden."

I turned to Dr. Klitsberg. "Can't you get him to pull his lips together?" I asked.

"He needs the release," said Dr. Klitsberg.

"Maybe it's time to release this," said Dylan. I walked to the other side of the small room just as he farted. Dr. Klitsberg's body stiffened as if she'd been hit with a load of buckshot.

It was into this tense and rather fetid ambience that Sergeant Cooperman's large, scowling visage intruded itself. His eyes glinted a peculiar mix of disbelief and raw malice. He closed the door behind him, shook out a Gauloises from his pack, and lit it with his Zippo. He looked haggard from chasing death, and mean as hell.

"I'll take a cheeseburger," said Cleve to Sergeant Cooperman.

When all the excitement died down, Cleve, along with Dr. Klitsberg, was on the other side of the door and Cooperman was stomping out his Frog fag on the floor as if it was a rattlesnake.

"Fuckin' skell," he said. He shook out another Gauloises and lit it with an almost poetic economy of motion. Cop ballet.

Dylan, Panama, and I waited and watched. For some superstitious reason I didn't vocalize my thoughts about McGovern, but Cooperman must've read my mail.

"Your pal McGovern may make it," he said. "They've taken him to the hospital but he hasn't come to yet. We'll be guarding him. He may have something interesting to say. The other one—what's his name?"

"Skycap," I said.

"That's a good name for him," said Cooperman, "because that's where he is."

Panama chained another Kent. Dylan took off his sunglasses. I sat down in a chair and felt like crying but no tears came. We mourn for ourselves, I thought.

Cooperman left the room for a moment and when he returned he was carrying two plastic bags. He put them on the desk. I got up from the chair and walked over to look. Inside one bag was a note, handwritten in big block capital letters. It read: "WAS IT WORTH IT?" In the other plastic bag was a little yellow rubber duck like a kid might play with in a bathtub.

Cooperman said: "The note was found in the left pocket of the sport coat Skycap was wearing. The duck was found in the right. Mean anything to you guys?"

We looked at the strange and pathetic objects in the little plastic bags. Then we looked at each other.

"It means," said Dylan, "that it's time for dis band to disband."

71

The stewardess on Continental Airlines was young, attractive, honey-blond, and sounded as if she had a hint of an Australian accent. Her name tag said, "Terri."

"How do you take your coffee?" she asked.

"Black," I said. "Like my men." She handed me the cup and gave me the Jackie Kennedy frozen funeral smile number forty-seven. She asked the guy in the next row how he took his coffee. Definitely an Australian accent, I thought. It was early Sunday morning, a "Bloody Mary morning," but on this occasion I was sticking with black coffee whether Terri liked it or not.

The plane was headed for San Antonio, Texas, with a stopover, of course, in Dallas, home of the majestic memorial plaque to President Kennedy which had about the size and spiritual impact of a commemorative stamp. Out my nonsmoking window, New York was beginning to look pretty much like a commemorative stamp as well, and what it had commemorated recently wasn't especially nice. But as I sat back in my seat and sipped the tepid coffee, I felt more at peace than I had in months. After all, I knew who the killer was, and unless I missed my bet, I'd be seeing him soon.

72

The solution to the puzzle of who was killing the Texas Jewboys had not come easy. It'd taken almost three days of wandering the streets, hitting every gin mill in the Village, until the Swiss cheese effect was totally in control of my mind, and little particles were suddenly able to get through the intellectual Seine all of us have been constructing since kindergarten. Like the song, I was convinced that little things mean a lot. When strung together, they shone like highway reflectors on a rainy night and led me down the mental road to the identity of the killer. Now all I had to do was prove that I was right.

McGovern was still in a coma. The doctors at St. Vincent's had told me that only the family could see him. I told them that there wasn't any family. They said then that nobody would be able to see him. I didn't trust the doctors at St. Vincent's. Dylan Thomas had died there, and though he might make McGovern's idea of perfect company, I didn't want McGovern to get any ideas about joining him yet. The world needs its McGoverns. There's damn few of them as it is. Guys who don't own a television, a car, or an answering machine are hard to find in New York unless you look in the men's shelter. The world always needs people who won't let their apartment go co-op even when everyone else in the building is for it; who trust a guy who owns a little pizza joint to work out their taxes for them; who take on a dangerous assignment from a friend so diligently that now they lie in a coma at St. Vincent's. There's lots of guys in this world with MBAs or BMWs, and many, probably, with both, but none of them ever thought to brush their hair before meeting a racehorse.

There was nothing I could do for McGovern, I realized, that I hadn't already done. I'd been a friend, hadn't I? Maybe I could've been a little better one, a little kinder one, but if I'd been very much different McGovern probably wouldn't've been my friend in the first place. By the time somebody's in a coma or in a box it's a bit late to worry about what you can do for them. "Seeing" them or sending them flowers is a poor excuse for living. As Allen Ginsberg says: "Love when you love."

I pushed the vision of McGovern's bright Irish mind lying brain-dead in his large, sad, comatose body out of my thoughts. Clap your hands if you believe a guy like McGovern can make it in this world. I didn't hear anything but the engines and the guy behind me droning on about real estate values someplace he was never going to live. On to more practical things, I thought.

I'd spoken to Kelli late Saturday night and I replayed part of the conversation so I could hear her voice.

"You're saying it's okay to come back now?"

"Yeah."

"And Travis?"

"He's not in New York, Dancer."

Marcie had spent a lot of time in Mexico, was fluent in Spanish, and had connections with the Mexican Red

Cross. When I talked to her I asked her to check a little matter out for me, though I thought I pretty well had the answer. Might as well cross the *i*'s and dot the *t*'s.

On Saturday I'd also called Rambam's lawyer and told him I'd be leaving for Texas sometime this week-end and if anything should happen to me Rambam could have my Smith & Wesson knife and my Caruso tape. I'd talked to Dylan, too, and asked him if he wouldn't mind sticking around a couple of days to take care of what was left of the band. Some guys had already split apparently, and some were still hanging around the city. Dylan said he'd stay.

"I'm leaving the cat in charge of the loft," I said to him, "and you in charge of everything outside the loft."

" 'Nobody feels any pain,' " said Dylan, " 'tonight as I stand inside the rain.' "

The only thing I did all weekend for my own per-sonal therapeutic amusement was to call my old friend Nick "Chinga" Chavin, the country music porn star turned highly successful ad exec. I had him mail a copy of his essay "Prison Rape As a Positive Experience" to Dr. Allison Klitsberg.

I chuckled dryly to myself and the next thing I knew I was in one of those semiconscious eight-mile-high dream states rolling across the Arizona desert in an old red pickup truck. My pal Jerry Rudes was at the wheel and we had in our possessions what Chet Flippo in *Rolling Stone* magazine had called "the quasi-legend-ary living-room tapes" of the Texas Jewboys. It was the swerving tail end of the sixties and we were on our way to California, on a path more crazy and circuitous than either of us had dreamed. Jerry'd been living in the south of France for almost twenty years now—Christ; could it've been that long?—and I'd been living the life of a jet-set gypsy. I could see that red pickup truck flyin' down the freeway into L.A. and I smiled. At least, I hoped it was a smile. When you're in a semiconscious eight-mile-high dream state it's sometimes hard to tell if you're smiling or mourning for yourself.

They say Texas is a state of mind and maybe it is. It provides the physical and spiritual "elbow room" that Daniel Boone was always looking for. The Texas tradition of music is so deep and multilayered it would require seven archaeologists with seven brooms seven years just to clear away the dust. When they got to the bottom, after digging through village upon village, they'd probably find Bob Wills's cigar lying next to Mance Lipscomb's guitar.

The influence of music upon Texas and of Texas upon music is enormous and farther-reaching than you might think. Not only did Buddy Holly influence the Beatles and T-Bone Walker influence the Rolling Stones, but Texas's early singing cowboys reached higher into the firmament than they might've known. A girl named Anne Frank, with just a fountain pen, reached the conscience of more people than the entire propaganda machinery of Hitler's Third Reich. After the war, local authorities checked the secret annex in which she and her family had lived. In Anne's little corner of the annex, pictures of American cowboy stars were still fluttering from the walls where she'd left them.

In small, unconscious ways all of our lives were as insulated as Anne Frank's. I'd made an educated guess as to the killer's identity and his current location. If I was wrong, Kelli was in danger, the remaining Texas Jewboys were in danger, and I was in for a long ride back to New York. If I was right, it could even be worse.

As Slim had said: "You never know what the monkey eat until the monkey shit."

245

73

The usual flotsam and jet-
sam of well-wishers and teenaged geeks in overgrown
cowboy hats was surging around the gate as we de-
planed in San Antonio. I scanned the crowd partly out
of recent and long-term New York paranoia, and partly
out of wishful thinking. I'd had a lot of airport rendez-
vous in my time. Some of the broads were good at missing planes and all of them were good at messing up my
life. There was something about airports. Especially
airports the way they used to be. The last memorable
thing I could think of that happened at a Greyhound
station was when Holly Golightly said good-bye to
Buddy Ebsen in *Breakfast at Tiffany's*. And I wasn't
doing a lot of steamship travel these days. So if something unexpected was going to happen it was probably
going to be at an airport and this one didn't let me down.

I didn't say romantic. I said unexpected.

Right between an obscenely obese Mexican lady in
a "Fat Is Beautiful" T-shirt and a fervent young man
holding some flowers was a dark, familiar face that had
once had a pretty fair tavern tan. The face was support-
ing a Yankee baseball cap that was precariously tilted
over one eye. The rest of the guy was decked out in full
camouflage battle fatigues complete with combat boots.
A green military duffel bag was hanging from his left

shoulder with a pair of red Israeli paratrooper's wings on it.

It was Rambam.

"Got tired of swatting mosquitoes down in Guatemala," he said. "Thought a little backup might be in order."

"So you just dropped in?"

"Didn't like the sound of what you told Wolf Nachman." Wolf Nachman, I thought, was either the world's best or the world's worst lawyer, if there was any difference. The jury was still out.

"So how the hell'd you know I'd be coming in this morning and what flight I'd be on?" It was a logical question.

"No problem," said Rambam. "You told Wolf you'd be coming to Texas sometime over the weekend. I just had a friend of mine hack into the airline's computer system."

"Can you do that?"

"Easier than jaywalking in Beverly Hills."

As we went through the terminal and out into the parking garage, it felt better and better having Rambam along for the ride. I wasn't exactly sure what I would find on this trip, but if I found it I was very sure it wasn't going to be an egg cream soda. I'd asked Max to drop off the old ranch pickup truck for me at a designated place and to leave the keys on top of the right rear tire. That's what Todd Miller, the owner of the "Happy Hooker 23-Hour Wrecker Service" in Kerrville, always did. Hadn't got my *Playboy* calendar from Todd yet this year, I thought. When he gives you a calendar he always says: "Twenty-four tits." We found the truck and we found the keys.

"Is this truck dusty or is it gray?" Rambam asked.

"A lot of both," I said as I started her up. There was no accelerator pedal in the truck. You just put your foot down and it usually went. I was gratified to see that it hadn't forgotten how.

"I like that 'Eat More Pussy' bumper sticker," said Rambam admiringly. "Where'd you get it?"

"My friend Bob McLane sent it from Shreveport. Bob used to be chairman of the Gay Texans for Connolly Committee. Now he sells bumper stickers at Grateful Dead concerts and bikers' conventions in South Dakota. It's pretty lucrative, he says, but bikers who're getting tattooed sometimes come up and ask him, 'How do you spell Aryan?' "

"I can think of a number of ways to spell Aryan," said Rambam.

"That's because you're not an Aryan," I said. But I wasn't thinking about Aryans. I was thinking about tattoos.

We got onto I-10 West, set our ears back, and made it to Kerrville in a little under an hour. On the way I filled Rambam in on where we were going and what I thought we might find when we got there.

"Sounds like good ol' Texas fun," he said.

By the time we were rolling through the streets of Kerrville, people were already coming out of church. I pointed out a few of the local tourist attractions to Rambam as we drove past.

"That building over there's the oldest Methodist Church in Kerrville. Recently, they lopped the cross off of the steeple and put in an aluminum drive-up window. Now it's a savings and loan."

"Now, *that's* progress," said Rambam.

"Some things change," I said, "and some remain the same. You'll be pleased to know that on the posted regulations of the Kerrville Bus Company over there it's still prohibited to transport bull semen by bus."

"What they need," said Rambam, "is a law prohibiting Texans from transporting bullshit by mouth."

"We'll get there some day," I said. "You New Yorkers are just more progressive."

I took Rambam to the Del Norte Restaurant for

lunch, and, like all Yankees, he ordered a chicken-fried steak. I went through the buffet with about forty good little church workers, almost all of whom were senior citizens.

"Great demographics in this place," I said as I rejoined Rambam at the table. "Always makes me feel young."

"The Prime of Miss Kinky Friedman," said Rambam.

"Last time I was here they had these hunting brochures that advertised Christian hunting guides. I guess they ran out of brochures. Hunting season's over."

"Not for us," said Rambam.

Later, in the Del Norte parking lot, I was deeply dismayed to find that, while Rambam and I were having lunch, someone had ripped off my "Eat More Pussy" bumper sticker. The culprit had left a note under the windshield wiper which I read aloud to Rambam in the cab of the truck. I read as follows: " 'Your bumper sticker is, or was, most disgusting and I assure you that the wrath of the God of Israel is going to be on you either now or forever more.' "

"Why doesn't the guy make up his mind," I said. I continued: " 'I do not wish to explain your bumper sticker to my five-year-old kids.' "

"They'll probably think you want to eat their cat," said Rambam.

"He ends it on a nice note," I said. " 'Repent and be baptized for the remissions of sins.' "

"I didn't know Jimmy Swaggart lived in Kerrville."

"Jimmy wouldn't mind an 'Eat More Pussy' bumper sticker. He might get a little upset about a 'Look at More Pussy' bumper sticker."

"Maybe it's an out-of-work Christian hunting guide," said Rambam.

As we drove out of the parking lot and headed for Highway 16, we tried to decide what to do with the note. Rambam wanted to burn it. I wanted to frame it and put it on my hero wall. Rambam then suggested rolling it into suppository form and seeing if I could fly. Finally, we put the note in the glove compartment, forgot about it, and watched the Texas countryside gently roll away.

But the wrath of the God of Israel, unfortunately, wasn't the kind of thing we were going to shake that easily.

74

Like a biblical curse, the mid-afternoon skies had grown dark and threatening, and, when we turned off the highway, thunder rolled across the heavens as the dusty pickup rolled across the old cattle guard. Rambam, by this time, was smiling and drumming his fingers on the window frame, ready for action. I was smoking a cigar and thinking about serial killers.

Sergeant Cooperman once, in a rare moment of sharing and caring, had given me a cop's-eye view of the anatomy of a serial killer. Leaving out some of the police jargon, here's the gist. When a man smokes his first victim, according to Cooperman, he may find he likes it more than he expected. He may feel the same exhilaration a kid feels the first time he rides a bicycle or learns to swim. Only more so. Maybe the killer never intended to go any further than whacking one person.

Probably you don't start out thinking you'll be a serial killer. But when you discover how easy it is sometimes to take a fragile human life, how powerful and Godlike it makes you feel, something like blood lust comes over you. By the time you cap the second victim and the third victim, you find you're really starting to enjoy your work and you become more brazen. Big-time serial killers often record or even videotape their performances these days. They begin to feel a veil of invulnerability falling over them. They may start to challenge or to bait the police or the newspapers, or to leave behind deliberate clues. It's almost as if the serial killer is saying: "Look, Ma. No hands!" Judging from the condition in which certain of the victims were found, that statement is sometimes literally true.

As we rolled along the dusty county road past several ranches, over three or four cattle guards, I grimly contemplated what I might find three miles or so ahead. I'd finally been able to assemble the chain of clues, some of them deliberate, some of them not, and it seemed to hold together close enough for color television. I was correct about the identity of the killer, I thought. The only question was whether he'd be here in person or just leave another clue, like a grotesque adult scavenger hunt.

Just as the storm broke and rain and hail began pelting the windshield, we pulled up to the place. There were steep cliffs on one side of the little valley, and a river on the other with two beautiful waterfalls that I remembered from long ago. The old house and the forlorn-looking garage that used to be a barn seemed pretty much the same as they had before. Maybe it was the storm and the dark, rolling clouds that made them appear so desolate and foreboding. There was no sign of an automobile and no sign of any people. A gate on a rusty hinge swung closed somewhere in the vicinity of the old barn. It sounded like part of a soundtrack for a

251

mystery program on the old-time radio. I stopped the truck on the gravel drive in front of the weed-infested yard.

"Place looks deserted," I said.

"They always do," said Rambam.

"I'll check the house," I said. "You check the barn."

"Fine," said Rambam. "If I run into Norman Bates I'll give him your regards."

We both got out of the truck into the driving rain. Rambam took off in the direction of the barn and I ran for the safety of the overhang of the house. I didn't quite get there in time to prevent my cigar from getting soggy. The door was unlocked. I walked into the front room. The place looked like it'd been uninhabited for a long time. I shook the rain from my hat and walked into the old living room. It really took me back.

The walls were covered with cobwebbed memorabilia from the seventies. A mirrored poster from Bob Dylan's Rolling Thunder Revue. A handbill from Willie Nelson's Homecoming at Abbot, Texas. I'd been so wired and inspired on that performance I'd almost strangled myself putting on my guitar. I remembered Sammy Allred of the Geezinslaw Brothers telling the crowd: "All right. We'll get Kinky to do a few numbers. Then he'll sing some songs for you."

There was another poster from a show we'd done with David Allen Coe. It's funny what you think about when your mind is on other matters. I recalled asking Willie Nelson if there was any truth to the rumor that David Allen Coe had a snake tattooed on the tip of his penis. "I don't know," said Willie. "It's never come up."

A lightning flash and a loud clap of thunder shook me out of my little reverie. There was a smell in the air that did not seem to be all that pleasant. My beezer hasn't been working too well for about seven years, but when I do detect an odor filtered through all the cat hair, cigar smoke, and Bob Marley residue, you can usually bet

252

that it ain't nothin' nice. I followed my nose into the bedroom.

There, on a little cot, was the body of a woman. She was wearing a white Mexican wedding dress. Her hands were folded beneath her breast, holding something that might've once been a flower. Her face was bloated like a moon pie and several species of insects seemed to be having a convention in her wide-open, sightless eyes. The only name she'd ever answer to now was dead.

"I believe you two know each other," said a familiar voice. It wasn't Rambam.

I turned around and saw a figure wearing an Indian headdress, a sickening smile, and red war paint that appeared very much like it might've once had a cholesterol rating. The figure was holding a double-barreled shotgun.

"I hold all of you accountable," said the voice, "but you, Kinky, I hold personally responsible."

On the backs of his ever-whitening knuckles I noticed the tattooed words *L-O-V-E* and *H-A-T-E*. *L-O-V-E* was the one that pulled the trigger.

75

"Then I heard two deafening blasts," I said as I paced McGovern's little hospital room. With McGovern's large form schlafed out in the bed with tubes and things still in him, there wasn't a hell of a lot of room left to pace. I did my best.

"As I hit the floor I saw these colorful feathers flying everywhere. It looked like the Jolly Roger had scored a direct hit on Long John Silver's parrot. Then I heard a voice echoing across the world and I didn't know if it belonged to God or Satan. It said: 'This property's protected by Smith & Wesson.' It was Rambam, of course."

A little smile came to McGovern's lips and he almost laughed. His eyes followed me as I paced.

"When I found the puppet head behind the refrigerator I should've known I'd been looking at things all wrong. That was the first major tip-off, so to speak."

"So it *was* Tequila," said McGovern in a weak, barely recognizable voice. It'd been a week since his little fall from grace and the doctors now assured me the prognosis was excellent for full recovery.

"Yes," I said. "You correctly ID'd him for the cops a few days ago when they showed you the old Jewboy photos. Tequila *was* talking about a train when he was overheard arguing with his wife in a hotel room years ago. He was accusing her of "pulling the train." In other words, hosing everybody in the band. That was the one experience all of us had in common."

McGovern nodded his head and kept following me with his eyes. I was heartened to see that McGovern's eyes looked clear and alert and filled with intelligence, just like my cat's.

"Marcie checked her Red Cross sources in Mexico and found that Tequila had been in prison there for ten years. That's when he got the tattoos and also, apparently, went around the bend rather irrevocably. The thought that he'd been cuckolded by the entire band sautéed what was left of his brain. When he got out he took a small fortune he'd stashed away from black-market schemes and began his crusade. He didn't care how much it cost him to exact his revenge. The twenty thousand samoleans he left behind in my loft was only a portion of what he had, but it was enough to put us all on the wrong track. The Sixteenth Avenue business only indicated that he'd come to New York from Nashville where he'd tried unsuccessfully to knock off Willie Fong Young. Unfortunately, he honed his act as he went along.

"The reason Travis Parnell blipped off the screen so completely was that he must've followed a tip from a loose-lipped lesbian and stumbled into my loft right after Tequila'd arrived and I'd left to get groceries. Tequila saw it as a perfect means to take himself out of the picture and proceed, quite unsuspected, with his ruthless campaign of revenge and death. There was a struggle between the two during which someone was thrown against the refrigerator, causing the puppet head to roll off. It was a little thing and it took me a long time to realize how significant it was. Tequila'd already had the water running and had stepped into the shower before I'd left. For him to have gotten out of the shower, struggled extensively with an intruder in the kitchen, then wound up dead in the rain room again with a hole shot through the curtain just didn't wash. Obviously, he'd finished showering and was back in the loft when Parnell wandered in and offered a perfect opportunity for Tequila to stage his own death by planting him in the bathtub.

"Which brings us, of course, to the little rubber duck and the note found in Skycap's pockets. The note said 'Was It Worth It?' meaning was it worth hosing Sharon, and the answer, after what we've seen, clearly was no. But put *duck* and the word *worth* together and you have *Duckworth*, the name of the ranch we once owned in Texas where the band first went to live, rehearse, and become inextricably intertwined in questionable karma."

McGovern seemed to be making little chirping noises with his mouth and pointing to the window. Watching each other was wearing both of us out.

"Oh," I said, "you want to know why Tequila hid in the hallway once he'd nailed my windows shut? Well, I eventually narrowed it down to either Tequila or Sharon, because she was the other one that might've had motive and means to be behind the whole thing. Even the puppet head clue didn't rule her out. She could've capped Tequila in the rain room. But, according to Skycap, she once held a stray cat in her arms and said: 'How do you like my pussy?' That lets her off the hook. Because the reason Tequila refused to wait inside the loft where he'd surely have killed me, and chose instead to lurk out in the hallway where, fortunately for me, he encountered Ratso, is quite simple. Tequila, you see, was allergic to cats."

McGovern stared at me for a long moment. "Let's take these cattle north," he said.

I thanked McGovern for his courage and invaluable help and, after I'd left, I felt very confident about his chances for full recovery. It wasn't because the doctors had said the prognosis was excellent. I never believed in doctors. And McGovern didn't look all that good. He still was weak, lethargic, and shockingly pale. But when I'd turned to say good-bye at the door I'd noticed something that lifted my spirits tremendously. Irish eyes were smiling.

76

Later that evening down at Gallagher's, I was having a drink at the bar with Dylan and James Clare when Billy Swan, Snakebite, Willie Fong Young, and Panama Red came into the place.

"I thought you guys had bugged out for the dugout," I said.

"Hell, no," said Snakebite. "We came here to play on a reunion tour of the Texas Jewboys and that's what we're going to do."

"The whole world is waiting for us," said Willie. "This is no time to woosie out."

"We'd need more guys," I said. "Roscoe West is doing very well as an artist these days. Washington Ratso is getting to be a big shot on television news in our nation's capital. Van Dyke Parks, as well as scoring motion pictures, is now a distinguished lecturer at Harvard. Country John Mankiewicz has become a big Hollywood producer. It may be hard to convince these guys that what they're doing isn't more important than pickin' in a country band."

Panama lit up a Kent. "Nothing in the world," he said, "is more important than pickin' in a country band."

With that sentiment in the air, James Clare bought all of us a round of drinks on the house. I thought of some of the great musicians I'd known and loved who'd gone to Jesus and would never play their music live again. Lowell George, Phil Ochs, Jimmie Don Smith, Mike Bloomfield, Ron Slater, Buffalo, Paul Butterfield, David Blue, Jesse Ed Davis. And I thought of Tom Baker, who wasn't a musician but who had beautiful music in his soul. And I thought of John Belushi who loved the blues.

I looked at Billy Swan. He shrugged. Then he smiled. Then I saw a million miles of road shining brightly back at me in his eyes.

"Well," I said, "what are we waiting for?"

" 'On the road again,' " said Dylan.

Around midnight Kelli came over to the loft. I was just pouring us a few drinks when Winnie called to thank me again for giving her the lovely portrait of Andy Warhol.

"All my girls adore it," said Winnie. "It's so compelling and sensitive. I don't know how the artist captured Andy so completely! It *was* done in oils, wasn't it?"

"Something like that," I said.

When I rang off with Winnie, I told Kelli the whole story about Tequila and Sharon and the Texas Jewboys and Travis Parnell. When I finished the story, I poured us both another stiff shot and made a toast.

"Here's to Anna Pavlova," I said, "the great ballerina whose last words were: 'Get my swan costume ready.' "

We both killed the shots.

Then Kelli asked: "How did you know about Anna Pavlova?"

"It's my business to know things," I said.

"Then there's something *I'd* like to know," said the Dancer. "You said all the guys in the band slept with Sharon. Did *you* sleep with Sharon?"

I walked over to the window and looked out as the Pacific Ocean embraced the nighttime California shoreline. Summertime. A little motel near Malibu. Another dancer's legs, lithe and steamy. A whiff of jasmine. A taste of the sea.

"*Did* you sleep with her?" said Kelli's half-pleading voice from over my shoulder.

My gaze strayed farther down the coast to a lone chinaberry tree. I turned around and looked in Kelli's eyes. Hope burned green in them. They wanted to believe. For an instant I saw the face of the child who'd once talked to the old Christmas tree ornaments. Maybe the back of the tree *was* an important place to be.

Life is moments, I thought. Disappointments, pleasures, tragedies, dreams, failures, and triumphs, all strung together like a bad puka necklace.

"No," I said.

Kelli smiled. Then she took my hand. Then she led me into the bedroom. Then we danced together for the very first time.